REVELATION

REVELATION

*An Original Novel by
Trevor and Gordon Dexheimer*

TATE PUBLISHING
AND ENTERPRISES, LLC

Revelation
Copyright © 2015 by Trevor and Gordon Dexheimer. All rights reserved.

No part of this publication may be reproduced, stored in a retrieval system or transmitted in any way by any means, electronic, mechanical, photocopy, recording or otherwise without the prior permission of the author except as provided by USA copyright law.

This novel is a work of fiction. Names, descriptions, entities, and incidents included in the story are products of the author's imagination. Any resemblance to actual persons, events, and entities is entirely coincidental.

The opinions expressed by the author are not necessarily those of Tate Publishing, LLC.

Published by Tate Publishing & Enterprises, LLC
127 E. Trade Center Terrace | Mustang, Oklahoma 73064 USA
1.888.361.9473 | www.tatepublishing.com

Tate Publishing is committed to excellence in the publishing industry. The company reflects the philosophy established by the founders, based on Psalm 68:11,
"The Lord gave the word and great was the company of those who published it."

Book design copyright © 2015 by Tate Publishing, LLC. All rights reserved.
Cover design by Donald Meyers, Trevor Dexheimer, and Nino Carlo Suico
Interior design by Shieldon Alcasid

Published in the United States of America

ISBN: 978-1-68164-765-4
1. Fiction / Religious
2. Fiction / Fantasy / Paranormal
15.07.31

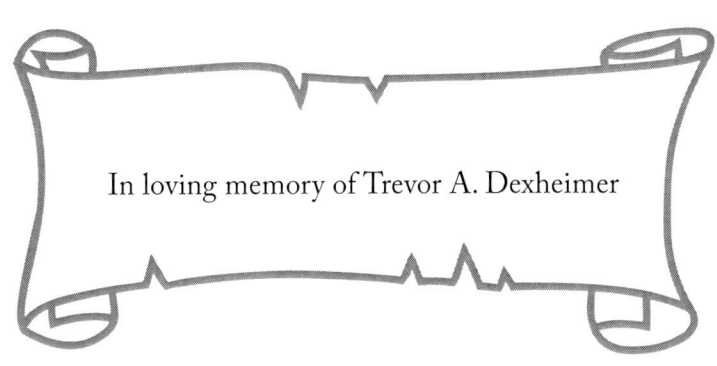
In loving memory of Trevor A. Dexheimer

Acknowledgments

REVELATION WAS AN idea my son, Trevor, had for a book we could research and write together. Unfortunately, his untimely death left the responsibility of finishing this story to me alone. I'm extremely thankful for the precious time I had with my son, Trevor, and I dedicate this book to him.

I'd like to thank my wife, Brenda, for her encouragement and for introducing me to Archbishop Alfred C. Hughes some years ago in New Orleans, Louisiana.

I am grateful to Archbishop Alfred C. Hughes of the Archdiocese of New Orleans for his encouragement and prayers.

Thank you to my good friend Donald Meyers in Memphis, Tennessee, who took the time to help create a terrific cover for *Revelation*.

A special thanks from both Trevor and me to our wonderful family.

When my son Trevor and I discussed writing *Revelation*, it was our sincere hope this book would accomplish much more than simply telling a story.

Contents

Prologue 13

1	Trevor	17
2	Katie	19
3	The House on St. Charles	24
4	The Procurator and His Wife	27
5	Dinner at Eight	31
6	Katie Steps into a Dream	39
7	The Malefactor	44
8	The Ghostly Encounter	47
9	Caleb and Judah	51
10	Breakfast in Audubon Park	54
11	Father Archer	61
12	Mystery at Loyola	64
13	Father Archer's House Call	67
14	Mystery in the Judean Hills	76

15	Father Archer and Trevor Talk	80
16	The Room Upstairs	86
17	The Painting	94
18	A King's Fortune in a Golden Chest	97
19	St. Louis Cathedral	100
20	The Sign	103
21	Jesus of Nazareth, King of the Jews	108
22	The Building Storm	113
23	Father Archer's Opinion	117
24	Death of a Prophet	122
25	A Wall of Sand	128
26	Father Archer's Plan	130
27	A Man of Light	135
28	Dr. Gallagher	140
29	The Empty Tomb	145
30	The Hypnotist	147
31	Desert Storm	161
32	Claudia Pleads with Pilate	166
33	Pilate Speaks with Lucanus	172
34	Dad	178
35	Lucanus Asks for Help	184
36	The Visit	189

37	Back to the Beginning	195
38	Buried Alive	200
39	The Riverwalk	203
40	The Coin	212
41	Mary	222
42	Stories to Tell	231
43	Dr. Gallagher's Idea	235
44	Going Out to Dinner	245
45	A New Plan	250
46	The Sanctuary	255
47	How It All Began	266
48	Luke Reports to Pilate	273
49	The Image	279
50	Luke Speaks with Paul	282
51	Pilate's Return	292
52	Recalled to Rome	295
53	Stabbed in the Desert	304
54	St. Agatha's	309
55	The Mysterious Woman	317
56	Revelation	322

Epilogue 333

Prologue

Is all that we see or seem
But a dream within a dream?
—Edgar Allan Poe

My name is Joseph Gallagher, and I am a Catholic priest. Admittedly, my affinity for a certain poetic line written by Edgar Allan Poe may seem quite unusual and misplaced for a man of God. As it turns out, thinking about this little verse was, in a large part, what led me away from the church. However, I eventually found my way back through the misty fog of my doubts—thanks to one very remarkable young man named Trevor.

Some years ago, I became disillusioned with what I perceived to be restrictions on nonsecular research and scientific study concerning the centuries-old teachings and beliefs of Christianity in general and the Catholic Church in particular. A close reading of Matthew, Mark, Luke, and John created for me more questions than answers. What seemed to me to be many inconsistencies from reading the work of one Gospel writer to another created more and more concerns in my own mind that, perhaps, what I was reading was nothing more than what Christianity and the church *wanted* me to read. Perhaps these writings, held to be accurate and sacred for centuries, had over time actually been altered from their original forms into something much less accurate and trustworthy—something designed instead to promote some agenda promulgated by the First Council of Nicaea by order of Roman Emperor Constantine in 325 CE, or by those in power during the early centuries of Christianity and of the Roman Catholic Church.

The very thought that what Christians have been led to believe concerning the life, death, and resurrection of Jesus Christ might not be true after all affected me deeply—not only as a priest but as a Christian. Without doubt, anyone who has lost a loved one hopes to see that person once again in the kingdom of heaven! For one who does not abandon God, the promise of eternal life is fulfilled through the crucifixion and death of Jesus and His resurrection from the dead. But what if the resurrection of Jesus from the dead, the very cornerstone of Christianity's teachings, never really occurred? What then?

Needing to believe unequivocally in the resurrection of Jesus from the dead in particular and what was recorded in scripture in general, I decided to pursue a deeper knowledge of all the writings and historical evidence concerning

Jesus of Nazareth I could find—including those historical references, writings, and documents not recognized and, in some cases, even forbidden by the church. In my search for truth, I made the difficult decision to leave my vocation as a priest. I sincerely hoped to find a better way to serve God and mankind by pursuing an unrestricted academic, scientific, and religious search for evidence supporting the resurrection of Jesus from the dead, as well as evidence to support the accuracy of the Gospels. It was during this time that I was first introduced to Trevor by a very dear friend. It would be through Trevor, who had doubts and concerns of his own, that I would be led to answers concerning many of the questions I had. These answers, hidden for two thousand years or more, would be uncovered at last—answers that undoubtedly would affect millions of people.

What follows is Trevor's astonishing *revelation.*

Trevor

Then said Jesus, Father, forgive them; for they know not what they do.

—Luke 23:34

As MOONLIGHT SLIPPED silently through silky curtains in mystical beams of subdued light, faintly illuminating the room, the rhythmic *ticktock*, *ticktock*, *ticktock* of an unseen clock offered the only breach of the silent hour. Abruptly the methodic ticking sounds were interrupted by whispering voices of a man and a woman. The figure of someone began to stir in the vague outline of a bed.

"He doesn't know," the man whispered. "He's lying again."

The woman's voice sounded impatient. "Just answer the question."

"He doesn't know," the man whispered.

The woman's voice was no longer a whisper. "Pontius Pilate."

The person moving in the bed had become startled and started to awaken.

The man's whispering voice faded into nothingness. "Stabbed in the desert…stabbed in the desert…stabbed in the desert…"

The figure in the bed reached for a lamp and switched it on. Trevor was a young man in his early thirties. His breathing was labored, and he was perspiring noticeably. He had a startled, frustrated look on his handsome face. As his eyes adjusted to the light, he sat up and looked curiously about his bedroom. It was clear he was alone. Trevor rose to his feet and looked at the door, which was locked and chained from the inside. He walked over to the window and pulled back the curtains. The window was closed and locked.

The sound of a ticking grandfather clock, located somewhere deep within the house, began to grow louder and louder and louder. Trevor put his hands up to cover his ears as he counted the striking of the clock. The strikes sounded like thunder—*bong, bong, bong!*—3:00 a.m.

Trevor spoke aloud in frustration, "What crime has this man committed?" As he sat down on the edge of his bed, he felt disoriented, his mind swirling. "What evil has this man done?"

The woman's voice whispered, "Wait! He is beginning to remember!"

Katie

"It happened again last night. I swear it is the most confusing, nonsensical dream anyone might imagine!"

Katie looked at Trevor over her coffee cup. "You say you have been having these nightmares for more than a year?"

Trevor took a sip of his coffee and sat back in his chair. "Well, they started shortly after my dad died—that's when I remember having the first one." Trevor leaned forward and spoke in a low voice, "These dreams, or nightmares as you call them, were very infrequent then. I maybe had a couple in a month, but lately it seems it is nearly every night!"

Katie first met Trevor in college, and they became fast friends. Trevor was extremely intelligent, and everything seemed to come easily for him, everything but trying to understand these nightmares he was having. He looked tired, and it was obvious to Katie that he wasn't getting much sleep. Trevor and Katie had always made it a pact to meet for coffee on Friday afternoons at Laveau's, a little coffee shop they enjoyed going to while they were in college. It was one of the oldest coffee shops in the French Quarter, but today the coffee didn't seem to be helping Trevor much.

"Is there anything I can do, Trev? Do you think it would help if someone else was in the house to watch over things while you tried to get some sleep?"

Trevor took a deep sigh. These dreams had become so frequent and so strange that he had found himself wandering around his old Victorian house and not realizing it. He had almost fallen over a stair railing outside his second-floor bedroom in the darkness one night, which would have been a twenty-foot fall to the hardwood floor in the foyer below. Another night, just a few nights before that, he came to realize he was sitting out in the garden, wearing his nightclothes, and he didn't remember even leaving the house.

He lived in the Historic Garden District just off St. Charles Avenue, and as beautiful as it was, Trevor was well aware of the bad things that can happen to a wandering soul at night—particularly a sleep-deprived wandering soul who wasn't aware of what he was doing. He couldn't remember ever sleepwalking before, but as a precaution, he had a lock and a chain installed on his bedroom door.

Katie reached out and touched her friend's hand. "Trevor, you're falling sleep!"

Trevor shook his head and looked a bit embarrassed. "Am I? I'm sorry, Katie. I'm just so damn tired."

"Trevor, did you hear what I said? Would it help you any if I were to stay in your house with you for a day or two so you could try to get some rest?"

Trevor looked at Katie thoughtfully. "I don't know, Kate. I suppose it couldn't hurt to try if you have the time to babysit."

Katie smiled. "Of course, I have the time! It wouldn't be babysitting either. I'd just be there to watch over things so you had one less thing to worry about. Maybe you could take a few days off from the university?"

"Maybe." Trevor nodded. "But it's not the best time." Trevor thought a moment about what he was about to say. "Kate, please don't think me crazy, but I'm actually beginning to believe I'm a part of these dreams somehow. But that can't be possible, can it? It's almost like they are scenes from an old movie, only they're not on a screen but all around me."

"Maybe that is what they are, Trevor—scenes from an old movie. I seem to remember you really love movies. You quote lines from them all the time!" Katie smiled. "So what do you think about my idea?"

"I'm really tempted to take you up on it. Maybe you're right. Maybe if there was someone else in the house for a couple of days, it would help me take my mind off things. I do worry about wandering off and getting into some type of trouble ever since I started walking in my sleep."

"I promise, with me in the house, I'll make sure you don't wander off if I have to sit up all night in front of the door."

Trevor grinned. "I don't think it will be that serious. Maybe my imagination is just getting away from me, not that it hasn't happened before."

"What do you mean?"

"Oh, I don't mean anything really, other than I have been told I have a vivid imagination. Maybe I'm just imagining all this because I'm tired, like you say." Trevor spoke the words but wasn't too sure he believed them.

"Listen, Trevor, do you want me to take you home right now? You do look tired, and I don't want you falling asleep on the streetcar."

"Oh, come on. I'm sure I can stay awake for ten minutes on the streetcar!"

"I'm not so sure of that. You fell asleep in here a couple of minutes ago. Besides, it would be no trouble. I do have a few things I need to take care of after I run you home, but then I'll come by around seven o'clock or so and make you dinner. How does that sound?"

Trevor sighed softly. "That sounds fine, Katie."

"Good. Then, after your dinner settles, you can go to your bedroom and get some sleep for a change with no worries. Oh, and no more coffee for you today, do you promise? I wonder if all that coffee you drink might be part of your problem."

Trevor nodded as he pushed his coffee cup away. "Whatever you say, Ms. Morpheus, whatever you say."

Katie looked in her bag for her car keys and, when she found them, pushed her chair back and rose from the table. She paused a moment as she looked at Trevor then shook her head, visibly concerned. He had already dozed off.

The House on St. Charles

Trevor waved from the front porch of his house as Katie honked her horn and drove off in her little Volkswagen. It was a comfortable feeling to know she wanted to come back, prepare dinner, and spend a little time. Trevor loved all the freedom and seclusion offered by the house he inherited from his father, but it was a very large house for one person, and it could be very lonely at times.

He fumbled with his keys for a moment and then grasped the one for the dead bolt his father had installed years ago. His father had felt badly about installing it because he wanted to keep the historic integrity of the house and enjoy the old-world charm of opening the front door with nothing more than a skeleton key. Unfortunately, times had changed, and his father had decided he needed to make the old doors and windows more secure. The skeleton keys would still work in the ancient locks, but with a little luck, someone could find such a key in a curio shop, which were many in New Orleans, and that was a chance Trevor's father was not willing to take.

A moment later, Trevor entered the foyer of the house, closed the door behind him, and turned the switch to once again lock the dead bolt. He told Katie he would just leave the door unlocked for her, just in case he fell asleep before she returned and he wouldn't hear the doorbell, but she wasn't at all comfortable with such a plan. "That is just too dangerous, Trev," she had warned him. So at her insistence, he had given Katie the keys to the old servants' entrance at the rear of the house.

The grandfather clock in the foyer chimed the half hour. It was 4:30 p.m., and Katie had told Trevor she would be by around 7:00 p.m. With a little luck, he might catch a couple hours of much-needed sleep before Katie arrived. Trevor thought it would be nice if he could sneak a little nap so he could at least be awake and coherent for dinner and a little conversation with his friend.

Trevor was starting up the main staircase to his bedroom when he thought he heard a woman's voice. He stopped on the stairs and listened for a moment. There it was again—a woman's voice, but it was muffled, as if she were whispering.

No one could be in the house. The door is locked! Trevor quietly made his way up the stairs, stopping momentarily when one of the steps made a loud squawk. As he listened, he could distinctly hear a woman's voice, which was barely more than a whisper. Trevor felt his pulse quicken as he began walking up the stairs once again. He didn't recognize the voice, but he was certain that it was coming from his bedroom. As Trevor reached the second-floor landing, he could still hear the woman's whispering. He held his breath and listened as he crept toward his bedroom. *There is a woman clearly whispering just beyond the door!* Trevor took a deep breath then opened the door abruptly and stepped inside, ready to confront the intruder. He stood there a moment, shaking his head in disbelief. There was no one in the room but him.

The Procurator and His Wife

"Leave me!" Pilate snapped. "I'll send for you when I need you."

The two young soldiers gave a slight bow in unison, turned sharply, and walked away in the setting sunlight. It had been a cloudy and cool late afternoon, as it had been much of this day. The day had begun early with a light rain, which was barely enough to settle the dust. There wasn't much of a breeze, just enough to cause little whiffs of dark smoke to swirl about from a reed pipe that Pilate held in his left hand. As if in deep thought, he paced back and forth in a garden corner of the courtyard.

I will never get the dust of this forsaken land out of my throat nor rid myself of this cough, Pilate thought as he drew smoke deep into his lungs from the reed pipe he held to his lips. *Dried tussilago will help. Is that not what the physician said?*

Pilate continued to pace along the stone wall separating his palace from the rest of the city. He was mindful to stay within the shelter of the olive trees. What had he done to deserve this place? These people were on the verge of a revolt, he could feel it. There was something he could sense, something he felt was about to happen, something he really had no desire to become involved with. *If I am not very careful*, he thought, *this place and these people will prove my undoing*.

"Where are your guards, my husband?"

Pilate turned with surprise to look at his wife, who seemed to have just appeared from nowhere. "Claudia! I didn't hear you approach."

"You look so preoccupied, my love."

Pilate nodded. "You are right. I am preoccupied. I sent the guards away. Why should I need guards within our walls?"

"Come inside," Claudia urged her husband. "It is getting late, and you should not be here alone. You know there is much dissent."

Claudia was beautiful and deserved much better than this horrible place. She was right. There was much uneasiness. Perhaps if he could calm these people, put their minds at rest somehow, perhaps then he would be assigned to a more hospitable place. But how could he calm them when he didn't understand what it was that caused their restlessness? "I need to finish these leaves, and then I will join you."

"So that is what creates this horrible smell?" Claudia looked at her husband as he continued to inhale the thick smoke into his lungs. "Why do you burn these leaves?"

"My physician claims this will help my throat and my cough, although it seems my cough is getting worse, and not at all for the better."

Claudia shook her head and smiled. "Why put that vile smoke into your chest, my husband, if it makes things worse?"

Pilate looked at his wife and laughed. "That is a most fair question, but I must do as Lucanus suggests if I hope to free myself from this affliction. He is the physician, and I am no more than a soldier."

"You are so much more than a soldier, my love, but I can see you are deeply troubled by something more. What is it that so darkly clouds your mind?"

Pilate looked beyond the wall as the sun sank deeply into the horizon. "It is this place and it is these people that trouble me. It is this unrest they have. I do not yet know what it is, but something makes me very concerned. I have this deep foreboding that whatever it is, if it indeed happens, I may not be able to put a stop to it."

Claudia touched her husband's arm. "There is no difficulty you cannot handle. You have done so before, and you will do so again."

Pilate noticed the leaves in the reed pipe had quit burning, so he dumped the ashes into the sandy soil and ground them under his heavily woven boot. "Come," he said as he held his hand out to his wife. "Let us go inside. Perhaps this ill feeling will leave me and remain here beneath this old olive tree."

Claudia smiled as she placed her hand atop her husband's. Together they walked through the garden and across the courtyard, disappearing inside the stone palace.

Dinner at Eight

As Trevor opened his eyes and looked around his room, he noticed the tantalizing aroma of shrimp and seasoned beef wafting up from the kitchen downstairs. He looked over at the clock on his bed stand and was surprised to see it was nearly eight o'clock. *Katie has been here almost an hour, and I didn't even know it!* As he sat up on the edge of the bed, he stretched his arms. *I'm sleeping better already in spite of the dreams*, he thought. *But right now I'm hungry!*

It didn't take very long for Trevor to make his way to the kitchen. Katie was busily preparing the dinner she had promised, and Trevor thought how nice it was to have someone actually making a real dinner in the house again. It had been a long time.

Katie turned around as she heard Trevor come into the room. "Well, sleepyhead, maybe you won't need me here after all!"

"That's nonsense! Just knowing you were coming over has helped me immensely!"

Katie made some adjustments on the stove then opened a cupboard and began taking down some dishes. "Your house is wonderful, Trev! It's almost like a museum!"

Trevor laughed. "Well, thank you very much."

Katie closed the cupboard and turned, smiling at her friend. "You know what I mean! This house looks like it must have looked over a century ago when it was built. Except for a few modern appliances, everything looks, well, antique."

"My father loved this house. I remember the first time I came here to visit him, I thought the same thing. He preserved it the best he could and often bought things at auctions that he thought fit the decor and general ambience of the place." Trevor turned and pointed to a large photograph just visible beyond one of the kitchen doors. "Do you see that photograph in there? That was taken of my dad and me a few months before he died. I loved him, you know. I only hope he knew how much I loved him. As much as I told him, I often wonder if I told him enough."

Katie put her hand on Trevor's shoulder. "It's a very nice photo, Trev. You favor each other. You even show similar mannerisms, like crossing your legs the same way as you sit and the way you are both smiling and holding your coffee cups in your left hands."

Trevor looked at Katie with a bit of surprise. "That's a lot to notice for a first glance, Kate."

"Well," Katie confessed, "it's not exactly a first glance. I looked at it earlier when I was exploring your first floor. You've never invited me here before. Why is that?"

Trevor looked puzzled then a bit embarrassed. "I don't know. I suppose I never really thought of it. Come to think of it, I don't believe I've ever invited anyone here. It's just home, I guess. A place I come back to at night."

Katie suddenly felt her comment may have been an intrusion on Trevor's privacy and quickly wished to change the subject. "So tell me more about your father. What did he do for a living?"

"Well," Trevor began, "my dad wanted to be an actor. He acted in stage plays as long as I can remember, and toward the end of his life, he even had a few small movie roles. When I first came to visit him, he had a small part in a movie called *Walk the Line*. It was being filmed up in Memphis, and he suggested I go up there with him. I went, and I ended up getting cast myself in a small role. My dad was really proud of that."

Katie shook her head. "Trevor, I never knew you were a movie star! Why don't you tell people some of these things?"

Trevor laughed. "Hardly a movie star, I'm afraid. Like my dad and I used to say, if you looked into your popcorn at the wrong time, you'd miss us completely. But it was fun and a nice memory of something we did together. It is something he and I will always have."

Katie checked the oven then turned and sat on one of the kitchen stools at the counter. "Dinner is not quite ready. Sit down and tell me some more while we're waiting. There is obviously a lot I don't know about you!"

Trevor sat down next to Katie. "There's not all that much you don't know about me. My dad, though, would be a different story. Did you ever meet him?"

Katie thought for a moment then smiled and nodded her head. "Yes, I did! I knew I recognized him in the photograph! Your dad was there when we graduated from college! I remember now. He came up to us when you and I were talking after the ceremony. I remember him smiling and shaking my hand then turning to you and giving you a big hug."

Trevor smiled sadly. "Yes, I had almost forgotten about that. He was good that way. I remember I was mad at him after he and Mom divorced. I was a junior in high school, and I didn't forgive him for a long, long time. But he was always there when I needed him or wanted him to be. I know now how much he really did care."

"So he made his living as an actor?"

Trevor shook his head. "No, although I think he always wanted to. He did a lot of different things. He taught English in college back in North Dakota where I was born and even taught high school English at a rough urban school in Memphis, Tennessee. He was a television announcer and radio disc jockey before that." Trevor looked at Katie. "Didn't you tell me once that your father was a lawyer?"

Katie nodded. "Yes, he was."

"Well, so was my dad. He went to law school while he was a disc jockey and also while he was teaching English at his old alma mater. He practiced law for nearly thirty years, but he never liked it."

"You're kidding!"

"No, it's all true. He loved writing and actually wrote a lot of stories, a few screenplays, and some poetry, but he never tried very hard to publish or sell any of it. In fact, one of the last conversations I ever had with my dad was about an idea I had for a story."

Katie looked surprised. "An idea you had?"

Trevor laughed. "Well, don't look so shocked! I told you I had an imagination, didn't I? I really did care about my father, more than I admitted to him for a long time."

Katie reached out and touched Trevor's arm. "He seems like he was a nice man, just like you are, Trev."

"Thanks, Katie. He was. He made some dumb mistakes in my eyes, like when he divorced my mother, but in spite of that, he was a good father." Trevor ran his hand through his thick hair and sighed deeply. "I suppose, as I think about it, my father and I were alike in a number of ways. My dad's middle name was Anthony, which was my grandfather's first name. Mom and Dad gave me the middle name Anthony as well. Both Dad and I were left-handed. We were both six foot four, and we both admired Abraham Lincoln. Dad even nicknamed me Tad, after one of Lincoln's sons."

"Your nickname is Tad?"

Trevor chuckled. "Well, Dad's nickname for me was Tad. I think he was the only one who ever called me that. He and I had similar interests in history, literature, and art. We both enjoyed writing, and we both tried to play guitar. Of course, there were things we didn't share. I wasn't all that crazy about the acting bit, too much standing around and doing things over and over. My interest in acting ended after a couple of roles. Dad also tried to get me interested in stamp and coin collecting, but I never quite picked up on that either. I do still have most all of the coins he gave me." Trevor reached inside his shirt and pulled out a bronze coin on a chain that hung around his neck. "This is one of them."

"You wear one of the coins your father gave you around your neck?"

"Dad told me it was an error coin, and he explained to me what coin errors were. He told me an error could often increase a coin's numismatic value, and he said there was definitely something quite unusual about the error in this coin. Apparently there was a *C* instead of a *K* in the inscription, which meant it was either a very rare error or a forgery. He later found out that similar coins with the

C instead of the *K* had also been discovered, and he was then able to have this coin verified as authentic. Dad had a jeweler mount it, and he gave it to me for Christmas the year before he died."

"That's an interesting story!" Katie looked at the coin, which was enclosed in what appeared to be a simple silver bezel and attached to a heavy silver chain. "What kind of a coin is this? I've never seen one like it before."

Trevor looked at it fondly. "No, I don't suppose you have. Dad told me it was a Roman coin nearly two thousand years old, from around 30 CE."

"Wouldn't a coin that old be worth a lot of money?"

Trevor shrugged. "Well, I'm sure it is worth something. Dad never told me what, only that he thought there was something very special about it." Trevor smiled. "Of course, he probably told me that so I wouldn't lose it."

Katie smiled. "Was this the only Roman coin he had?"

Trevor shook his head. "Oh no, he had other Roman coins, even older Greek coins from as far back as 300 BCE. A number of the coins he collected from these time periods were made of silver."

"That's absolutely amazing. I never knew anyone who collected coins that old before. Whatever happened to them?"

"I have them. When my dad died, he left his coin and stamp collections to me, along with everything else in this house. I look at them now and then, but that is about all. I wouldn't have the first idea about collecting them or what they might be worth, not that I would ever sell them. However, I did take two other Roman coins that Dad had in his collection. I took them to a jeweler and had a necklace made for each of my brothers, just like the one Dad had made for me. They were Kyle's and Rob's Christmas presents from Dad and me this past Christmas. I thought Dad would have liked that."

"That was a unique idea, Trev. Maybe you can show me some of the other coins sometime? I'd really love to see them!" The stove buzzer interrupted their conversation, and Katie jumped to her feet to turn it off. "It looks like dinner is about done after all. If you can set the table for me, it will be ready to eat in a few more minutes."

Trevor tucked the ancient coin back into his shirt as he got up and stepped over to the dishes Katie had set on the counter. "You don't have to ask me that twice. It all smells delicious, and I'm starving!"

Katie Steps into a Dream

KATIE SHIVERED AS she sat in a leather recliner near the fireplace. It was windy tonight, and the wind made a whirring sound as it echoed through the cold chimney and through the spaces surrounding the antique fireplace cover, which concealed the fireplace opening. What an ornate massive brick and mahogany fireplace it was—nothing like one would ever hope to find or duplicate in houses built in the last fifty years or so. Katie had never seen a fireplace cover before. This one was of antique metal and a rustic iron finish. The detail was remarkable, featuring a forged design with the image of a young woman in a Victorian dress. Behind the woman was a French fleur-de-lis and family crest. The wind continued making its lonely whirring sound—almost like some wild animal howling in the far distance.

Katie shivered again as she got up from the chair. *This is a frightening place at night*, Katie thought as she walked into the next room, which was the library. She wondered how Trevor could live in such a huge and lonely house all by himself. She reached out and pushed the lower button on the wall switch, and a marvelous chandelier hanging from a twelve-foot ceiling ignited the room with light. Trevor had taken her into the library to look at his father's coin collection after they had finished dinner. *Poor Trevor*, Katie thought, *had struggled to keep awake as he paged through his father's collection.*

Katie walked to the desk and looked down at the volumes of coins that Trevor had arranged there after dinner. Katie looked at the plastic pages contained in one of the three open ring binders that Trevor had seemed to show the most interest in. Each page had a number of pockets on it, each pocket containing a little cardboard square with a plastic film at the center covering a single coin. Among the several binders Trevor had retrieved from the shelves above the desk, there appeared to be a great number of these pocketed pages. *There has to be hundreds of coins in this collection*, she thought.

Katie looked more closely at the page Trevor was explaining just before he had gone up to his bedroom. He was telling her that all the coins on this page were nearly two thousand years old and from the same time period as the coin he wore around his neck—the coin his father had given him the last Christmas before his dad died. Katie marveled at how coins so old could look as good as these coins looked. Trevor explained that some were bronze, like the one he wore, and some were made of silver. Katie touched the page pocket of one of the coins, and even through the protective plastic, she could feel the design on the coin. As crudely made as most of them were compared to modern coins, these coins were really *beautiful*!

The sound of a voice startled Katie. She looked up, as if expecting to see Trevor standing in the doorway, but there was no one there. As she walked around the desk, she thought she heard the voice again. *It's coming from upstairs*, she thought as she made her way toward the main staircase. As she ascended the stairs, she stopped. *My God, there are two voices now, and one is definitely a woman's voice!* Katie hurried quietly up the stairs and stopped briefly at Trevor's bedroom door to listen again.

After being unable to stay awake in the library, Trevor had been so sleepy that Katie had walked with him upstairs to make sure he made it safely to his room. His door was still ajar as she had left it when she returned downstairs. Katie paused outside the door and listened. There clearly were voices—a man's and a woman's—but they were so soft Katie could not understand what was being said. Katie took a deep breath then slowly pushed open the door and stepped inside.

In the dim lighting, Katie looked over at the bed and could see that Trevor seemed to be asleep. She walked to him and noticed all the bedcovers had been drawn back. It was then Katie realized how unusually cold it was in the room. Trevor shivered as he slept, and his breathing seemed labored. Gently Katie covered him up with the bedcovers and looked over at the windows. She could see the curtains moving and could hear the wind.

She walked to the windows, and as she drew back the curtains, she gasped. *The windows are closed!* Katie looked around the room and listened. She couldn't hear anything now, no wind and no voices. The curtains were no longer moving, although the room remained extremely cold. *Where is this cold coming from?* She walked around the room, looking for a reason. *What about the voices?* Katie knew she had heard voices coming from this room. *Is there a radio that has been on somewhere?*

Without warning, the bedroom door slammed shut. Katie turned abruptly, uttering a startled gasp at what she saw. Standing in front of the door was a woman, dressed in a flowing white robe. The woman was looking at Trevor as she seemed to glide silently to where he was sleeping.

Katie was frozen, unable to move or even utter a sound.

"He doesn't know," a man's voice whispered. "He's lying again."

Where is the man? I only see this woman, Katie thought as she stood there paralyzed with fear. *Where is the man?*

"Just answer the question," the woman demanded.

Katie was frozen, unable to move or utter a sound.

"He doesn't know," the man whispered.

"Pontius Pilate."

Katie looked on with horror as Trevor slowly sat up on his bed and turned his head toward the apparition.

"Stabbed in the desert," Trevor whispered in an unnatural tone.

Almost mechanically, Trevor and the woman turned and looked at Katie as if they both just realized she was there. The woman moved toward Katie silently until they were face-to-face and whispered to her, "Wait! He is beginning to remember!"

As the room began to swirl, the last thing Katie would remember was Trevor walking toward her and her alarming realization that she could still see him lying asleep upon his bed.

The Malefactor

"What could they possibly want at this hour of the morning?"

"I am sorry, my lord," the centurion apologized. "They say they have a man who is a malefactor. They say they fear, unless they bring him to you, it may be wrongly believed that this man speaks for them."

Pontius Pilate sighed deeply. "Who is it they have brought here, and what evidence of wrongdoing do they have against him?"

"They say that he claims he is a king."

Pilate scoffed at the notion. "A king! A king of what, pray tell?"

"I have said what I know."

"Well, let's not keep *a king* waiting. Have them bring their king in here now!"

The centurion appeared to hesitate then spoke in a cautious tone. "I am afraid they want you to come to them."

"They want me to do what?"

"They seem to believe if they enter this palace, they will be defiled and unable to take part in their rituals of Passover."

"They seem to believe that, do they? Well, they need to fear more than that if they believe they can order me about! How many are they? Assemble the guard!"

"My lord, if you please, you yourself have told us there is much hostility in the hearts of these people," the centurion carefully spoke. "And if you send them on their way, it may turn matters worse."

Pilate moved toward the centurion with contempt but stopped himself before he spoke. As he thought about what the centurion said, he realized he was right. He was well aware of the unrest and the constant threat of revolt among these people. With many thousands of these people now in the city and barely a half legion of three thousand soldiers at his disposal, things could get out of hand quickly. If that indeed happened, Rome would not be pleased with his report. He and he alone had been entrusted to maintain the peace in this troublesome city. It is why he made the journey to Jerusalem from Caesarea each year at this time. "Very well. If they fear coming in here to me, then I will go out there to them."

With that, the centurion was relieved. "Do you still wish me to assemble the guard?"

"Not yet, but don't rule out the need. For now, we will rely on what we have. Take me to our early-morning visitors and let us meet their king."

8

The Ghostly Encounter

"Katie? Wake up! What are you doing here?"

Katie opened her eyes and saw Trevor looking down at her. She immediately pulled away. "No, get away from me!"

Trevor rose to his feet, a puzzled look on his face. "Katie, what in the world is the matter with you? Are you all right?"

Katie, now sitting up on the floor of Trevor's bedroom, put her hands to her head and tried to think. "Trevor, I'm sorry. I…I don't know what's wrong. I…"

Trevor knelt down by his friend and put a hand on her shoulder. "Katie, what happened? What are you doing on the floor of my room?"

Katie looked at Trevor and then looked around the room. Everything seemed perfectly normal in the morning light. "Trevor, I'm not sure. I remember hearing voices and coming upstairs to see if you were all right. It was cold in your room, and you were shivering, but the windows were closed, and then there was this woman..." Katie stopped for a moment, thinking Trevor would wonder if she were crazy.

"Katie, slow down. Calm yourself and take this a little at a time. You saw a woman?" Trevor asked incredulously. "What woman?"

Katie shook her head. "I saw a woman in a white robe. She was talking with you about someone knowing something and something about Pontius Pilate and being stabbed in a desert."

Trevor shook his head. "Well, so much for taking things slowly."

Katie looked at him and couldn't help but smile in spite of the fact that she was feeling quite upset. "I'm sorry. It was just so unexpected and so frightening."

Trevor sat back on the floor beside Katie and looked at her for a moment. "I think we need to talk about this, Kate, but not here, and certainly not before we have some coffee."

"Coffee? Are you serious? After what happened here last night, and you want to have some coffee?"

Trevor smiled and nodded. "Yes, Kate, I want to have some coffee. It's too early to have bourbon."

Kate shook her head in disbelief. "I don't believe you. Everything is just a joke?"

"No, it's not a joke," Trevor answered with some reassurance. "Tell you what, let's get ourselves together, and

I'll take you out for breakfast. Then we can talk about all this after we've had some time to think more about what might have happened."

Katie rose to her feet. "You don't believe me! You think I'm being foolish, that I imagined everything."

Trevor stood up and looked at Katie, this time with a serious look on his face. "I do believe you, Kate, which is why I want to get out of this house and find some coffee and some breakfast and talk about this."

Katie shook her head. "I think you are just saying that. How could you possibly believe what I just told you?"

Trevor put his hands on Katie's shoulders and looked directly into her eyes. "I believe you, Katie, because what you just told me you witnessed last night was very similar to what I dreamed about."

Katie looked at Trevor with a wave of fear creeping over her. "What? But how is that possible?"

Trevor shook his head. "I have no idea, Kate, which is why we need to think about this and talk it out. Maybe I've been telling you too much about these dreams of mine, and you—I don't know—are beginning to have them yourself?"

Katie frowned. "This was no dream, but even if it were, how could I have the same dream?"

Trevor shook his head again. "I don't know. I don't." Trevor gave Katie a reassuring smile. "Come on—let's get out of this house for a while. I really could use that cup of coffee."

Katie nodded. "All right. Give me a few minutes to freshen up?"

Trevor smiled. "Take all the time you need. I'll be waiting for you on the front porch."

Katie shook her head. "Oh no, you don't! You wait for me right here. I'm not spending one minute alone in this house of yours!"

Trevor looked troubled. "That's fine. I'll wait for you downstairs. But trust me, Kate. There's nothing in this house that can hurt you."

Katie suddenly felt a bit foolish but honestly wasn't sure if Trevor's reassurance was quite true. "I'm sorry, Trev. I guess I'm still a bit rattled about what happened."

"That's all right, Kate. I'll just be downstairs. There are some fresh towels in the bedroom down the hall that I made up for you." Trevor smiled. "But apparently, you never had a chance to spend any time there."

Trevor walked out of the room, and Katie could hear him walking down the stairs. She now wished she hadn't mentioned anything about being afraid to stay alone in the house. She had come here to help reassure him and give him a chance of getting some much-needed rest. Now she wondered if she hadn't caused him more harm than good.

Caleb and Judah

SITTING ON A rocky slope in the Judean hills a few miles outside Jerusalem, Caleb unconsciously dug in the sandy soil with his staff as he watched his flock of sheep grazing in the morning light. It would be hot soon, and Caleb would need to move his animals to the lower ground, nearer to the water and the sparse shade found there.

"Caleb! Why do you daydream so?" It was Judah, another shepherd who roamed these same hills with his flock day after day.

Caleb smiled. "I just was thinking of the city."

Judah sat beside his friend. "The city is trouble, Caleb. It is always trouble. We are better being here with our sheep."

Caleb laughed. "You, Judah, might be better here with your sheep. I don't want this for my life. I want to learn things and see places I have not seen. If I can get a good price for my animals, I will move into the city. Maybe I will even go to America."

Judah shook his head at his friend's words. "America! Now that is very big trouble!"

"America is where you are free to do anything you want, maybe even have a big house and car."

"Big house, big car." Judah scoffed. "How are you going to get to America and get a big house and big car? Selling your scrawny sheep? We are shepherds, Caleb. Our fathers were shepherds, and their fathers before them. There is no life for us but the desert."

"My sheep are fatter than those dogs of yours!" Caleb playfully pushed Judah, and the two of them started wrestling and laughing as they rolled down the slope. Suddenly Judah cried out in pain, and Caleb looked concerned. "Judah, what is wrong?"

Judah sat up and put his hand on his lower back. The two young men looked at Judah's hand in surprise as they could see there was fresh blood on it. "I am hurt, Caleb. Something hurt my back."

Caleb quickly looked at Judah's back and could see a deep jagged cut. The blood was oozing slowly, and Caleb quickly tore a piece of cloth from his tunic and pressed it against his friend's back. "The blood is slow, which is good. It looks like we will be going into the city after all, Judah."

Judah got up on his feet and held the cloth to his back. "I will go into the city. You must stay here with the sheep and get them to the lowlands."

"Do you think you can get there without my help?"

Judah smiled. "I can get to the city without your help. But can you take care of our animals without my help?"

Caleb nodded. "Of course, I have done so before and many times." Caleb knew his friend was right; he had to stay with the flocks. "You better be on your way and hold that cloth tightly."

Judah started down the hill toward Jerusalem. "Do not worry about me. You just take care of our sheep. I will not be gone long."

As Caleb watched his friend walk away, he noticed a glint in the sunlight of something jutting out of the ground where the two had been wrestling a few minutes before. Caleb knelt down and began brushing away the sand. Whatever this was, it was made of metal, and the protruding edge was sharp. *So that is what hurt Judah.* Caleb picked up his staff and began digging, trying to see what the object was. There was some writing on it, whatever it was. He brushed away some more sand, and as more of the writing began to appear, Caleb knew he had discovered something important. Although he couldn't read and understand what the writing said, he had seen this type of writing many times. It was Greek—the language once used by the ancient Romans.

Breakfast in Audubon Park

Katie sat on the park bench and removed the lid from her coffee cup to let the coffee cool. "You sure spare no expense taking a girl out to breakfast."

Trevor grinned as he sat down beside Katie. "I thought it would be better this way, more private. I wouldn't want anyone to think we were both crazy." He sipped his coffee then put down his cup and opened the paper bag he held in his other hand. "So do you want the bacon and egg biscuit or the egg and bacon croissant?"

Katie shook her head. "Does it matter whether I have bacon and egg or egg and bacon?"

"Do you want a croissant or a biscuit?"

Katie sighed. "Was the croissant with the bacon and egg or the egg and bacon?"

Trevor laughed. "The croissant is with the egg and bacon."

"In that case, I'll have the biscuit."

Trevor and Katie sat for a long time as they ate their sandwiches and sipped their coffee without saying a word, just looking out at the beautiful trees and watching people milling about with their morning activities in popular Audubon Park.

Trevor loved this park and enjoyed either walking from home or riding the streetcar along St. Charles Avenue, which bordered part of the park, to Loyola University, where he currently taught English literature. Following his morning classes, he enjoyed walking across St. Charles to enter the park and have his lunch there. It was the perfect place to sit and think about things as he listened to the birds and watched the interesting people who frequented the area. He would often read and grade student papers as he sat, and occasionally, he would try to write a poem or do some other writing of his own.

"You seem deep in thought." Katie was the first to break the silence. "Just what was it that happened at your house last night anyway?"

Trevor looked at Katie for a long moment. "I don't know, Katie. You tell me. You were the one who was seeing things."

"Seeing things? I thought you believed me?"

Trevor became serious. "I do believe you. Tell me again about the woman you saw. What did you say she looked like?"

"Well," Katie began, trying to think, "she was a young woman, dressed in a flowing white robe. She seemed to glide, or float—I don't know, Trev—but I *saw* her! And what's more frightening than that, *she* saw us!"

"Did you recognize her at all? Was she familiar to you in any way?"

Katie shook her head. "No, I had never seen her before. I know what this sounds like, and common sense tells me she couldn't possibly have been real, but she *was* real, Trevor!"

"How do you know she was real?"

Katie swallowed hard as she looked into Trevor's eyes. "The two of you *talked* with each other, Trevor. Don't you remember that?"

Trevor shook his head. "No."

"Well, you did, and then you and this woman looked right at me. She came to me and said, 'Wait! He is beginning to remember.' And that was when you walked over to me too, only it wasn't really you."

"What do you mean it wasn't really me?"

"Trevor, the person who looked like you, the one who walked over to me last night, couldn't have been you because *you* were still sleeping on your bed!"

Trevor looked at Katie for a long moment before saying anything. "I…I'm not sure I understand what you are trying to tell me here."

"Trevor, this woman and this man were like…" Katie stopped short.

"They were like a what?"

"They were like ghosts."

"What?"

"Trevor, they looked like ghosts, or what I imagine ghosts would look like." Katie paused as a young woman rode by them on a bicycle, looking in their direction. As the young woman passed, Katie leaned closer to Trevor, almost whispering, "They were transparent, Trevor. I could see right through them!"

Trevor took a deep sigh and leaned back on the bench. "Kate, I want to believe all this, but I have never seen any transparent ghosts."

"But you have seen both the woman and the man in your dreams!"

"I have seen a man and a woman in my dreams, Kate, in my dreams." Trevor paused for a moment then spoke cautiously, "Please don't misunderstand, but I wonder if just maybe your imagination has—"

"No," Katie interrupted. "It was not my imagination!" Katie got up from the bench and walked a few steps toward a flower garden. Then she turned and looked at Trevor. "I could see right through them, Trevor!" Katie took a deep breath and turned away. "Oh, I don't know! Maybe I *did* imagine it. I have to admit, I was a little uneasy sitting downstairs by myself after you had gone to bed."

Trevor got up from the bench and walked over to Katie, putting his arm around her shoulders and giving her a gentle hug. "Well, you heard *something*, which brought you up to my room, that's for sure; and when you got upstairs, you apparently *heard* and *saw* something."

"I heard a woman's voice first and then a man's voice. When I got upstairs and walked into your room, it was cold in there, and then I saw the woman. The two of you talked to each other, and then she spoke to me. It seemed so real."

Trevor looked at Katie. "When you dropped me off at the house yesterday afternoon, I went upstairs to take my nap and…" Trevor hesitated.

"What happened?"

"I heard a woman's voice coming from my room."

"What! You didn't tell me that!"

"Katie, I thought I was just overtired or dreaming again. I'm still not convinced that's not the case, but you are right. If this is all a dream, how *could* we be dreaming the same thing?"

Katie looked at Trevor. "What *did* you dream last night?"

Trevor knelt down by the flower bed and took a closer look at a small snake slithering silently among the flowers. "I dreamed what I often dream. There is this woman in a flowing white robe, and she asks a man who is with us a question. I'm not certain who this other man is, but for some reason, I don't want her to believe the answer he might give her, so I tell her, 'He doesn't know. He is lying again.' The woman says, 'Just answer the question,' and I tell her again, 'He doesn't know.' She says, 'Pontius Pilate,' and then this other man says, 'Stabbed in the desert.' That's it. I have no idea what any of it means. I have had the same dream from time to time since my dad died. It just doesn't make any sense."

Katie looked at Trevor and felt herself grow pale. "That is exactly the conversation I heard last night, except it was you who said 'stabbed in the desert,' although your voice was different—so different it frightened me!"

"But, Kate, I have told you about my dreams before. Just yesterday I told you I had it again."

"Yes, but you have never told me the specific words of any conversation."

Trevor thought a moment. "Are you sure about that?"

"I am very sure. Trevor, I don't think either one of us were dreaming at all. I think this is really happening!"

"How can that be possible? There is no woman in a white robe floating around in my dad's house! Why haven't *I* ever seen her, except in my dreams?"

"Trevor, you have told me before that when you have these dreams, there are other people in them, including the man this woman talks to. Do you recognize him, or do you remember what he looks like?"

"No, I don't remember much about him. I've never seen his face. He is dressed like an ancient Roman senator or official of some kind. I never quite see his face, although he sometimes smokes a long, thin pipe. There is also something familiar to me about his voice."

"His voice is familiar to you?"

"Yes, somewhat, but I can't tell you why."

"Do you remember anything else?"

Trevor walked back to the park bench and sat down. "Well, bits and pieces of this man's conversations with the woman and a soldier, I think, but I can't tell you what any of them actually say. The only words I can really remember are the ones I told you about—the words you tell me you heard yourself last night." Trevor ran his hands through his hair and let out another deep sigh. "Like I have said, it just doesn't make any sense!"

Katie sat beside Trevor on the bench and touched his hand. "Would you mind if I spoke to one of my friends about this, just to get a sort of professional opinion on what might be happening here?"

Trevor looked at Katie with a bit of suspicion. "You want to get a professional opinion? Do you mean a shrink? Do you think I'm nuts?"

Katie smiled and shook her head. "No, I don't think you're nuts. If you are, then so am I. No, he is just a very good friend of mine who may have some expertise in this sort of thing. He might be able to help us figure it all out."

Trevor looked at Katie with some reservation. "Who is your friend then if he's not a shrink?"

"He's a Catholic priest."

Father Archer

FATHER ARCHER MADE the sign of the cross with his rosary then kissed the crucifix as he stood up quietly from the tile step and gently put the rosary into his coat pocket. He gazed for a moment at the altar, genuflected, then turned and began walking away from the altar steps toward the front doors. His footsteps echoed in hollow tones as he walked through the centuries of the historic St. Louis Cathedral, the oldest active Catholic cathedral in America. As he walked through the first set of doors and then the next, he stepped out into the late-morning daylight and quickly began to blend into the crowd of artisans, locals, and tourists making their way through Jackson Square in the heart of the French Quarter.

Father Archer took a deep breath and then looked about the square. He smiled in his thoughts and softly chuckled to himself. What was it that Archbishop Hughes said during his homily some years before, only a few months after Hurricanes Katrina and Rita caused such havoc on the Gulf Coast and, particularly, in New Orleans? Oh yes, now he remembered: "Some say that the hurricanes were God's punishment for New Orleans, but don't you believe them," the archbishop had said with a twinkle in his eye. "For if God wanted to punish New Orleans, why would he have spared Bourbon Street?"

Bourbon Street, infamously notorious for its debauchery, was indeed spared by the hurricanes. The archbishop's reasoning for why God could not be blamed for imposing the disaster as some form of punishment was certainly sound. Long an embarrassment for the Christian faithful who believed Bourbon Street to be a modern-day equivalent of Sodom and Gomorrah, the French Quarter attracted thousands of tourists and millions of much-needed dollars to New Orleans every year—particularly at Mardi Gras time. When the New Orleans Saints defeated the Minnesota Vikings in the play-offs and ultimately won the Super Bowl, tourism and the money it brought into the city exploded to near pre-Katrina numbers.

"Father! Father Archer! Hold up a moment!"

Father Archer turned in the direction of the woman's voice calling to him, and recognizing his old friend's daughter, he smiled warmly and stopped near the large bronze monument of Andrew Jackson sitting on horseback.

"I was just coming to see you at the cathedral, and the lady in the gift shop told me you had just left. I thought I may have been too late to catch you." Katie took a series of deep breaths, perspiration visible on her brow. "I'm so lucky to have spotted you before you disappeared in the crowd."

Father Archer had known Katie since she was a young girl. Her father had been one of his closest friends, and he missed the lively debates they used to have about biblical history. Katie's father, a lawyer who demanded solid and irrefutable evidence for everything before he could believe or trust in it, had tried very hard to fully embrace the church's teachings but regrettably remained agnostic to the day he died.

"What can I help you with, Katie? You look mildly perplexed. Is there something wrong?"

"It's a friend of mine, Father. His name is Trevor. You met him once, a year or so ago, when I convinced him to attend Sunday-morning mass with me at the cathedral. I introduced him to you and to the archbishop outside on the front steps afterward."

Father Archer laughed. "Well, Katie, I'm afraid my old memory isn't quite that good. I can't place him at the moment, but perhaps if I met him again? Come over here for a minute and sit down. You look flushed." Father Archer walked a few steps over to one of the benches and invited Katie to sit there with him. "Now, tell me what I can do for you and for your friend Trevor on this glorious Saturday morning."

12

Mystery at Loyola

It will be a very warm day today, Trevor thought as he stepped down the remaining steps of the Gothic-style building that housed his campus office. As he walked across campus toward St. Charles Avenue, Trevor smiled at a few students and faculty he recognized. *Saturdays are typically quiet days on campus, but with finals a little more than a week away, this Saturday is certainly a different story.*

"Professor." It was one of Trevor's students. "Do you have a minute? I need to ask you something."

Trevor stopped and looked in the direction of a young man, tall and thin with a shaved head. *I'll never understand why these kids shave their heads*, Trevor thought. "Sure I have a minute, Monty. What's the question?"

"I'm working on my paper about Edgar Allan Poe, and I wonder if he was, well, sort of weird?"

Trevor laughed. "I hope you aren't using that vernacular in your paper!"

"Huh?" Monty asked, puzzled. "What's *vernacular*?"

"Well." Trevor smiled. "Let's just say you know how to use it. Edgar Allan Poe certainly had a unique quality about him that was reflected in his personal life and in his writing. There are a great number of sources you might review, which should answer any questions you have about him."

"Oh, so I don't get any freebies from the teacher on this one, huh?" Monty asked, disappointed.

"It is your paper, Monty. I want your impressions from the research you do and not a rehash of anything I told you."

"All right, Professor, thanks. I just thought I'd ask."

Trevor watched as Monty sauntered off in the general direction of the library. *I just bet the first thing he looks up is vernacular*, Trevor thought.

"Trevor?" It was Father Potter. "May I show you something?"

Trevor nodded. "Of course, Father."

"Come with me to the chapel. It is one of the most extraordinary things I have ever seen! I can't imagine who could have done it, or when!" Father Potter moved swiftly, taking long strides toward the chapel doors. "I just found it a few moments ago!"

Trevor followed the priest, wondering what it was he was about to see that could create such excitement in the elderly cleric. As he stepped inside the chapel and his eyes adjusted to the change in light, Trevor looked in the direction of where Father Potter was pointing. "What is it I'm looking at, Father?"

"Don't you see?" Father Potter asked anxiously. "Look there!"

As Trevor looked more closely at a painting of the Crucifixion, which the old priest was pointing to, he turned to Father Potter and smiled. "I'm sorry, Father, but I am still not sure what it is I am supposed to being looking at here."

"You are supposed to be looking at this painting, my boy," the elderly priest answered excitedly as he gently touched the very edge of one of the figures in the painting, showing the tip of his finger to Trevor. "Look at this! Why, don't you see? This Roman was never in the painting before! This is new, my boy. The paint is still drying!"

Trevor had never spent much time in this chapel, so there was little reason he would recognize anything new about the painting. The occasional times he would come here were when he just wanted to get away from the outside world for a while—not to pray as most visitors would do but just to think. As he looked closely at the face of this freshly painted Roman official, kneeling some distance from the cross of Jesus in the painting, a sudden chill crept over him. As he moved even closer, Trevor realized he was looking at a portrait of what appeared to be his own father!

13

Father Archer's House Call

Father Archer walked up the steps of the porch of Trevor's large Victorian house, situated some distance from the wrought iron fence and gate that separated the property from St. Charles Avenue. As he knocked on the ornate door, he thought about how Katie insisted he had once met Trevor, but he had met so many people over the course of his years at St. Louis Cathedral he just couldn't seem to recall specifically who Trevor was. Perhaps, since Trevor was introduced to him by the daughter of his old friend, he should have made a better mental note of the encounter.

It was Katie who answered the door. "Thank you so much, Father, for stopping by. Did you have any trouble finding the place?"

Father Archer shook his head. "No, not at all. Your directions and description of the house were precise."

"Trevor just came home a few minutes ago, and he is upstairs. He'll be down in a few minutes. Come in, come in!"

As Father Archer stepped inside the foyer, an odd sensation seemed to come over him at once; and although he couldn't quite explain what it was, Father Archer felt unusually calm and relaxed. "This house gives a person a rather pleasant and relaxed feeling, doesn't it, Katie?"

"Do you really think so?" Katie asked, somewhat surprised.

Father Archer smiled. "I really do—at least I certainly feel quite comfortable and welcome here."

As they walked past the staircase and entered the parlor through the glass-paned French doors, Katie motioned to the leather wingback chairs. "Have a seat, Father. Trevor told me to make you feel at home, so can I get you a drink?"

Father Archer looked about the room and noticed the painted scene on the twelve-foot ceiling. "Good Lord, is that a page from the Sistine Chapel?"

"Not quite." Katie chuckled. "But I must admit I thought the same thing when I first saw it."

The ceiling was beautiful, with angelic beings cheerfully smiling as they frolicked in the midst of the clouds surrounding the celestial throne of God.

"This is absolutely amazing! Tell me, Katie, how much of the history of this house has your friend told you about?"

"About as much as I know myself." It was Trevor, stepping down into the foyer from the foot of the staircase as he buttoned the sleeve of his shirt. "This was my father's house, and although he was quite proud of it, he never told me very much about its history." As Trevor stepped forward into the parlor, he smiled warmly and held out his right hand. "You must be Father Archer. Katie thinks quite highly of you, Father, and she seems to think you can help me."

Father Archer took Trevor's hand and returned a hearty handshake. "It must be the collar that gave me away?"

Trevor and Katie both laughed. "Yes, I'm afraid the priest's collar *was* a clue," Trevor responded. "As well as the fact that Katie allowed you to come into the house. She is convinced I should keep my doors and windows tightly locked at all times."

Katie sighed. "Father, Trevor is terrible about keeping his doors locked—all except the one upstairs in his bedroom."

Father Archer reacted with surprise as he sat down into one of the leather chairs. "Oh? Dear me, that may be a bit more information than I need to hear!"

Trevor laughed aloud. "Father, it's not quite like that. You see, I have walked in my sleep recently, and I had a couple of locks put on my bedroom door to keep me from wandering out into the New Orleans night." Trevor took a chair across from Father Archer and smiled. "Katie has been good enough to stay here—in a separate bedroom, I might add—to keep an eye on things, as well as on me, like a mother watching over her child."

"Excuse me, gentlemen, but Katie is still here." Katie shook her head. "Men think women are bad for jumping to conclusions."

Father Archer chuckled. "I was momentarily taken by surprise, that's all." Father Archer cleared his throat. "Did you mention something a moment ago about getting me a drink?"

Trevor turned to Katie and winked. "Maybe you better make it a double, whatever the good father would like to have."

"If you have bourbon, I'd like that on the rocks, Katie, although a double won't be necessary."

"A bourbon on the rocks sounds good to me too, Kate, although I would like you to make mine a double. I have a feeling before the night is over, I'm going to need it."

Katie sighed. "Fine, two double bourbons on the rocks. Just promise me you two won't talk about anything important until I get back."

Trevor looked seriously at Father Archer as Katie left the room. "Tell me, Father, are you some sort of exorcist or something? To be honest with you, this is Katie's idea and not mine. I'm not quite sure what the plan is here."

Father Archer leaned forward and looked directly at Trevor. "There are only a very few priests who perform the ancient rituals of exorcism, and then only with the approval of the archbishop. I *am* one of those priests, Trevor, only there is no plan for an exorcism here at your house. Katie's father and I were very good friends, which is why she came to me.

She simply thought it might be beneficial to you if I were to come by and discuss these dreams you have been having and the other, well, phenomena that have occurred here lately."

"Father, I do appreciate Katie's concern and the fact you are willing to come here and discuss these things. However, I have to be honest here. I am not as convinced as Katie is that there is anything or anyone haunting this house. I don't even believe in such things!"

Father Archer sat back in his chair, and as he did so, he noticed a large volume on the coffee table. It was *The Complete Works of William Shakespeare*. "I see you read Shakespeare, or is that book simply part of the ambience of your remarkable home?"

"Actually, it is both. Almost everything you will find in this house belonged to my dad. He left it all to me, along with the house, when he died. That book is right where he left it. I have read some of Shakespeare's plays and sonnets, however. Dad and I shared a number of interests."

"Is *Hamlet* one of the plays you read?"

Trevor smiled. "I suspect I know just the line you are thinking of: 'There are more things in heaven and earth… than are dreamt of in your philosophy.' Did I get that right, Father?"

"I *am* impressed, Trevor! You do know your Shakespeare!"

"Thank you, but I suppose I am my father's son. I believe I also know what you are suggesting here, Father—that I need to keep an open mind? Is that it?"

"Correct again, Trevor! You have a very quick mind."

"Two double bourbons on ice, or rocks, or whatever you call it." Katie handed Father Archer his drink from a tray then turned to Trevor and gave him his. As she sat down in one of the remaining leather chairs, she placed the tray upon the small table situated in front of the chairs. She then picked up her own drink, which was lemonade, and took a sip from it, leaving the bottle of bourbon and an ice bucket on the tray. She looked at the two men and smiled. "What did I miss?"

"You missed a rendition from *Hamlet*, and a quite impressive one if I may say so." Father Archer shook his drink, the ice noticeably tinkling against the glass. "Ah, the Angelus," he said, smiling, as he sipped from his bourbon. "Very nice. Very nice indeed."

Trevor laughed. "I see you have a rather quick mind yourself." Trevor looked at Katie, who seemed to be anxious that he started telling Father Archer about his dreams. "Kate here wants us to get down to business, I'm afraid. So if you are ready, where would you like me to start?"

Father Archer looked at Trevor a long moment, sipped his drink again, and put the glass down upon the table. "These dreams, Trevor, Katie tells me you have had them since around the time your dad died?"

"I had my first one shortly after that, yes."

"And they are of some type of religious theme, is that correct?"

Trevor seemed surprised. "I…I don't know if they are religious or not. I suppose they could be. There's mention of the name Pontius Pilate, so I guess that at least might have something to do with religion."

"You are Catholic?"

"I was raised Catholic, sort of. We didn't go to church all that often when we were growing up, except in later years when we went to Catholic school."

"You told me your father is deceased. What about your mother?"

"Mom is doing well. She lives up in Minnesota—the house we moved into a few years after Mom and Dad divorced."

"Are you an only child?"

"No, I have two brothers. My older brother, Kyle, lives in Saint Paul, Minnesota, and my younger brother, Rob, lives in New York. There was one older brother, Troy, who died shortly after birth."

"I see. Tell me, Trevor, do you go to church on a regular basis?"

"No, I don't go to church very often at all. I've gone a few times—once with Katie when I met you a while ago now and occasionally when I feel like it, but I'm not a churchgoing person."

Father Archer seemed puzzled and looked at Katie for a moment then back at Trevor. "Yes, Katie told me about the two of us meeting. I'm sorry, though, I just can't remember it."

Trevor smiled. "I'm glad to hear that, Father, because, to be honest, I can't remember meeting you either. I do remember meeting Archbishop Hughes."

Father Archer nodded. "Yes, everyone who has ever met Archbishop Hughes remembers him. He is truly a holy and memorable man. He is mostly retired now, you know."

"Yes, I heard or read something some time ago about there being a new archbishop."

"Do you still consider yourself a Catholic, Trevor, someone who believes in Jesus Christ?"

"Once a Catholic, always a Catholic, I suppose. As far as believing in Jesus Christ, I believe there was a well-meaning prophet by that name some two thousand years ago. I can also accept that he may have been crucified as some sort of criminal, but I find it very difficult to believe this Jesus actually rose from the dead. That is something that seems quite unlikely."

Father Archer sighed. "I see."

Trevor looked at Katie and smiled a bit uneasily. "You didn't bring the good father here to make me a believer and get me back into the good graces of the church now, did you, Katie?"

Katie felt a bit embarrassed by the question. "Of course not. What you do about your faith is your business."

"I'm only asking these questions, Trevor, to help us understand why you might be having these dreams and experiences." Father Archer spoke in a soft, reassuring tone.

"Typically, people who have dreams and experiences like you have had—the types of dreams and experiences Katie has described to me—are deeply religious people."

"As you can probably see by now, I don't consider myself religious, Father. Maybe you can't help me after all."

"Oh, give him a chance, Trevor!" Katie pleaded. "Father Archer knows a lot about these kinds of things."

"Trevor, if you wouldn't mind, why don't you tell me about these dreams of yours? I'd really like to hear more about these experiences you are having as well—the ones that have prompted you to put locks on your bedroom door."

Trevor finished his drink then looked at Katie and quipped, "Maybe it's good you brought the bottle, Kate." Turning to Father Archer, Trevor said, "Drink up, Father. I have a feeling you're going to want more than one of these."

14

Mystery in the Judean Hills

As DAWN BEGAN to break, Caleb stood and looked in the distance toward Jerusalem. *Where could Judah be?* Caleb wondered as he walked among their sheep. *He said he would not be long. I hope he found a doctor.*

"Remind me not to leave you alone to watch the animals ever again, Caleb! If you did not see me coming, how can you protect them?"

"Judah! I was just wondering what had happened to you! Why have you been so long? Are you well?"

Judah sat down by what remained of Caleb's fire and rubbed his hands above the fading glow of the dying embers. "It is cool this morning. I am fine, Caleb, but it is very strange what happened. Come, sit down, and I will tell you."

Caleb walked to the fire and sat down by his friend. "What is strange?"

Judah looked at Caleb, this time with a serious look. "Caleb, you saw the cut on my back, did you not? You saw the blood that came from it?"

"Of course, I did! I tore my tunic to slow the blood, remember? Why do you ask me that?"

Judah sighed and looked at his friend. "When I got into the city, I went to my mother's house. The bleeding had almost stopped, and I thought I would ask my mother if I needed to see a doctor."

"But, Judah, that cut was very deep. I saw it. Remember one of our animals got a deep cut like that one time? The wound had to be sewed shut. Of course, you needed to see a doctor!"

"Caleb, I really did not! That is the strange thing that has happened. When I got to my mother's house, she looked at my back. There was no cut, not even a mark, and there was no blood."

Caleb looked at his friend in disbelief. "That is not possible, Judah. I saw the cut! We both saw the blood! I even found the metal that cut you in the earth. Let me see your back!"

Judah turned his back toward the fire and lifted his tunic. "Do you see I am telling you the truth? See, there is nothing!"

Caleb looked closely at his friend's back in the dying light of the fire and the first light of the new dawn. He reached out and touched Judah's back and shook his head in disbelief. "This is not possible, Judah! I saw the deep cut, and we both saw the blood!"

Judah turned and faced his friend. "I know what we saw, Caleb. But my mother did not believe me. She asked why I would make up such a story. I could not believe it, not after what you and I had seen and after the pain I felt as I walked to the city. I was very tired, and my mother asked me to stay until this morning. She had not seen me for a time. I hope you do not mind?"

"I do not mind that you stayed, Judah, and I am happy you are well. Yet I do not understand how the wound and the blood could vanish!" Suddenly Caleb had an idea. "Judah, do you have the part of my tunic that I tore to help stop the bleeding?"

"Yes, Caleb, I do. I thought we might use it for something else, maybe if one of the sheep got hurt. Why?"

"Bloodstains! There would be bloodstains to show we are not foolish and that we saw what we say we did!"

Judah shook his head as he looked in his pack and pulled out the torn piece of Caleb's tunic. "I thought of that when I tried to tell my mother about what happened. Here, look for yourself."

Caleb took the cloth from Judah and held it into the light, staring at it in disbelief. "There is nothing! There is no stain, nothing!"

"There was nothing on my back and nothing on my tunic either, just sand and the dust of the earth."

Caleb stood to his feet and looked out over the sheep as they began to stir at the break of daylight. "This just cannot be."

Judah stood and put his hand on his friend's shoulder. "Caleb, you say you found what cut me in the earth?"

"Yes, I did. It is old, Judah, with Greek writing on it. I tried to dig more of it out. It looks like it could be an old bronze chest of some kind."

"Can you find it again?"

"Yes, I marked it so I could show it to you when you came back."

"Come, let us build up this pitiful fire of yours and fix something to eat. Then you can take me there. I want to see what this thing is for myself."

"I wonder, Judah, if we should go there again after this strange thing that has happened. Maybe we should leave it alone. What is hidden there in the earth may be something very good or something very evil, and I worry which it may be."

Father Archer and Trevor Talk

"So you have no idea of the history of this house?" Father Archer asked. "For example, your father never told you about this painting on the ceiling above us?"

Trevor smiled. "My dad was interested in trying many different things, Father. Yet he would have been the first to admit that he was not an expert on any of them. I do know he tried to paint, only because it was one of a number of things he tried to interest me in." Trevor chuckled. "My brothers and I used to joke that whatever Dad gave us for our birthdays or Christmas was probably going to be something educational."

"Do you think your dad painted this ceiling?"

Trevor shook his head. "I doubt it, although it is possible, I suppose. He has some things in his room upstairs—palettes, brushes, easels, those sorts of things. I really doubt he could have painted this. He tried, but he was certainly no Michelangelo."

Father Archer looked admiringly at the painting above. The painting was certainly no Michelangelo, but it was not a novice attempt either. "Well, if your father did paint this, I hope there are more of his paintings around somewhere."

Trevor felt proud of his father, though he realized he may not have mentioned that fact to him very much when he was alive. He felt sadness at the thought that, at least in the present world, he would never again have the chance to tell him how much he admired and loved him. A thought suddenly occurred to Trevor. "Father, do you know Father Potter by any chance?"

"Are you speaking of Father Potter who serves at Loyola University? Of course, I know him. Why?"

"Well," Trevor began, "I just find it a strange coincidence that you would be talking to me about the origin of this painting, particularly after what I experienced earlier today."

Father Archer sat up straight in his chair and took another sip of bourbon. "Oh? What happened earlier today?"

"You haven't spoken with Father Potter?"

"No." Father Archer shook his head. "I haven't spoken to Father Potter in the last—oh, I don't know—few months, I suppose. Why do you ask?"

Trevor took a last sip of his drink, rattled the ice at the bottom of the glass, and then added two pieces from out of the ice bucket. "I think what I'm about to tell you calls for a refill."

"It's all that bad, huh?"

Trevor poured himself another drink from the bottle of bourbon that Katie had left for them. As much as she had wanted to stay, she realized she had promised to help her sister on the West Bank. It was already late, after 10:00 p.m., when she left. Trevor had suggested she just stay with her sister overnight since it would likely be after midnight before she returned. Katie reluctantly agreed after making Trevor promise to lock *all* the doors after Father Archer left and to give his word he would tell her about anything she missed while she was gone.

"Would you like another, Father?" Trevor asked.

"I shouldn't. I am driving, but a small one couldn't hurt." The priest held out his glass, and Trevor put two cubes from the ice bucket into it and poured the bourbon until Father Archer clicked his glass against the neck of the bottle.

After putting the bottle down and leaning back in his chair, Trevor took another sip from his glass and sighed. "Earlier today, as I was walking across campus, Father Potter flagged me down. It seems he had discovered something in the chapel that he hadn't noticed in there before. It appears someone had painted in the figure of some type of Roman official on a painting of the Crucifixion."

"Oh my," Father Archer responded in a low tone. "Vandalism in a holy chapel."

Trevor shook his head. "Not exactly vandalism, although I suppose you could call it that."

Father Archer reacted in surprise. "What else would you call it?"

Trevor chuckled. "Father Potter called it a miracle."

"A miracle!" Father Archer exclaimed. "How could vandalism possibly be a miracle?"

"As I said, Father, it was not exactly vandalism. The addition to the painting was very professionally accomplished. Even on close inspection, I doubt anyone but a professional or someone who is around the painting every day could tell the figure was added. Father Potter saw it right away because he does see the painting every day. I couldn't tell until he pointed it out to me, yet once I looked closely at it…" Trevor stopped short of finishing his sentence.

"Go on! Don't leave me hanging on a cliff like that!"

"Father," Trevor spoke softly, a much more serious tone now evident in his voice, "as I looked closely at the freshly painted figure, I could see a most remarkable resemblance to my dad."

"What? The freshly painted figure in the painting reminds you of your father?"

"Actually," Trevor answered cautiously, "I almost believe the newly painted figure in the painting *is* my father, as incredible as I know that must sound."

Father Archer looked at Trevor and could see he appeared thoughtful as he looked into the distance and rattled the ice in his glass. "These dreams that you have, is your father in any of them?"

Trevor looked thoughtful another moment then shook his head. "No, I don't believe so. There is a voice that seems familiar to me in my dreams, but I don't think it is my dad's voice. It is odd that I have these dreams about people running around in Roman armor and togas, and then I see my dad dressed like a Roman senator in a painting of the Crucifixion."

Father Archer sipped his drink and thought a moment about what Trevor just said. "Katie tells me you have been very tired, that you haven't had much sleep. She is rather worried about you, of course, which is why she asked me to come by."

"I know. She is a sweetheart to worry, but this is just something I have to work through."

"What are you trying to work through, Trevor? Do you know?"

"I'm not sure. I suppose I have always had my bouts of depression, but ever since my dad died, I can't seem to get him out of my mind—not even for short periods of time. Don't get me wrong, I want to remember my dad, and I have some wonderful memories of him, but I have become obsessed. Everything I see or think about seems somehow linked to him."

"I'm no psychologist, Trevor, but don't you think that might explain seeing your father in that painting earlier today?"

Trevor shrugged. "I suppose it might explain it, but what's up with this ancient Roman theme I suddenly seem to be surrounded by?"

Father Archer looked again at the painting on the ceiling above. The art period was distinctly Roman. Was it coincidental that the painting Father Potter had shown Trevor earlier today was of the Crucifixion of Jesus Christ? *I wonder*, Father Archer thought, *if there might be some explanation*. "Trevor, just out of curiosity, could I ask you to show me something?"

"Sure, Father. What would you like to see?"

Father Archer finished his drink and then got to his feet. "I'd like to see more of this beautiful old house of yours if I may."

Trevor stood and faced his guest. "Well, you might see more in the daylight, but if you don't mind seeing it at night, I'm ready if you are. Where should we start?"

Father Archer looked at Trevor as he thought carefully about their discussion the past few minutes. "I'd love to see your entire house at some point, of course, but as you say, daylight would perhaps be best for the full tour. I know it is getting late. However, if you don't mind, I'd like you to at least show me one part of the house."

"Sure, Father. Which part would you like to see?"

"I'd like to see your father's room."

16

The Room Upstairs

As Trevor topped the stairs and headed down the hall, dimly lit by electric light candelabras along the walls, Father Archer followed a short distance behind. It was as if Father Archer had stepped back in time, which is not an uncommon feeling at all for someone in New Orleans to experience; but here in this house, there was an ambience of a different sort—one Father Archer couldn't quite identify. There were photos and paintings hanging along the walls, some of which were on lengthy wires hung in the way a museum might display them, which was allowed by the very high second-floor ceilings. The shadows cast by the electric candles among the various wall hangings created a somewhat eerie sensation to everything. Many of the photos were likely of family, some of them appearing to be from many decades before. There were quite a number of other photos and pictures, interspersed with some of historic significance, as well as a few religious prints and paintings.

Father Archer stopped and looked at one large and very beautiful painting of the Nativity scene. It was set traditionally in a rustic stable with Mary and Joseph admiring the baby Jesus lying upon a bed of hay in a manger—with cattle, sheep, and shepherds looking on and an angel floating above the scene lit by a celestial light from the ancient Bethlehem sky. Yet there was something different about this painting, something Father Archer sensed immediately yet couldn't quite identify.

"My dad loved Christmas. It was his favorite time of the year. As kids, my brothers and I looked forward to it too, only for different reasons." Trevor smiled. "We could usually count on finding what we had asked for under the tree, along with the usual clothes and a few surprises. Mom and Dad never had a lot of money when we were little, but they usually managed not to disappoint us somehow." Trevor chuckled. "Except I remember one year my brother Kyle wanted an aquarium. There was this huge box wrapped under the tree with his name on it, and for days, he just knew what it was. As it turned out, there were many smaller boxes containing random books for weight, one inside the other, in that huge box. I can't remember what he ended up getting, but it wasn't an aquarium. Mom and Dad meant it to be a little joke, intending all along to let Kyle choose his own aquarium and fish after Christmas, but he wasn't too amused at the time. It wasn't long after Christmas that Kyle had his aquarium and assorted fish."

"That's a great little story—a nice memory of Christmas." Father Archer looked again at the painting of the Nativity. "There is something different about this painting, something I just can't quite figure out. Do you notice anything?"

"What is it with you priests and paintings?" Trevor laughed. "First, Father Potter, and now you ask me to look for something in a painting." Trevor stepped in close to the canvas and looked more intently at the scene. "I'm sorry, Father, but I only see the same painting I have seen for as long as I can remember."

Father Archer sighed. "Perhaps I'm just imagining something, expecting to find something there that should or shouldn't be there, like your brother Kyle imagining his Christmas gift was an aquarium and instead getting a box full of other boxes and books."

"That could be, Father." Trevor looked at his watch. "I'm afraid it is getting late. Do you still want to take a look at my dad's room?"

"Yes, I'm sorry. I guess I allowed myself to become a bit distracted."

The two men continued along the hallway, which didn't really seem as long as it really was because of the little twists and turns built into it. Father Archer assumed the builder's reason for building the house the way he did was to create rooms that weren't uniform in size, as well as to create the illusion that the hallway was much shorter than it actually was, thereby disguising the enormity of the house.

"Here we are." Trevor turned the ornate brass doorknob, and the door made a slightly perceptible squawk as it swung open. Trevor turned on the lights to reveal a very large room with what looked to be another smaller room off to one side. "Dad's room is very much like the one I have, two bay windows and a small closet. It's odd that in these old houses, they built the bedrooms so large and the closets so small. The only difference, however, is that there is this other room off to the side that my room doesn't have." Trevor walked over to the other room—which had a doorway with the door having been removed—stepped inside, and turned on another light.

Father Archer stepped into the room behind him, and his attention was immediately drawn to a large stained glass window featuring the Gospel writer Luke. "This is amazing! Was this always here?"

"No, that is something Dad had installed a short time before he died."

"Where did he find this, do you know?"

Trevor shook his head. "I don't know for sure, but I seem to remember him telling me it was from a church that had been damaged or destroyed in the hurricane. I do remember how excited he was the day it arrived at the house. It was in the foyer downstairs for several days until Dad could find carpenters to install it up here. He insisted when it was installed that it had to look like it had been part of the original house. They did a good job of it, don't you think?"

Father Archer gently touched the framing of the window; then he looked with wonder at the artistry of the stained glass scene. There were no perceptible flaws that he could see, and the image of Luke appeared as if he could step down at any moment into the present century. "This is absolutely marvelous!" Father Archer looked at Trevor. "I too salvaged some things from churches that were damaged or destroyed by the hurricane. It appears your dad found this beautiful stained glass window before I did." Father Archer turned his attention again to the window. "I imagine it is quite beautiful with daylight streaming through it."

"Yes, it is quite nice in the daytime. In the last months of his life, Dad seemed preoccupied with this writer of the Gospels. I never fully understood why as, I told you before, we weren't a particularly religious family. I never knew my dad or my mom to read the Bible or have an interest in something like this."

"Your father must have mentioned something?"

"He didn't talk about it much at all, but I do know he read and reread the two books of the Bible credited to Luke, and he did a lot of other research. He seemed fascinated by it all. Once, when I came home, Dad was so excited about something he had found he felt certain it would change completely what people believe about life after death."

Father Archer turned to Trevor. "Did he tell you what it was he found?"

Trevor shook his head. "No, only that he couldn't believe that in nearly two thousand years, everyone—biblical historians, scholars, and those in religious vocations—seem to have missed something that was right there before them the whole time. I didn't ask anything more about it because, to be honest, at that moment I wasn't that interested. Although I have often questioned the whole life-after-death business, I had other things on my mind. Besides, Dad loved telling and writing stories, so it wasn't unusual for him to get some wild idea about something or another. I just figured, when the time came, he would tell me all about it." There was now sadness in Trevor's look and his voice. "I didn't realize time would run out for us as quickly as it did."

"Do you think he wrote down any of what he was researching somewhere?"

Trevor smiled. "Knowing Dad, he probably did. I'd have to check his laptop and see if there's something on it. Come to think of it, he was working on his laptop quite frequently near the end of his life. He spent quite a lot of time those last days in his library downstairs."

"That would be most interesting to read if you found something."

"I'll have to take a look when I get the chance, though I may need to figure out his password if he had one. You have me wondering about this now too."

"That would be nice, when you find the time."

"Maybe I'll even get to it tomorrow since Sundays can be a bit long and dull sometimes. Although, come to think of it, I promised Katie I would go to mass with her at St. Louis Cathedral in the morning and treat her to lunch afterward somewhere in the French Quarter."

"There's no rush. I'm glad to hear you are going to mass."

Trevor chuckled. "Well, to be honest, it's more Katie's idea than mine. I haven't been to church for quite some time."

"It's a start." Father Archer looked around the smaller room and saw a few small shelves with books, a recliner, a floor lamp, and some cigar boxes stacked neatly in one corner. There was also a table, an easel, and some painting materials in another corner of the room. "Is this where your father tried his hand at painting?"

"Mostly, I guess, although he would sometimes paint out on the front porch. He and I painted—or should I say, *tried* to paint—out there a time or two."

Father Archer stepped over to the table and began looking at some of the items upon it. "I don't see any paintings. Did you put them away?"

"No, there weren't any. I came up here and looked for some one day, shortly after Dad died. I don't know what I expected to find, but I was hoping I'd find something. I rummaged around up in the attic too but found no paintings. If he painted anything during his last days, I have no other idea where to look."

"Trevor, when was the last time you were in this room?"

"I don't know. I never came in here very much, even when Dad was alive. He and I would usually talk downstairs in the room you and I were sitting in, or in the library, or out on the porch."

"You haven't been doing any painting yourself lately?"

Trevor laughed. "No, Father Sherlock Holmes, I haven't. Why do you ask that?"

Father Archer held up his hand to show Trevor the paint on his fingers. "I was just looking at the brushes on this table. It appears there is some wet paint on them."

17

The Painting

As Trevor watched Father Archer drive away in the darkness, he sighed as he looked at his watch. *It is nearly midnight. Wait until I see Katie tomorrow. Father Archer is a nice enough fellow, but he doesn't seem to know when to go home.* As Trevor stepped back inside the foyer, he closed the door and began walking about turning out the lights. *Wait, I promised Katie to lock all the doors.* Trevor went back to the door and turned the lock. Trevor knew it was a good idea to lock the doors, especially in a city like New Orleans, but sometimes he just neglected to do it.

After turning out the rest of the lights, Trevor walked up the stairs. He was tired. A nice warm bath, and then he'd go right to bed. Katie would be picking him up for church in the morning. How long had it been? Suddenly it dawned on him, and he wondered how he could have possibly forgotten. *The last time I remember going to church was for Dad's funeral.*

It wasn't long before Trevor had settled back into a tub of soapy warm water. *Ah, that feels good. I could sleep right here.* Trevor thought through the events of the day. What a strange day it was! As Trevor thought about all that had happened, he began to realize it was all somehow oddly connected to the dreams he had been having. Katie's involvement was easily explained, and so was Father Archer's. After all, it was Katie who had confided in Father Archer and had asked him to stop by.

I'm not sure how much good it did, Trevor thought. *But it was an interesting visit.* The part that Trevor couldn't explain was when Father Potter stopped him outside the chapel and took him inside to show him the altered painting. *The likeness of the freshly painted figure in that painting was remarkably like Dad, wasn't it? And what was with the wet paintbrushes in Dad's room? How likely was it that Father Archer would not only ask to see Dad's room but find brushes with wet paint on them—all that after we had been discussing paintings! It all has to be coincidental, yet how could those brushes be wet?* Trevor shook his head. He wasn't going to figure it out tonight—he was simply too tired. He was falling asleep and knew he had best be getting to bed.

There was a thud, as if something had fallen to the floor down the hall, in the direction of his room. Trevor stood up from the tub, shivering and wondering how his bathwater had turned cold so soon as he reached for a towel. *What is that noise? Has Katie come back after all instead of staying with her sister like she planned?* Trevor quickly dried himself off and put on his robe. As he stepped out of the bathroom and into the hall, he turned the lights on and walked toward his room. As he turned the corner by his father's room, Trevor stopped short and felt his heart begin to beat faster.

There, on the floor and leaning against the wall, was the painting of the Nativity that Father Archer had been talking with him about. As Trevor knelt down before it, he could see that the fall hadn't damaged either the frame or the painting in any obvious way. He gently pulled the top of the painting toward him and looked behind it. The wire had snapped in two, as if it had been cut. *How could this have happened?* Trevor wondered. *I have never seen such a thing happen before!*

Trevor eased the painting back against the wall and looked at it more closely. *What was it Father Archer noticed that he couldn't identify?* Trevor looked intently at the canvas, and then he saw something. There was a large area of the stable that he didn't remember seeing. There was a stone trough with water and a larger pile of hay beside it. Trevor looked at it more closely, and a chill swept over him. *That wasn't there before! Wait—the three kings! Where are the three kings?* Trevor reached out gently with his left hand and touched the unfamiliar trough. Then he drew his hand back quickly and looked at the tips of his fingers. They were wet with fresh paint!

A King's Fortune in a Golden Chest

"See, Judah?" Caleb asked his friend as he pointed to a small pile of rocks on the rocky slope where they had been the day before. "Do you see that little pile of rocks there? That is where it is buried."

Judah chuckled and teased his friend, "Only you, Caleb, would use such a tiny pile of rocks on a slope covered with rocks to mark something. I am surprised you have found it at all!"

Caleb reached his little pile of rocks and smiled. "I am wiser than you think, Judah. This is the place. I did not want to make it so clearly marked that others passing by might find it. I knew just what to look for."

Judah nodded. "You are right, Caleb. That was a wise thing for you to do after all. Come, let us find out what it is that lies beneath this sandy soil."

Caleb looked at the distant sky. "We must hurry, Judah. We must get the sheep to the lowlands soon. It is very warm again today, and it looks like there may be a storm coming."

Judah knelt down and began removing the rocks. He could see the sharp edge of the object and that Caleb had begun digging it out. He began digging with his staff and with his hands. "Come help me, Caleb. You have already made a good start. I think we can get this from the earth in no time!"

Caleb looked again at the sky then at the sheep lazily grazing along the slope before kneeling down beside his friend. "All right, Judah, but remember, we cannot stay too long. I do not like the look of the sky."

It was as if Judah did not hear him. "Look, Caleb!" Judah cried with excitement as he continued to dig. "You are right! This is an ancient chest of some kind! But, Caleb, I do not think it is bronze as you said."

Caleb looked at his friend and smiled. "You do not think this is gold, do you, Judah? What would this much gold be doing out here, where only sheep and poor shepherds live?"

"Do you not see, Caleb? You yourself said this writing on the chest is in Greek, the language of the ancient Romans. The ancient Romans were very, very rich, Caleb. I do not think this is bronze at all. I do think this is gold!"

"But why would a valuable thing such as a golden chest be buried here, Judah?"

"Think of it, Caleb! There have been all sorts of treasures found in this land over the centuries. You and I just have not found any before now. That is all. If I am right, and if this chest is made of gold, it must hold something inside that is very important and very valuable. Caleb, what you and I have found could be worth a king's fortune! Imagine, Caleb! You and I, poor shepherd boys, might just have found a king's fortune in a golden chest!"

St. Louis Cathedral

TREVOR WALKED DOWN the aisle of St. Louis Cathedral, just behind Katie, and he stopped as Katie genuflected and entered the pew she had chosen. He too genuflected before entering the pew. However, unlike Katie, he did not kneel down in prayer but chose to simply sit down instead. As Katie prayed, her head bowed, Trevor looked at the number of empty pews. *Strange*, Trevor thought as he looked at his watch. *It is only a few minutes before mass is to begin, and there are so few people.*

An altar boy stepped out upon the altar and began systematically lighting the candles. Trevor remembered, what seemed a long time ago, when he was an altar boy at Sacred Heart Catholic Church. He was carrying a cruet of sacramental wine during the entrance procession to the altar. He hadn't particularly been interested in being an altar boy, but his dad had been one when he was a boy, so Trevor thought it might be interesting. It was interesting all right. The cassock he wore was too long, and as he reached the steps to the altar, he tripped and fell. Wine was everywhere! A few elderly ladies and a nun in the front pew gasped aloud, and he remembered the nun making the sign of the cross. He had spilled the precious blood of Christ! In his embarrassment, he had the distinct feeling his days as an altar boy were numbered. After mass though, in the sacristy, the kindly priest assured him that all he had spilled was wine.

"That's all right, Trevor, the transubstantiation had not taken place yet. Such things happen." The priest then smiled his reassuring smile. "Your cassock will just need to be hemmed so it doesn't trip you up again—hemmed, that is, after the wine stains have been removed from it, of course."

Then the most remarkable thing happened. The priest laughed! He actually laughed! It seemed odd to Trevor that a priest would actually laugh about what had happened, but he did. Trevor and the other altar boy began laughing too, and suddenly he didn't feel quite as embarrassed as he had been feeling. Trevor always liked that priest after that day. He felt badly when the priest was assigned a short time later to another parish.

Katie made the sign of the cross and sat back on the pew. "Where are you?" Katie whispered. "You look like you are miles away from here."

Trevor smiled. "I was," he whispered. "Miles and years away from here."

Katie gave Trevor a puzzled look as the organ music began and everyone stood up and began singing the opening hymn. Trevor looked around and was surprised to see how full the church seemed to be all of a sudden. *When did they all get here?* he wondered.

As the strongest voices began to grow louder, the thurifer walked by on his way to the altar, rhythmically swaying a thurible forward and back as it clanked gently upon its chains and filled the air with the pungent smell of incense. Just behind the thurifer, a second altar boy solemnly carried a large crucifix, followed by two more altar boys walking side by side bearing lit candles. A deacon was next, holding aloft a large Book of Gospels. He was followed by two priests, hands folded, singing with hearty voices. Finally it was the archbishop himself, dressed in his ornate robes and wearing a beautiful gold and silver colored miter. He carried his pastoral staff and strode confidently among his flock.

The archbishop is celebrating the mass, Trevor thought. *Only this is the new archbishop.* He wondered if he would be as interesting as Archbishop Hughes had been on Trevor's first and only other visit for mass at St. Louis Cathedral—the mother church of the Archdiocese of New Orleans.

20

The Sign

Lucanus quickly brushed his paint upon the small sign, writing what Pilate had asked him to write. Greek, Latin, and Hebrew—all were familiar to him, although he much preferred Greek for his own writing. Pilate had been aware for some time that Lucanus liked to paint, so who better to paint this sign? Painting seemed to relax him and give him some momentary peace in this troubled place. *There, it is written, just as Pilate wants it.* As he took up the sign and looked at it more closely, he thought about what he just painted upon it. *This is most certain to cause confusion and anger among some of those who will see it!*

Lucanus rose to his feet with the sign, the paint on it not yet quite dry enough, and he hurried across the courtyard and out into the road. They were all some distance ahead now, but there was still time to catch them. He could hear the shouting in the distance. As Lucanus made his way, he could see people standing along the road, some of them sobbing openly. On the road itself were spots of blood. *Too much blood*, he thought. *Surely this Jesus was growing weak and might even die before the soldiers could crucify him. That would make Pilate's newly painted sign unnecessary.*

"Stand back, all of you!" A very large Roman centurion raised his short sword and made broad, sweeping motions toward the gathering crowd. "Stand back, I tell you!"

Lucanus recognized the centurion as Longinus who, nearly blind from his years of service on the fields of battle, had been relegated to command a small detachment of soldiers charged with the horrible duty of crucifying those unfortunates whom Pilate condemned to death. Lucanus held up the sign he had painted, and Longinus, squinting his eyes and eventually recognizing Lucanus with some difficulty, waved him forward.

"Let this man through by order of Pontius Pilate, prefect of Judea," the huge man bellowed as Lucanus made his way past the crowd. "Let this man pass!"

As Lucanus approached the other soldiers, he could see one of them raising a hammer and bringing it down soundly on a metal spike. This man Jesus screamed in pain as the spike went through his wrist and into the wooden beam beneath him. One look at his face, and Lucanus knew this man was not likely to live much longer.

The soldier holding the hammer stood and turned to Lucanus. "What can I do for you?"

Lucanus offered the sign to the soldier. "Pontius Pilate wants this sign to be placed above this man on the cross."

The soldier motioned with the hammer for the beam to be raised, and with a jolt, the ropes attached to the large rings on either side of the beam raised the beam and this man they called Jesus up from the ground. Jesus cried aloud in his agony as the beam slammed against the upright pole and as he was dragged up near the top of it.

The soldier took the sign and gave it to one of the other soldiers. "Nail this sign above the prophet." Turning to Lucanus, he asked, "Is there anything more?"

"No." Lucanus watched as the soldier took another spike and, with the help of another soldier standing nearby, crossed one of the man's feet over the other. The soldier again raised the hammer, and with a solitary and powerful blow, he struck the spike deeply into the man's feet. A horrible cry came from Jesus, and his head dropped to his chest. *That surely finished it*, Lucanus thought. *The prophet is most certainly dead.*

As the soldiers, Lucanus, and the others looked on, Jesus raised his head and looked at them with tears visible in his eyes. After what seemed a long period of silence, he raised his tearful eyes to the heavens. Then said Jesus, "Father, forgive them, for they know not what they do." Jesus looked directly at Lucanus, and their eyes met. Never had Lucanus witnessed anything like this! This man was praying for those who were torturing and killing him! He was praying for those who stood there and watched, many of whom were mocking him and cursing him. He wasn't praying for himself; he was praying for them!

One of the soldiers climbed up behind the cross and fastened the sign, which Lucanus had hastily painted, above the head of Jesus. "This is the king of the Jews." Some of those who had gathered shouted their protest at reading the words. "Take it down! That is blasphemy! This blasphemer is not our king!"

The centurion and some of the other soldiers angrily confronted the crowd.

"Be quiet and get back," Longinus, the centurion, shouted with authority. "The sign is by the command of Pontius Pilate himself! Get back!"

Lucanus felt suddenly ashamed. He was a Roman citizen, and he was ashamed. He stumbled back and realized his eyes were burning from the sting of his own tears as he looked at this Jesus of Nazareth agonizing and dying on the cross. There were two others who had also been crucified along with Jesus, one on either side. One of the men, who himself was dying, mocked Jesus. The other man, also dying, admonished the first man for his mockery. And he said unto Jesus, "Lord, remember me when thou comest into thy kingdom."

Jesus looked at the second man, and Jesus said unto him, "Verily I say unto thee, today thou shalt be with me in paradise."

Jesus looked at Lucanus, and once again, their gazes met. As Jesus looked at him, Lucanus felt his knees grow weak as he knelt to the ground in shame for his part in this innocent man's death. Blinded by his tears, Lucanus hung his head and wept.

Jesus of Nazareth, King of the Jews

INRI—Trevor remembered reading James Joyce's *Ulysses* in college, which was one of his father's favorite books. There was a copy of it in the library at the house, which his dad kept from his college days. What was it Leopold Bloom thought as he looked at those letters during a visit to mass? Oh yes, now Trevor remembered: INRI—iron nails ran in. Trevor somehow would occasionally think of that passage, yet he never quite understood why. It seems he thought of it lately whenever he saw a large crucifix. Although the sign was purported to have been written in letters representing the three languages common in Jerusalem at the time of Jesus, *INRI* were the letters representing Latin, weren't they? Didn't those letters stand for *Iesus Nazarenus Rex Iudaeorum*, which—translated into English—meant *Jesus of Nazareth, King of the Jews*?

Unexpectedly, Trevor looked on in horror as Jesus, nailed upon the cross above the altar, opened his eyes, and tears of blood began to trickle down his face. The blood dripped into the gold chalice the archbishop raised to catch his blood. Then Jesus looked directly at Trevor and fixed his tortured gaze upon him, and Trevor felt his sorrow burn deeply into his very soul. Then said Jesus, "Father, forgive them, for they know not what they do."

As Jesus looked at him, Trevor felt his knees grow weak as he knelt to the ground in shame for his part in this innocent man's death. Blinded by his tears, Trevor hung his head and wept.

"Trevor! What's the matter with you? Are you all right?"

Trevor looked up at Katie, who was kneeling beside him. As he looked around, he realized he was on his knees in the middle of the aisle, and he could see that mass had stopped. Everyone, including the archbishop, stared at him. The cathedral was deathly quiet. He looked for the large crucifix hanging above the altar, but to Trevor's astonishment, the crucifix was not there! "Katie, I…what happened?"

Katie looked at Trevor with a bewildered expression on her face. "Trevor, come. Let's go outside and get you some fresh air."

As Katie helped him get to his feet, Trevor remembered once again how he felt when he spilled the wine as an altar boy. He felt that way now, confused and embarrassed by what had happened and not knowing what to say or to whom to say it. Somehow he didn't think the archbishop would laugh about this incident later to make him feel better, as the kindly priest had done when he spilled the wine as an altar boy and disrupted mass so long ago. As he and Katie walked down the aisle and made their way toward the cathedral entrance, he could feel everyone's eyes upon him. He was somewhat relieved when he heard the archbishop continue with mass as he and Katie reached the first set of doors. Moments later, they were outside and walking across the street into Jackson Square. It was a beautiful morning, and soon he and Katie had reached a park bench and sat down. There were a number of people milling about, but Trevor hardly noticed them.

"Trevor," Katie began in a worried voice, "are you all right?"

"I'm fine, I think. What happened? How did I get into the aisle like that?"

"Don't you remember?" Katie asked, perplexed.

"No, I…I think I must have fallen asleep, maybe? I was looking, or dreaming I was looking, at a large crucifix above the altar. I was thinking about the sign at the top of the cross, and then suddenly Jesus came to life and looked at me. There was blood running down from his eyes and dripping into the chalice the archbishop was holding up to him to catch it all. Jesus just kept looking at me, and then you were there, and everyone was looking at me."

Katie sat stunned, looking at her friend. "Oh, Trevor, what is happening to you? There is no large crucifix above the altar! You imagined it all!"

"What did I do?" Trevor asked. "How did I end up on my knees in the aisle?"

"You were standing by me in the pew as the archbishop held up the chalice in final preparation for communion. Suddenly you stepped out into the aisle and called out to the archbishop, saying something like, 'My lord, with tears in his eyes, he looked to the heavens and asked his Father to forgive us for what we had done.' And then you fell to your knees and began to weep."

Trevor looked at Katie in disbelief. "I did all that? I don't remember anything but what I told you. I thought I was just thinking or daydreaming. I don't remember doing or saying anything!"

"Come on, Trevor. Let's take you home. We'll talk about this some more later, and then we can figure out what we should do."

Trevor looked at Katie, and she could see he had tears welling up in his eyes. "Katie, do you think I'm losing my mind?"

Katie shook her head. "No, I think you are terribly sleep-deprived, that's all. People do strange things when they don't get enough sleep. Come on, let's go."

Trevor stood and looked at Katie doubtfully. "I hope that's all it is, but something tells me it's more than that."

As they began walking in the direction of where Katie had parked her car, Trevor stopped suddenly. "Katie, what else have I done that I don't remember?"

Katie smiled weakly. "Nothing, maybe the sleepwalking business you spoke about, but nothing else, I'm sure. Let's forget about all this for now and get back to your house. You'll feel better once we've had something to eat, and then we can talk some more."

"All right, whatever you think is best. I just hope I haven't done anything we don't know about."

"I'm sure you haven't," Katie said reassuringly. "Or we would know about it by now, don't you think?"

Trevor smiled and gave a small sigh of relief. "I hope you're right. It seems I have enough to worry about as it is. It's bad enough I'll have to avoid the cathedral for a while now—like the rest of my life maybe."

Katie took Trevor's hand in hers with a reassuring grasp. "Don't be silly! Of course, I'm right! Now, come on. Let's get out of here before mass ends, or we'll be stuck in traffic."

As they walked to her car, Katie tried to hide her concern about Trevor and wondered to herself if she really was right after all.

The Building Storm

As the wind picked up, Caleb looked at how restless the sheep were beginning to get. The sky was getting much darker now, yet the heat of the day seemed as hot as it always was at this time of day. "Judah, look at the flocks! Look at the sky! Do you not see? We must go now."

"Caleb, we cannot leave this now. It is almost free. We must keep digging. It is heavy, but we can move it a little now. With just a little more work—"

"No, Judah, we must go now." Caleb stopped digging and stood up. "The sheep are restless, and the storm is near. We have no more time. We should have left hours ago. We will be lucky to reach the lowlands as it is. Let us cover this up with more rock, and we will come back to it again."

Judah stopped digging and looked at his friend. "I am sorry, Caleb, but I cannot leave this behind, not now. You must take the sheep yourself. I will catch up with you. I think this chest may be made of gold as I have said, and if it is made of gold, who knows what may be inside it?"

"This chest is not going anywhere, Judah, and with the storm that is building, I will need your help with the sheep. We have waited far too long already."

"But I believe this is gold, Caleb! You are the one who wants to stop being a shepherd someday, the one who wants a big house and big car in America. This chest, if it *is* gold, may be the way you can do those things you dream of doing!"

"It is true I have dreams, Judah, but you and I have responsibility to our sheep, and you do not know this is gold. It may be only brass like I think it is, and it may be empty. It is very old, and it has been here a very long time. It can wait a day or so longer."

"No, Caleb, someone else may find it now. We have almost dug it out. We cannot hide it now, not with some little pile of rock like you did before. No, Caleb, I cannot leave this now. You must take care of our flocks. You have done so before. You have told me so. You just took care of them yourself when I was hurt, or we thought I was hurt, did you not?"

"That is another thing, Judah," Caleb answered with a slight trembling in his voice. "How do we explain you being hurt on this thing in the earth, and yet it turns out you were not hurt at all?"

Judah shook his head as he kept digging. "There is no explanation. You and I have discussed it."

"We also talked about this thing being something we should not play around with. We do not know if it is good or if it is evil."

Judah laughed at his friend. "Do not be so foolish, Caleb. It was you who talked about that, not me. How can a *thing* be good or evil? You go. You take our flocks to the lowlands before the storm. Leave one of the donkeys and some rope for me. I will catch up to you with the chest. You will see. We will be rich, Caleb!"

As Judah continued to dig, almost as if he was possessed by the thought of the ancient chest and what it might contain, Caleb knew it was no use to try to convince him any longer. Judah would not leave until the chest and whatever it held was freed from the earth. "Very well, Judah, I will go. I just hope I can manage without your help. The sheep are very restless now, and the storm is soon upon us. You are being very foolish, Judah. I hope we are not making a big mistake."

"It will all be fine, Caleb. You hurry and take the sheep to the lowlands. I will not be long behind you."

Caleb looked to the darkening sky as he caught one of the donkeys and tied it to some brush near where Judah continued his madness. The donkey tugged at the rope, probably because it did not understand why it was being left behind and not going with Caleb and the sheep and perhaps fearful of the coming storm.

As Caleb walked among the sheep and the three remaining donkeys, trying to keep the animals on the path to the lowland, he began to worry. The sheep and even the donkeys were really reacting nervously, but perhaps it was not too late. He would hurry now and do what he could do to reach the lowland and find some shelter and protection before the storm struck. As he looked back one last time, he could see Judah still digging desperately to free what was buried on the rocky slope. It was not like Judah to abandon his flock. Something told Caleb that he should not have marked the place where this thing they found was buried after all. He had a very bad feeling about it all now, and he was worried—not only about the animals but also for his friend.

23

Father Archer's Opinion

As FATHER ARCHER drove up in front of Trevor's house and pulled into the driveway behind Katie's Volkswagen, he could see Katie swinging in a glider on the front porch. As he shut off the engine and got out of the car to make his way toward the porch steps, Katie waved, and he waved back. In a few moments, he was seated across from her in a comfortable rocking chair.

"Trevor isn't available right now, Father. He had a very restless night and is still trying to get some sleep. I checked on him a few minutes ago. He's restless but seems to be sleeping."

Father Archer sighed and looked almost relieved. "That is all right, Katie. It is you I really wanted to see. I would have stopped by to speak with you yesterday after mass, but considering what happened, I thought it best to wait until today and try to speak with you alone."

"Father, I am so worried about Trevor. I just don't know what to do! He thinks he's losing his mind."

"Did he explain himself to you, Katie? I mean, about what happened at the cathedral yesterday?"

"He doesn't remember much of it—only that he was thinking or daydreaming about a crucifix above the altar and the body of Jesus coming to life with blood dripping from His eyes. He didn't realize he had done anything until I asked him on the aisle what he was doing."

Father Archer shook his head. "There is no crucifix above the altar."

"I know. I told him he imagined that too."

"This is all really becoming quite difficult to sort out, isn't it?"

Katie looked at Father Archer hopefully. "Father, did you come to any conclusions during your visit here Saturday night?"

"Well, yes and no, Katie." Father Archer leaned forward and spoke softly, "There really isn't anything particular that I noticed about the house, as much as it was what I began to realize after I had left."

Katie shook her head. "I'm not sure I understand, Father. Surely you must think it is this house—that it is haunted or possessed or whatever it is that Catholics believe about such things—and it is affecting Trevor in some way."

"Katie, I really don't believe this house is haunted."

"Then what is going on here, Father?"

"Katie, whatever is causing these dreams and other things to happen is not because of this house. I think it is something in Trevor's own mind."

"You think it's something in Trevor's own mind!" Katie said in surprise. "You can't be serious!"

"After what happened at the cathedral yesterday? I'm very serious and more convinced than ever that, whatever the cause is, it is triggered by something that lies solely with Trevor."

Katie shook her head. "But I don't understand!"

Father Archer leaned back in the rocking chair and looked at Katie for a long moment. "Katie, Saturday night, when I spoke with Trevor, I had the feeling at times he wanted to tell me something."

"Tell you something like what?"

"I don't know, but it almost seemed at times that he was preoccupied. On the one hand, he seemed the perfect skeptic, but on the other, he seemed genuinely concerned—almost frightened."

"Well, of course he's concerned, Father," Katie answered. "I'm concerned too. I'm also a bit frightened by all this, and I'm worried about Trevor. It is this house, Father—I just know this house holds the answer. I mean, look at this place! It is big and old, and I can tell you now from personal experience it can be a frightening place at night!"

"Katie, you told me you heard voices and saw a ghost?"
"That's right. I did."
"Where were the voices you heard coming from?"
"I heard the voices upstairs, in Trevor's room."

Father Archer nodded. "And this ghostly woman you saw? Where did you see her?"

"I saw her in Trevor's room, upstairs." Katie looked at Father Archer curiously. "What are you getting at, Father?"

"Was Trevor awake when you heard these voices and saw the ghost?"

Katie shook her head. "No, he was asleep. Why? What difference does that make?"

"What about yesterday? What happened during mass? Didn't Trevor tell you he thought he was dreaming?"

"I think what he said was that he was *thinking or daydreaming*, Father."

"But that suggests he wasn't in the moment, am I correct? He wasn't, was he? His thoughts were somewhere else."

Katie had to agree with the logic. "I suppose so, but the question is why? I'm still convinced it all has something to do with this house."

"Trevor was at the cathedral yesterday. Does it have something to do with the cathedral too? Do you think maybe the cathedral is haunted?"

Katie smiled facetiously. "Well, I suppose it could be. Aren't there stories about a priest and about the voodoo queen Marie Laveau making ghostly appearances there from time to time?"

Father Archer sighed. "Come now, Katie, let's be serious."

"I know, Father. It's just that I can't quite come to grips with all this."

Father Archer stood up from the chair and sat down again on the glider beside Katie. "Katie, listen to me. This isn't something I ever thought I'd be discussing, but have you ever heard of a telepath?"

Death of a Prophet

Lucanus stood in the distance as he noticed the centurion and the soldiers under his command talking as they looked at the sky. The sun was setting, and it would soon be dark—again. Lucanus recalled that it was about noon when a sudden darkness came over the land, which lasted for three hours. The sun had been completely eclipsed.

Lucanus overheard members of the Jewish council, who had been watching the crucifixion, being told shortly after three o'clock that the veil of the temple had been violently torn in half. It was at that very time that Jesus looked again to the heavens and, with all his remaining strength, cried out in a loud voice, "Father, into your hands I commend my spirit."

As Jesus took his last ragged breath and his head dropped to his chest, the darkness that prevailed from the sixth to the ninth hour passed, and the sun reappeared from beneath its shroud. Lucanus moved a little closer, and he heard Longinus, the centurion, say in a low voice, as if to himself, "Truly, this was a righteous man!"

At long last, nightfall came quietly with the setting sun as this most horrible of days was finally near an end. Most of the onlookers had left or were leaving, and only a few, in addition to the Roman soldiers, remained. One of the men, who had stood much of the day among those whom Lucanus perceived to be the family and followers of Jesus, was now walking toward him.

"You are one of Pilate's household, are you not?" the man asked.

"I am the physician of Pontius Pilate. Do I know you?"

"I do not think so," the man answered. "I am Joseph of Arimathea. I have a request to make of Pilate."

"Why come to me? You must go to him directly with your request."

Joseph nodded. "I know, Physician, yet I do not know if he would speak with me. I am quite certain he wants little to do with anyone who is a member of the Jewish council at the moment."

Lucanus reacted in surprise. "You are on the council? *You* are one who demanded Pontius Pilate crucify this Jesus of Nazareth?"

"I am on the council, yes, but I did not agree with the actions taken by the others. I did not consent to it, and I argued against it, but the number of those who considered Jesus a blasphemer was just too great."

Lucanus felt uneasy. "Why do you come to me? As I have told you, I am only Pilate's physician."

"Perhaps, in your position, you can get me an audience with him so I can make my request?"

Lucanus shook his head. "I know nothing about this request of yours and have no interest in taking you to him if you believe he will not welcome you."

"My request is a simple one. The body of Jesus of Nazareth still hangs upon that cross. I would like to ask Pontius Pilate to allow the body of Jesus to be released to me."

Lucanus looked at Joseph in surprise. "Release the body of the prophet to you? For what purpose would you make such a request? Surely you must know it is not the practice of Rome to release the bodies of crucified criminals to anyone. They are usually left upon the crosses as a warning to others and for the wild animals to dispose of."

Joseph nodded. "I am sadly aware of that barbaric practice. But this is a different matter. Jesus was not a criminal. My purpose is to allow the family and friends of Jesus time to prepare the body for proper burial. I have a tomb close by, which I had intended for myself, that may be used now for Jesus. Physician, you know Jesus did not deserve this death."

Lucanus was startled by what he just heard. "How is it you tell me what *I* know in this matter?"

"I watched you. You were moved by his death. You wept as you fell to your knees in your remorse. You have been here since they nailed him to the cross—just like the rest of us who believe in him and who have remained here."

"Believe in him? Believe in him for what?"

Joseph looked compassionately at Lucanus. "Do you not know? I think you do."

Lucanus wanted to walk away from this Joseph of Arimathea but found that he could not. There was something in what he said that Lucanus knew in his heart to be true. It was true that he had remained throughout the crucifixion, but why? What was it that affected him so deeply? "I do not know what to say to you on this matter, so I will say nothing."

"That is all right to say nothing, my son, but will you help me? Will you take me to see Pontius Pilate?"

Lucanus heard at that moment an agonizing scream and looked to the top of the hill, where a Roman soldier had just broken the legs of one of the thieves crucified with the prophet. "They are breaking their legs now that the sun has finally set. That will hurry along their deaths and end their suffering."

"Jesus is already dead."

Lucanus shook his head. "It will not matter. They will want to be sure he is dead. Look," Lucanus said, pointing toward the top of the hill. "They will break the legs of your Jesus of Nazareth next."

"No, my son. For you see, it is written that 'not a bone of his shall be broken,' so these soldiers will not break the legs of Jesus."

"What are you talking about? Look for yourself! See there? Look!"

As the two men watched, one of the Roman soldiers standing before Jesus on the cross was raising a club to smash Jesus's legs when Longinus, the centurion, suddenly stepped up and stopped him. Longinus then took a spear and pierced the prophet's side instead.

"Do you see?" Joseph said knowingly. "It is also written that 'they will look upon him whom they have pierced,' which we all are now doing. Now, will you take me to see Pontius Pilate?"

Just then, the other thief screamed in agony as one of the soldiers broke his legs with a club. Lucanus felt a wave of fear come over him as he looked at Joseph in disbelief. "Who *are* you? How did you know the soldiers would not break the legs of Jesus but that the centurion would pierce his side with a spear instead?"

"It was long ago written in the holy scriptures that 'not a bone of his shall be broken' and that 'they will look upon him whom they have pierced,' whose prophecy has now, before our very eyes, been fulfilled."

"Who, Joseph of Arimathea, was responsible for this writing?" Lucanus asked.

"Physician, there will be much more written now. Because of what we have witnessed here this day, death is now *only* the beginning." Joseph looked at Lucanus with an intensity that gave Lucanus an extraordinary feeling. "Perhaps even you, being an educated man, will write what you have heard and observed about Jesus one day. After all, was it *not* you who wrote Pilate's words for him that hang above Jesus on his cross?"

Lucanus looked up and saw the sign he had painted at Pilate's command only hours before. "This is the king of the Jews." He felt at once ashamed as he looked again at Jesus and the two thieves hanging upon their crosses atop the hill. He looked at Joseph and nodded. "Come, I will take you into the palace courtyard and give you introduction to Pontius Pilate's personal guards on duty, but from there, you must be on your own."

A Wall of Sand

A SUDDEN GUST of wind caught Judah by surprise as he almost lost his balance. As Judah looked into the distance, he realized the sky had a strange hue to it, and he could feel tiny grains of sand beginning to pelt his face and sting his eyes. *Caleb was right*, Judah thought. *There is a storm coming!*

The last few hours had been difficult for Judah to dig. The sand was packed tightly and almost like solid rock. Judah had made progress, but it was slowgoing. Judah was determined to free the treasure as he dug feverishly, exposing a little more of the ancient chest. *I am so close*, Judah thought. He tried once again to move the large chest, and this time, he found some success. "It is moving!" Judah cried aloud. "I must get the donkey!" Excitedly he got to his feet so he could get the trusty animal to help him pull the chest from the sandy grave where it had been hidden for so long. But as Judah turned to where Caleb had tied the donkey, he stopped short. The donkey was gone!

Judah realized the wind was very strong now, and he was horrified to see a wall of sand coming over the rise. There was no more time! He quickly moved to the little clumps of brush and piles of rock where the donkey had been tied, and he crouched behind the rocks and brush, which seemed to offer the most protection, as the massive sandstorm poured down upon him. Judah struggled with his kaffiyeh, trying to cover his face so he could breathe. Judah could no longer see anything around him—not even the brush and rock he huddled behind but which he could still feel with his hands. He stayed close to the rock and brush, trying to find the most shelter he could from the storm that had come so quickly and violently upon him.

The sand was swiftly piling around him, and Judah struggled to stay close enough to the rock and brush in order for him to breathe. He kept his eyes tightly shut, and his mind began to swirl as he listened to the howling wind. And darkness closed around him. Judah was frightened as it became more and more difficult for him, as he struggled for each and every breath. Slowly he began losing consciousness inside the massive and powerful wall of swirling sand.

Father Archer's Plan

Katie wondered as she stood along Canal Street, watching for Father Archer's car, if they were doing the right thing. She was still convinced it was the house that was causing Trevor's sleeping difficulty, and she couldn't quite accept Father Archer's idea that it was somehow all in Trevor's mind. *I heard the voices myself! I saw the woman in white! I saw Trevor sleeping on his bed and walking toward me in a transparent form at the same time!*

A quick honking sound startled Katie, and as she looked in the direction it came from, she saw Father Archer's car signaling and pulling near the curb where she was standing. There was a momentary lull in traffic as Katie quickly got into the car and fastened her seat belt.

"You were right where you promised to be," Father Archer said, smiling, as he looked in his side-view mirror and drove his car back into traffic. "I hope you weren't waiting too long?"

Katie shook her head. "No, I was there only a few moments actually." Katie looked seriously at Father Archer. "Are we really doing the right thing, Father? I mean, I am having trouble believing this is all in Trevor's mind—particularly when I have heard the voices and seen for myself what Trevor is dreaming about."

"Well, I'm sure my superiors would question what I'm thinking as well. The church has had some discussions on the theory of telepathy over the past few years, and the general consensus is that further study needs to be completed to determine whether such a theory is sound."

"Then why, Father, are we doing this?"

"Consider it further study, Katie. This is a rare opportunity to find out for ourselves whether there is merit in telepathy, don't you agree?"

Katie shook her head. "I'm not sure, Father. I don't like the idea of making Trevor some type of guinea pig in an experiment."

Father Archer chuckled. "No one is making anyone a guinea pig, particularly your friend Trevor. Trevor is troubled by a lack of sleep and dreams he cannot understand. I believe he's still very deeply affected by his father's death." Father

Archer glanced at Katie as he signaled a turn off Canal Street. "Trevor's father was apparently very interested in biblical history toward the end of his life, which I think is all a part of these dreams Trevor has been having."

"But why would his father's interest have anything to do with Trevor's dreams? If they are just dreams, then what was it I heard and saw the other night?"

"All good questions, Katie," Father Archer answered. "Which is why a visit to Dr. Gallagher's office might provide us with some answers."

"Who is this Dr. Gallagher anyway?"

"Well, he used to be a priest."

Katie looked at Father Archer with surprise. "We're going to see a fallen priest?"

Father Archer laughed aloud. "See a fallen priest? Where on earth did you come up with that notion?"

Katie looked serious. "I thought once you were a priest, you were always a priest? I've heard the ones who aren't were either kicked out of the church, or they left it because they wanted to get married or some such thing."

Father Archer shook his head and smiled as he signaled another turn and pulled into a large parking lot, stopping to wait for a parking stub. "Father Gallagher—I mean, Dr. Gallagher—was not 'kicked out of the church,' and he didn't leave it because he wanted to get married." The parking attendant handed him a parking stub, and as the control arm was raised, Father Archer drove forward and began looking for an open space to park in. "Dr. Gallagher wanted to pursue certain theories that the church did not embrace, so he left the priesthood in the pursuit of science, in addition to his religious beliefs." Finding an open spot, he parked the car and turned off the ignition. "He is considered a *former* priest, not a *fallen* one."

Katie sighed. "From the way my mother raised me, I'm not sure there's much difference."

As the two stepped from the car, Father Archer looked at Katie. "What would your father have thought about it, do you think?"

Katie smiled. "I would guess it wouldn't have bothered him a bit, but then you know as well as I that he had more doubts about religion than he did about science."

Father Archer nodded in agreement. "That is very true. Science could prove or disprove things, which your father always wanted the church to be able to do. Since the church couldn't prove or disprove many of its teachings, like science seemed to prove or disprove most of its theories, your father could never quite bring himself to just have an unquestioned faith in the church."

"My father was certainly not the only one who struggled with his faith."

"I know that's true," Father Archer agreed sadly. "There are many like your father—many who won't admit it as he did. Faith in what cannot be explained is very difficult, to be sure."

As they walked toward the office building, which stretched ten or more stories toward the sky, Katie renewed her question. "So aside from being a fallen—ah, *former*—priest, what does this Dr. Gallagher really know about telepathy and hypnotism?"

Father Archer reached out and opened the entrance door, standing aside for Katie to enter. "Let's go in and find out, shall we?"

A Man of Light

When he heard the news, Pilate summoned the elite members of his guard to arrest the centurion Longinus and his small detachment assigned to watch over the sepulcher where Jesus of Nazareth had been entombed. The men had been put in chains and brought before him in the judgment hall. "You realize, of course, that the penalty for falling asleep while on duty as a Roman soldier is death?"

The men were struck from behind by their captors, and they fell to their knees on the hard marble floor. As they knelt before Pilate, one of the men looked up at him and spoke, "My lord, we did not fall asleep at our watch."

Pilate scoffed in anger. "You dare speak falsely to me when I know what you did?"

"We did not fall asleep, my lord, but to tell you what did happen would not be believed. I cannot believe myself what happened, and yet I was there and saw with my own eyes."

"Saw? You saw what? What am I to do with you men unless you give me some reason to spare your lives? If you were not asleep on your watch, then what happened?"

The man who had spoken for the others just looked at Pilate, unable to speak further.

"Answer me!" Pilate shouted as he struck the man a heavy blow with the back of his hand. "Answer me or be put to death!"

Longinus, the centurion, spoke. "My lord, there was a man who appeared from nowhere deep in the dark night. This man had the strength of ten men, and he was bright white, as bright as the sun when it is highest in the sky, so bright it hurt my eyes to look upon him. We were all like dead men in his presence and could neither move nor speak. This man of light—by himself, my lord—rolled away the large stone that would have taken several of my men to move. Then, my lord, an even brighter light came from inside the tomb, and the sounds of a thousand voices rang out through the night sky. As I watched in fear, my heart beating hard and fast against my ribs, the man who had been placed dead in the tomb appeared! He walked out of the tomb and looked right at us! Then the man turned and walked toward Jerusalem. That was the last I saw or remember until the light of morning when, once again, I was able to speak and move my limbs. We looked inside the tomb and could see it was empty, except for the linen where the body had been. We dared not go inside the tomb but stood outside it, trying to understand what had taken place. We discussed among us what we were going to say that would be believed, but we could not believe ourselves what we have seen."

Pilate scoffed. "Longinus, you are practically a blind man! What could you have possibly seen that I should believe?"

Longinus looked beyond Pilate at a limestone tablet leaning against the far wall. "Do you see the writing on that tablet on the far wall behind you, my lord?"

Pilate looked behind him and then fixed his eyes upon Longinus once again. "I can see it, but I'm surprised you can."

"I can see the tablet and what is written upon it: 'To Tiberius Caesar from Pontius Pilate, Prefect of Judea.' Is that not what is written there, my lord?"

Pilate looked behind him once again and could scarcely make out the writing himself. He turned to Longinus in surprise. "That tablet was finished only days ago. You could not have seen it before. How is it that a nearly blind man can read what I myself can hardly read from this distance?"

"My lord, do with me what you will. I have no fear of death. But I speak the truth. As nightfall came on that terrible day that I, by your order, crucified Jesus of Nazareth, I took my lance and pierced his side to be certain his suffering had ceased. A splatter of his blood and water came into my eyes, and as I kneel before you now, my lord, I swear from that moment, my sight was restored to me! Truly, he was a most righteous man."

Pilate was astonished by the centurion's words and looked upon the trembling guards, who no doubt realized that their deaths were imminent. Pilate was angered and insulted by the story Longinus had told, but something in his heart told him that he could be speaking the truth of the matter—especially since he knew he and his men were about to die. Pilate felt a wave of fear come over him as he thought about this Jesus, who had stood before him on nearly this very spot just three days before. He remembered that same wave of fear then as he looked into the eyes of the prophet on that regrettable morning. Pilate was not about to make another mistake this time. Yet the centurion's story was so incredible! Could such things be possible?

One of Pilate's elite guards, who had taken custody of the men now kneeling before Pilate, stepped forward with his short sword drawn. "What do you want us to do with these curs, my lord?"

Pilate stood silently a moment then shook his head and waved the guard back with his hand. "I want you to free them."

The guard reacted in surprise. "You want us to *free them*?"

"What I said, I said." Pilate was certain the guards might think he believed this incredible story, and he did not want them to spread that belief. "I pardon Longinus and his men for this unfortunate incident, but if there is one word uttered about this 'man of light' or any other part of this absurd story outside these walls, the one who speaks it will forfeit his life."

They all looked at one another in bewilderment as Longinus and his men got to their feet, and the guards freed them from their shackles. One by one, the pardoned men acknowledged what Pilate had commanded and thanked him for his unexpected mercy. The procurator of Judea had never before been one to forgive such a breach of trust or to show such mercy.

"Longinus, you and your men are no longer in my service. I want you all gone from here at once. If I should see any of you again, the ones I see shall be put to death. Am I understood?"

Longinus looked at his men and then at Pilate. "You are understood, my lord. We will take our leave as you demand."

As Longinus and his men disappeared through the massive bronze doors of the judgment hall, Pilate turned to his elite guard, who stood in disbelief at what had just taken place. "There is one more thing. I want some of you to accompany me to this empty tomb. I want to see it with my own eyes."

Dr. Gallagher

As the secretary hung up the telephone, she stood up from her desk. "Dr. Gallagher is ready to see you now," she said as she smiled at Father Archer and Katie. "Please follow me." She led them down a hallway then opened a large mahogany door and stepped aside. "Here we are."

Dr. Gallagher was a man of about sixty years of age, a little heavyset, with a full head of wavy gray hair. "Thank you, Brenda. That will be all." He stepped forward and gave Father Archer a hearty handshake then turned with a broad Irish grin to Katie. "Come in, come in!"

In a moment, both Katie and Father Archer were seated next to each other on a large leather couch.

"It looks like you are doing very well for yourself, Joseph," Father Archer chided. "Science has been treating you very well indeed."

Dr. Gallagher opened up an ornate bar and turned with his wide Irish grin still intact. "What can I get you? Brandy, Scotch, a glass of wine perhaps?"

Katie looked at her watch. It was two o'clock. "I'll just have a soft drink if you have one."

"You'll have a soft drink! What kind of an Irish Catholic are you, child?" Dr. Gallagher bellowed a hearty laugh. "All right, a soft drink it is. Why don't you step over to that little refrigerator over there and choose your poison?"

"I'll have an Irish whiskey, Joseph, which I suspect you'll be having?"

"Ahhh, you know that is precisely what I'm having."

As Dr. Gallagher poured the whiskey, Katie made her way to the refrigerator, which was nearly full of every type of soft drink she could imagine. After making her choice, she returned to her seat on the couch as Dr. Gallagher handed a drink to Father Archer and sat down on the couch facing them. "Now then, tell me all about this young man you think may be a telepath."

Father Archer sipped his drink and looked at Katie then at Dr. Gallagher. "Katie here knows him best, so she will be able to answer more of your questions than I will, but let me see if I can bring you somewhat up to speed. The young man's name is Trevor. He's in his early thirties. His father died within the past year or so. He lives alone in a large Victorian house out in the Garden District. He is an adjunct professor at Loyola. He sleeps very little, and he dreams quite a lot about ancient Romans."

Dr. Gallagher shook his head and chuckled. "I hope your sermons aren't quite that succinct, Donald, but that does give me the framework." Dr. Gallagher sipped his drink and then turned his attention to Katie. "I assume you will now fill in that framework of this young fellow for me?"

Katie told Dr. Gallagher everything she thought important about Trevor, from the time they first met in college to the events of recent days. Dr. Gallagher seemed to take everything in stride with fairly mild interest until she described what had taken place a few nights before. It was when she described what she herself had heard and seen that he sat forward with a serious look on his face.

"*You* heard these voices and saw these apparitions *yourself?*"

Katie nodded. "Yes, I did." Katie looked at Father Archer and then looked again at Dr. Gallagher. "That is why I really think we might be wasting your time, Dr. Gallagher. If this is all in Trevor's mind, I don't see how it is possible that I can experience it too."

Dr. Gallagher leaned back on his couch and looked thoughtful for a moment. He stood up and began pacing back and forth then sat down again and looked at Katie as he spoke. "To begin with, telepathy is the ability of one mind to impress, or be impressed by, another mind. So from what you tell me, we have something here that is very interesting indeed! It would seem that Trevor may be opening an entirely new chapter in the study of telepathy!"

Father Archer looked at Katie cautiously as he spoke. "Joseph, I don't know about Katie, but I'm not following you. What are you saying?"

"Don't you see?" Dr. Gallagher said excitedly as he took another sip from his drink. "We aren't merely discussing a transfer of thought from one mind to another—what you could call a natural causality. From what Katie here has told us that she herself has observed, these experiences that Trevor and Katie are having suggest preternatural causality!"

Katie shook her head. "Wow, I'm afraid you've lost me completely now, Dr. Gallagher."

Father Archer stood up and took the last sip of his drink, suddenly looking as deeply in thought as Dr. Gallagher had looked a few moments before. "Preternatural causality, Katie, if I'm following Joseph here, would suggest that Trevor is receiving telepathic communication from the spirit world."

Dr. Gallagher jumped to his feet. "That is precisely correct, Donald! That is precisely what I'm trying to tell you!" Dr. Gallagher laughed his hearty laugh and turned to Katie. "You saw a real spirit, young lady! Your friend Trevor appears to have the ability to not only communicate with the living but also with the dead—and apparently, he can do *both* at the same time!"

"What? You can't be serious!"

Father Archer looked at Katie and put his hand on her shoulder. "Really, Joseph, don't you think you may be getting way ahead of yourself?"

"Not at all, Donald. You don't really believe that exorcists are the only people who have the ability to communicate with the spirit world, do you?"

"As a former priest, Joseph, you know full well our beliefs inside the church are much more restricted than they are outside the church."

"That is precisely why I'm no longer a priest, dear friend! Sometimes it is necessary to break the archaic bonds that hold us back from science and learning. Don't get me wrong—religion in general and the church in particular are still very important, but science helps to fill in the gaps. It's just such a pity we can't all play nicely together and reconcile the two." Dr. Gallagher rubbed his hands together and turned to face Katie, once again with his big Irish grin. "Now, dear girl, when do I get to put your marvelous young friend Trevor under hypnosis?"

29

The Empty Tomb

As Pilate stepped into the tomb behind two of his most trusted guards, he immediately noticed the empty linen shroud lying on a stone table. As he reached down and picked it up, he could see what appeared to be the image of the Nazarene on the cloth. He flung the shroud to the ground and stepped back in fear. "This cannot be!"

"What is it, my liege?" one of the guards asked, alarmed.

Pilate pointed to the heap of linen on the floor. "That burial shroud, I can see the face of the crucified man upon it!"

The two guards looked at each other, and then one of them picked up the shroud and looked at it. There on the cloth was indeed the image of a man. The two guards looked at it more closely, and one turned to Pilate and spoke. "We see it too. It is from his blood. Do you see here, my liege, that—"

"Roll it up! I do not care to look upon it again just now. I will look at it later."

As one of the guards began rolling up the shroud, something fell from it to the floor of the tomb. The other guard stooped down to pick it up. "Look, my liege, one of your coins!"

Pilate took the coin from the guard and looked at it. It was one of the bronze coins that he, as procurator, had designed and minted for use in Judea. As he looked at it more closely, he saw a spot of what appeared to be dried blood on it. Perhaps the guard was right, and the image on the cloth was nothing more than bloodstains.

"Do you want this napkin as well?" It was one of the guards, holding up a bloodstained smaller cloth that was likely used to cover the crucified man's face.

"Bring it. Bring the shroud and bring anything else you can find that might explain what happened here."

"Very well, my liege."

As Pilate rubbed the dried blood from the coin, he could see the coin was flawed. *This is not my design*, he thought. It was one of the bronze coins he designed, but one of the letters on the coin was wrong. He would remember to look into it and have it corrected, but for now, there were other matters that had to be attended to—chief among them, finding out what happened to the body of this prophet Jesus of Nazareth.

The Hypnotist

Dr. Gallagher took his seat in front of Trevor while Father Archer sat on one side of Dr. Gallagher and Katie sat on the other. "You have quite a magnificent house, Trevor! This parlor is just perfect! Do you have any questions, Trevor, before we begin?" Dr. Gallagher asked.

Trevor smiled and shook his head. "No, Doctor, just promise me you won't make me bark like a dog or do anything embarrassing if this hypnosis thing works."

"You may rest assured," Dr. Gallagher responded, "that hypnosis is not the type of mind-control experience some people believe it to be. I cannot make you do anything you don't want to do or that would be embarrassing for you. Our plan will be to make you relaxed and to focus your concentration and attention to a higher state of awareness, with the hope that, by achieving that goal, it will allow you to explore these dreams you have been having."

"Well, you certainly sound every bit of the hypnotherapeutic doctor Father Archer tells me you are."

"Thank you, Trevor, although I must confess I was a bit surprised Donald agrees with me to hypnotize you at all—hypnosis is not exactly a method that has been embraced as legitimate or, dare I say, even tolerated by the church."

"That's essentially correct, Joseph. Although in this instance, I'm hopeful hypnosis will help Trevor identify what the root of his dreams might be."

"So let me get this straight." Trevor chuckled. "If Dr. Gallagher here can get to the bottom of these dreams with hypnosis, I won't need your services as an exorcist?"

Dr. Gallagher looked with surprise at Trevor then at Father Archer. "You think we are dealing with some evil spirit here, Donald?"

Father Archer shook his head. "No, I don't believe there is any need for an exorcism. Though initially, that *is* what I first came to this house to investigate. As we discussed in your office, Katie asked my help because of her concern for Trevor, but I don't believe there is anything that would require an exorcism. I do, however, believe that there may be some connection between these dreams Trevor has been having and his late father."

"You mentioned something similar to that the other night when you were here. Do you really think my dreams have something to do with my dad?" Trevor asked, caught off guard by Father Archer's sudden revelation.

"Think about it, Trevor. You have mentioned you think of your father frequently, and you talk about your father a fair amount. You live in his house and among many of his possessions. You wear a coin around your neck that he gave you sometime ago, and you told me about a figure you saw recently in a painting at Loyola that you believe is a likeness of your dad."

"I suppose you are right, Father. I just never quite put all of it together in a laundry list like that before."

"Well, if I may," Dr. Gallagher interrupted. "I don't think it is wise to suggest possible reasons for the dreams before we actually attempt learning what we can through hypnosis—that is, if you still want to go through with the process?"

Katie spoke up first. "Oh, Trevor, let's try it? I know you are skeptical about all this, but I know you want some answers too, don't you?"

"Of course, Kate, and you are right that I'm a bit skeptical. But like you say, I want some answers here; so if you're ready, Dr. Gallagher, then so am I."

"All right, Trevor, now try to relax. Donald mentioned a moment ago that you wear a coin around your neck that your father gave you. May I see it?"

Trevor shrugged his shoulders. "Sure." Trevor lifted the silver chain up and over his head and handed the coin and chain to Dr. Gallagher. "Here you are."

Dr. Gallagher looked closely at the coin. "I see this is an ancient Roman coin. When was it your father gave it to you?"

"It was a Christmas gift, the last Christmas before he died."

"And you have worn it since?"

"Yes, I have. I've taken it off a few times when I didn't want the chain to get broken or the coin to get lost, but I've worn it most all the time since Dad gave it to me."

"When did you say you started having these dreams?"

"A short time after my dad died."

"Do you remember if the dreams occur only when you are wearing this coin?"

"I have worn this coin ever since Dad gave it to me, only taking it off for very short periods of time." Trevor smiled. "Why? Do you think this coin has something to do with my dreams?"

Dr. Gallagher sighed. "I don't know, Trevor, and I don't want to suggest that it does. One flaw about hypnosis is that too much prehypnotic suggestion might actually trigger false memories for you, and that is something we do not want to happen. Trevor, would you mind if I used this coin instead of my medallion when I attempt to put you into a hypnotic state?"

"You can do that? Just any old coin will work?"

"We'll see if your coin will work, if I have your permission to try?"

"Sure. Knock yourself out. Oh, wait, that's what you intend to do to me."

Dr. Gallagher, Father Archer, and Katie all laughed.

"You do have a quick wit, my boy," Dr. Gallagher said. "Just remember, you won't actually be unconscious. That's a myth. You will remember most things while under hypnosis—except perhaps for those things your unconscious mind might choose to protect you from. Are you ready?"

"I am if you are," Trevor answered. "Let's get the show on the stage."

"Very well, let's begin." Dr. Gallagher held the coin by the chain before Trevor's eyes and twirled it into a gentle, rhythmic spin. "Look at the coin, Trevor, and free your mind of anything but this coin. Concentrate on the way it spins and shimmers and gleams in the light. Let your thoughts drift back—back to a more pleasant time, a more happy time, as you and your father sat here in this room and talked and laughed together."

Trevor looked at the coin and concentrated on how it spun and shimmered and gleamed in the light, just as Dr. Gallagher asked him to do. Calm seemed to drift over him as the coin began to blur. Soon it seemed he was looking into fog and could no longer see the coin at all. There was something—no, someone—who began taking shape in the fog. As the fog began to disappear, a face gradually started to come into focus. Trevor thought he had seen this face somewhere before, but he couldn't recognize who it was.

Suddenly, Trevor could faintly hear the sound of a man's voice. "Dad, is that you?"

Katie gasped and put her hand to her lips as she, Father Archer, and Dr. Gallagher looked intently at Trevor. Trevor's eyes were open, and he looked extremely peaceful and relaxed.

Dr. Gallagher leaned close to Trevor as he put the chain and coin silently on the coffee table. "Is your dad with you Trevor?"

Trevor's voice seemed much softer and far away. "I can hear a voice—it sounds like my dad's voice, but I'm not sure it is really him."

"If it is not your dad, who is it, Trevor?"

"I don't know. There is someone else here too whose face is vaguely familiar to me, but I just can't place who it is."

"There is a man with you, but you don't know who he is?" Dr. Gallagher asked, looking at Katie and Father Archer, who both sat quietly and obviously concerned by what was taking place. "Trevor? Can you still hear me?"

Trevor looked at Dr. Gallagher as if he were a stranger then spoke in an unfamiliar voice. "I hear you, but I am not Trevor."

"Oh!" Katie spoke in a startled voice.

Father Archer looked at Katie and shook his head, putting a finger to his lips.

Dr. Gallagher spoke softly. "You are not Trevor?"

"No!" Trevor answered.

"Who are you?"

"I am Lucanus of Antioch."

"Why are you here with us? What is your purpose?"

"I have traveled to many places. My purpose later in life was to write a true narrative of what took place in Judea, during the reign of Emperor Tiberius."

"Tiberius Caesar! This is incredible, Joseph! Emperor Tiberius reigned during the time of Christ!"

Dr. Gallagher nodded. "Tell me then, if this is so, how is it you speak my language?"

"The Holy Spirit has allowed me to speak in many languages."

Dr. Gallagher looked with surprise at Father Archer. "The Holy Spirit?"

Father Archer sat back in his chair, stunned at what he was hearing.

Dr. Gallagher looked at Trevor with deepening interest. "Tell me how such things can be?"

"It is through the Holy Spirit I speak to you and to all Gentiles about the kingdom of our Lord and Savior Jesus Christ. Salvation is not meant for the twelve tribes of Israel alone but for all of mankind. I am a Gentile chosen to speak for this purpose."

"How is it that you were chosen, Lucanus of Antioch?"

"I saw Jesus crucified. He looked into my eyes as he hung dying upon the cross. His look gave me salvation. I have written what I have seen with my own eyes, heard with my own ears, and I have learned from those who walked with the Savior. I have come to you to tell you the Word is Truth, and the Truth is Jesus the Lord, Messiah and Savior of all mankind."

"What is it have you written, Lucanus?"

"As Lucanus, I was asked by my most excellent benefactor to learn all I could about Jesus of Nazareth. I was not only my benefactor's physician, but I was his confidant and his friend. He released me from his service and provided funds so I could do what he asked and write a true narrative of all I observed and learned about the crucified prophet. Little did I know in the beginning that I would find myself writing for a much greater purpose using the name Luke."

Dr. Gallagher and Father Archer looked at each other, dumbfounded at what they were hearing. Dr. Gallagher turned his full attention to Trevor. "You have written by the name of Luke? But why not by your own name?"

"As I began my inquiry concerning Jesus, I was given the name Luke, and I was instructed to write under that name by the will of God—even though I would not fully accept this God as my own until sometime later. I directed my narrative to my benefactor—the most excellent Theophilus—in order to conceal his true identity. Sometime later, I would find myself writing my narrative for all mankind."

Dr. Gallagher and Father Archer looked at each other—astonished at what they were hearing. "*Theophilus!*" Father

Archer spoke aloud as Dr. Gallagher and Katie looked at him in surprise.

"Why would you want to conceal the true identity of your benefactor by using the name Theophilus?" Joseph asked.

Trevor sighed, as if he were trying to remember. "Stabbed in the desert…"

Father Archer looked at Trevor. "Stabbed in the desert? Was someone stabbed in the desert? What was your benefactor's true name?"

Trevor sighed again as he appeared to be awakening from his hypnotic state.

"Ask again quickly! We must know!" Father Archer pleaded with Dr. Gallagher.

"What is your benefactor's true name? Who is Theophilus?"

"Theophilus," Trevor whispered as he began to shake his head. "Theophilus?"

Dr. Gallagher persisted as Trevor continued to awaken from his trance, "Yes, Theophilus—you just said Theophilus was your benefactor and your friend!"

Trevor looked directly at Dr. Gallagher, his facial expression now dark and troubled as he spoke in a different voice. "You propose to give me a name that means 'loved by God'?"

Katie gasped as she looked at Trevor and heard the change in his voice. "Dr. Gallagher, what is happening?"

Dr. Gallagher had a look of concern visible on his face. "It would seem another presence has taken the place of Lucanus."

Trevor shook his head violently. "What evil has this man done?" Suddenly he stopped and looked blankly for a few moments at Dr. Gallagher then at Katie and Father Archer. Then, smiling, he calmly spoke in his own voice, "So did I bark like a dog or do any embarrassing tricks?" Trevor looked at Katie then at Dr. Gallagher and at Father Archer. Trevor's smile slowly faded and was replaced by a puzzled look. "What's the matter with all of you? Did it work or not?"

Dr. Gallagher picked up the coin and chain from the coffee table. "It worked, perhaps too well, but in any event, welcome back, Trevor."

"Oh, Trevor, are you all right?" Katie threw her arms around Trevor's shoulders and gave him a big hug.

Father Archer gave a deep sigh. "We'll need to talk about what happened, whenever Dr. Gallagher feels it might be all right."

"Trevor, tell me," Dr. Gallagher said softly as he put the coin back down on the coffee table. "Do you remember anything, anything at all?"

Trevor thought a moment and then shrugged his shoulders. Not really, other than I believe I saw that face again, the one that is familiar to me but I just can't seem to recognize."

"That's all you remember, Trevor?" Dr. Gallagher asked, a somewhat concerned expression on his face.

"That somewhat familiar face is about all I remember, I'm afraid."

"Do you remember a voice?"

Trevor thought a moment. "A voice? Wait, yes, there was a voice—it sounded like my dad's voice, I think!"

"Do you recall what the voice was saying?"

Trevor seemed surprised. "No, I don't remember. That doesn't make much sense or help us very much, does it?"

"Well, Trevor, it seems you were speaking for two distinct persons." Dr. Gallagher sat back in his chair, deeply in thought for a long moment.

Father Archer broke the silence first. "Joseph, what are you thinking?"

"I'm puzzled by this, Donald," Dr. Gallagher answered. "I'm not quite sure what to think about it all."

Trevor and Katie looked at each other as Father Archer spoke up. "It does seem what we learned from Trevor raises even more questions."

"There appears to be the presence of two distinct entities that we can identify in our short time of having Trevor under hypnosis. The first, Lucanus, seems to be a benevolent presence. However, Trevor doesn't remember much of what occurred—except for seeing a somewhat familiar face he can't identify and hearing a voice similar to his father's voice. Then there is this second presence—a presence that seems to be much darker and more troubled than the first. It was when this second presence manifests itself that Trevor began coming out of his hypnotic state. This could suggest this second presence may be at odds with the first."

Trevor stood up and took a deep breath. "All right here, fellows. Let's not get so serious unless you let Katie and I know what you're getting so serious about."

Father Archer nodded. "Of course, Trevor, we're sorry. This has just been quite an enlightening and unbelievable evening."

"Yes, my boy, we're sorry. Please sit down for a few minutes so we can talk. You do present a most interesting case. Where would you like us to start?"

Trevor sat back down, looked at Katie and then back at Father Archer and Dr. Gallagher. "I've always been told that starting at the beginning is a good place, but I would like to know who these characters, Lucanus and Theophilus, are first, if you don't mind."

"Do you read the Bible, Trevor?" Dr. Gallagher asked.

Trevor smiled. "Not really, but then Father Archer and I had this conversation a few nights ago."

Dr. Gallagher nodded. "I see. Well, Trevor, I think it best then we start from the beginning."

"Start from the beginning?" Trevor sighed. "Just where might the beginning be exactly?"

"That is an excellent question," Dr. Gallagher responded. "Which will indeed take a little thought."

Trevor smiled. "Maybe we can start with what happened this afternoon while I was under hypnosis?"

"Trevor," Dr. Gallagher spoke in a serious tone, "I'm thinking we need to go back quite a bit further than this afternoon. I'm thinking, perhaps, back to when you first received this coin from your father."

"Do you really think this coin has something to do with all this?"

"Yes, I do. Under hypnosis, you mentioned the Roman Emperor Tiberius, who reigned during the time of Christ's crucifixion. As we all know, Christ was crucified by order of Pontius Pilate, who was prefect in Judea at the time. Pontius Pilate is also a name mentioned in your dreams."

Trevor looked at Katie and Father Archer, who sat silently, then turned his attention once again to Dr. Gallagher. "So this coin my dad gave me has something to do with all this because it's from about the time in history these people lived?"

"Yes, although your coin may be even more connected than you might think." Dr. Gallagher picked up the coin from the coffee table once again and handed it to Trevor. "When you first gave me the coin, I recognized it as a bronze *prutah*—a coin minted by Pontius Pilate himself in Judea around the time Christ was crucified. I am confident this coin of yours has *much* to do with all of this, Trevor." Dr. Gallagher sat back in his chair and sighed. "Now, if we can just piece together what clues we have and try to figure out why all of this is happening to you."

31

Desert Storm

Caleb had just reached an ancient sheepfold—mostly hidden by rock, scrubby growth, and thornbushes—in a small ravine bordered by a rocky slope on one side. There was an entrance to a small cave in the rocky slope, partially obscured by brush. The wind had noticeably increased enough in strength to create twisters of sand. Caleb held his kaffiyeh close to help protect his face from the pelting grains of sand and to help him breathe more easily as he herded the last of the flock through the gate. Here, behind the heavy stone walls built years before, the animals would at least be out of the wind. Caleb worked quickly to put the wooden posts in place to block the gate from inside as small amounts of sand sifted through the thornbushes atop the six-foot walls, and the blowing, drifting sand lightly rained down into the fold.

Caleb quickly began gathering some wood from the remaining pile as he wondered about where he was. He and Judah had roamed these hills for several years, but he could not remember this place. He was very happy to have stumbled upon it since he had become disoriented in the worsening storm and was uncertain of precisely where he was heading. He began picking up some scattered pieces of wood and stacking what he could find in front of the gate. He would build a fire now since nightfall was near. The fire near the only entrance to the fold would help keep any wild animals away, as well as provide a signal to help guide Judah to the fold in the darkness and the storm.

Caleb could feel grains of sand pelting his face as he crouched down near the rock wall and watched the strengthening wind creating blinding swirls of sand outside the gate. The sheep huddled in groups near the walls as the donkeys stood quietly watchful among them. The animals had become very restless by the time they had reached the fold but seemed now to be settling down somewhat. The wind howled through little breaks in the centuries-old rock walls as Caleb shivered, realizing the drop in temperature over the past hour or so.

There was a loud cracking sound, and as Caleb looked in the direction from where the sound came, he saw one of the donkeys kick its hindfeet and the sheep move away as a large branch from a gnarled centuries-old olive tree crashed down into the fold. Caleb got to his feet quickly and went to where the branch had fallen. The reaction of the donkey had scattered the sheep huddled near it and thereby prevented any of the sheep from being injured. Caleb looked to see if any breach in the wall had been created by the fallen branch, but he could see no damage. He looked about to see if there were any other trees that might cause problems in the gathering storm. The wind howled through the ancient olive trees, which had stood through countless storms over the centuries, as it tore violently at the thornbushes atop the rock walls. Caleb looked carefully about the walls of the fold but could not see any more immediate dangers.

Caleb turned his thoughts once again to building the fire. It was turning cold, and he worried about Judah finding his way, even with the donkey left behind. The fire would help, even though this storm was much worse than Caleb thought it would be. He had tried to convince Judah it would be a bad storm. *What was Judah thinking? He has always been so responsible when it came to the flocks and has never ignored the weather before.* It was that chest Judah thought was made of gold. That had changed Judah into a person Caleb did not know.

As Caleb moved the little pile of wood so it would be sheltered somewhat from the wind and began to start a fire, he heard a bray from a donkey outside the gate. "Judah!" Caleb spoke aloud as he stood up by the gate and looked out into the darkness and the storm. Caleb could see nothing beyond a few feet from the gate, and he shouted out to his friend, "Judah, the gate is here! Can you follow my voice? I have just started the fire. Can you see it?"

Caleb listened but heard nothing but the wailing of the wind and the sand pelleting the rock walls of the fold. "Judah, can you hear me? Talk to me, and I will help you!"

Suddenly Caleb heard the braying of a donkey, and there it was, right before him at the gate. Quickly Caleb removed the wooden posts that blocked the gate, and the donkey ran inside the fold. Caleb stood there for another moment and called out once again to his friend. "Judah, can you hear me? Are you hurt? Talk to me!"

Again Caleb listened and heard nothing but the storm. He replaced the wood posts to again block the gate and then went to the donkey he had left behind for Judah. As Caleb began removing the rope from the halter, he shivered—but this time, not from the cold night air. As Caleb looked at the rope, he could see the frayed end. The rope had been broken! The donkey had apparently broken free from where Caleb had tied it for Judah and had come on its own to rejoin the flock. That could mean only one thing to Caleb—that without the donkey and the pack of provisions it carried, including food and water, Judah was now alone and in very grave danger!

"All will be well, shepherd boy!"

Caleb, startled, turned to look in the direction the voice had come from. He was instantly struck with fear and couldn't believe his eyes! There, above the small cave, an angel dressed all in white, with robes blowing in the wind, seemed to just be floating above the entrance. Caleb called out to the apparition. "Who are you?"

"Fear not, for you and your animals will be protected here in this holy place. Rest, shepherd boy, rest. You will be needed tomorrow."

"But what about my friend? Do you know if my friend Judah will be safe in this storm?" Caleb looked around the sheepfold, but the angel was gone. *What and where is this place?* Caleb shivered as he sat by the fire, wondering how what he had just seen was possible—or whether he had actually seen it at all.

Claudia Pleads with Pilate

"You must do this for me, my husband, and for yourself. Neither of us will have any peace or any hope for salvation if you do not."

"Have any hope for salvation!" Pilate exclaimed. "Do you suggest *I* believe that this dead prophet came back from death?"

Claudia looked calmly at her husband. "Do you suggest that you do not believe it?"

Pilate walked to the window and looked out upon Jerusalem. He stared into the distance, toward Golgotha, where only a few days before, this man the people called Jesus of Nazareth had been put to death—a horrible death by crucifixion, which centuries earlier, had been used by the great Greek commander Alexander. The Romans now used it themselves, not only as a means of executing the condemned but also as a deterrent to anyone who witnessed its horror. This death—as terrible as it was—he, Pilate, had allowed to be imposed upon the prophet. Why had he succumbed to the wishes of those who brought this innocent man to him for judgment when he knew this Jesus had done nothing to deserve death, let alone the worst possible death the Romans could impose? So terrible was the death of being beaten and hung upon a cross by nails that it was forbidden for any Roman citizen to ever be subjected to it.

Claudia spoke in truth. How could he say with any true conviction that he did not believe, or did not at least have doubts, as to whether this Jesus may have actually returned from the dead? How could he say he did not believe it to at least be possible after what he himself had heard with his own ears and had witnessed with his own eyes? Pilate turned to his wife. "What would you have me do?"

Claudia rose to her feet and embraced her husband. "Perhaps you could speak with your physician?"

Pilate reacted in surprise. "For what purpose would I speak with my physician?"

"Show him the burial linen, the image of this man that you showed to me. Ask him how such a thing could be!"

Pilate shook his head and turned away. "What you and I speak about is not the same as what I might speak about to my physician in this matter."

Claudia looked at Pilate undeterred. "But why would it not be the same? You have often told me how much you admire and trust Lucanus. He has traveled with you for a number of years, and you have put your faith in him. Why should you not consult him about this matter?"

"He is my physician. He is not my confidant."

"Speak with him, if not for yourself, then for me? You have admired him as learned in many things."

Pilate sighed. He knew it was not a good use of time to debate with his wife. He had heard that some around him questioned why he *allowed* his wife to speak her mind so freely, yet he suspected they either did not know or had forgotten her kinship with the emperor in Rome. Indeed, there had been those who whispered the only reason he was procurator of Judea was because Claudia was his wife.

"For you, Claudia, I will speak with Lucanus and show him this image on the cloth. I truly wonder if anyone, even my trusted physician, can give reason for it." Pilate looked into his wife's eyes. "I have seen much death, but I have never seen anyone come back from death. Yet there are those who say they have actually seen this prophet walking among them, alive again. I have seen only his empty tomb and his likeness on the linen that wrapped his body after he died."

"Do you believe this man lives again, Pilate?"

"How, dear Claudia, can I believe such a thing? I cannot bring myself to believe it is possible, yet this Jesus was so different from any man I have ever encountered. To tell truth, I wonder what to believe on the matter." Pilate nodded. "I will confide in Lucanus."

Claudia smiled at her husband. "Thank you. Perhaps he will be able to help us. I have heard him speak of Jesus, even before he was brought to you for judgment."

Pilate looked at Claudia as if he had not heard her correctly. "What? Lucanus is not a Jew! What could he possibly know about this man that he could speak about?"

"Ask him when you speak with him. I can tell you that he was very much troubled by the events of these past few days. He has said as much to me when I told him of my dreams."

Suddenly, what his wife was telling him was too much for him to accept. "You told my physician about your dreams?"

"Yes! Oh, my husband, I tried to speak to you before you judged this poor man, but you did not hear me! I hoped your physician might know what to do, that perhaps he could speak to you, but he told me such was not his place."

"But I did hear you, Claudia!" Pilate recalled how his wife had asked him to have nothing to do with the judgment of Jesus, but what could he do? He found no fault in the man, but he could not risk what surely would have been a revolt among those who insisted the prophet be crucified and the thousands of Jews who were in the city for their Passover. After all, was not keeping the peace the reason he came to Jerusalem from Caesarea each year at this time with barely three thousand Roman soldiers?

"Pilate, I know you did not want the prophet to die, though you sent him to his death because you thought it was what you must do."

"I have sent many to their deaths and have felt little or no remorse, but my judgment of this man troubles me greatly. I knew he did not deserve to die, but his people were so resolute, and he did nothing to defend himself on the charges they brought against him. You should have heard them, Claudia! They sounded shrill, evil, and inhuman—like the wailings of a thousand demons! I was weak, Claudia. I even tried to pass the decision to Herod, but he was wiser than I and sent him back to me. I should have used my authority to release the prophet and should not have allowed him to be crucified. Yet there were so many demanding his death, and he gave me nothing—no plea, no reason, nothing! It was almost as if he wanted to die."

"Oh, husband," Claudia said tearfully. "You are not the only one to blame, but is there anything to be done now? The prophet has been put to death, and some say he lives again. I fear for all who took a part in shedding this innocent man's blood."

"Leave me for now, dear Claudia. I need to think. I will speak with Lucanus about these matters as I have promised you."

Claudia thought of saying something further but turned without another word and disappeared through the curtained entry to her chambers.

Pilate once again walked to the window and looked out upon Jerusalem. As he stood there silently, he thought about the events of the recent few days. *Who was this Jesus of*

Nazareth? Is it possible he truly returned to life after dying on the cross and after being placed in his tomb? Suddenly Pilate thought of something he could do to find truth. Perhaps his trusted physician might prove valuable in these matters after all!

Pilate Speaks with Lucanus

"You wanted to see me, my lord?"

Pilate rose from his chair and took a gulp of wine from the goblet he held in his left hand. "I did. Have some wine?"

Lucanus stepped up to the table and poured wine into a silver goblet. "Is your cough still troubling you?"

Pilate waved his hand in the air and shook his head. "I will always have that cough, I fear. It is the dust of this place, and it may also be those foul leaves you give me to burn."

Lucanus looked at Pilate in surprise. "The leaves do not help you?"

"I do not know about the leaves. They may help, or they may do nothing. I do not know, but that is not why I want to see you." Pilate motioned to a chair near his. "Come, sit with me and drink your wine. I have much to discuss with you."

Lucanus waited until Pilate sat before seating himself and drank from his goblet only after Pilate once again drank from his. "May it please you, what is it you wish to discuss, my liege?"

Pilate looked at Lucanus for a long moment, thinking again of whether it was wise to involve his physician in what he had discussed with Claudia. He had promised her, and he knew she would hold him now to that promise. "Lucanus, tell me what you know of this man—this Jesus of Nazareth."

Lucanus moved uneasily in his chair, wondering how to answer Pilate's question. *Pilate condemned the prophet to death, did he not? Why ask this question now? I must be careful of what I speak.* "I am not sure what you ask of me, my lord."

"Come now, Physician. I want you to tell me what you know of this man! My wife tells me you were greatly troubled by his death."

"Am I allowed to speak freely, even if my answers may displease you?"

Pilate thought a moment. "You disagree with my decision to crucify the prophet then? Is that what troubles you, Lucanus?"

"It is not my place to question you or your authority, my lord."

"What is it then? You have been in my service for a number of years, and I want to know why you are troubled by the death of this Jesus."

Lucanus knew Pilate had a temper, and to anger him would not be wise. "My lord, I saw him die."

Pilate sat up in his chair. "You saw him die? But how could you witness that?"

"Your sign, my lord, the one you asked me to paint. The soldiers had already taken him away to Golgotha when I finished it. I took it there myself."

Pilate drank from his wine goblet then looked intensely at his physician. "Tell me, Lucanus, how did this man face his death?"

"My lord, with tears in his eyes, he looked to the heavens and asked his Father to forgive us for what we had done."

Pilate rose to his feet and threw his goblet across the room. "Forgive us for what we had done! What about his own people who were not satisfied with anything less than his death?"

Lucanus stood up and took a step toward Pilate. "He sought mercy for us all. His own people were there, some taunting him, some demanding your sign be taken down as they protested he was not their king. He died a better death than I have ever seen any man die."

Pilate walked to the window and looked out toward the hill where Jesus died. He spoke, but this time, softly, in almost a whisper. "What have I done, Lucanus? I knew this Jesus to be innocent, yet I succumbed to the will of those angry people of his. His own people cried out for his crucifixion, Lucanus!"

"I know they did, my lord. I heard them. They feared him, I believe. We destroy what we fear, do we not?"

Pilate turned toward Lucanus. "Tell me, my trusted physician, do you believe this Jesus was destroyed?"

Lucanus looked at Pilate as if he hadn't heard the question correctly. "I know not what you mean."

"Haven't you heard? There are those who say Jesus of Nazareth has risen from death and walks among us, even now. Some swear they have seen him! I have heard the soldiers guarding the tomb where his body was placed tell an incredible story of what they swear on their lives took place there. I myself, Lucanus, have seen his empty tomb."

"My lord, I too have heard these stories."

Pilate looked at Lucanus. "Here then is my question for you. Do you believe this Jesus of Nazareth lives again?"

Lucanus knew if he were to answer truthfully, he must choose his words with great care. "My lord, before I watched Jesus of Nazareth die upon that cross, I would have said I do not. Yet, after having witnessed what I saw, having heard what I have heard these past few days, I must tell you that if any man can live after death, Jesus of Nazareth *is* that man."

"Do you hear what you are saying? You are as much telling me it is possible the dead can come back to life?"

"My lord, if I may be so bold, what are your thoughts on the matter?"

"My thoughts are that when a man is dead, he stays dead!" Pilate looked at Lucanus then sighed and sat once again on his chair. "But, in truth, I am beginning to have great doubt about my previous thinking. You may think me mad, but I do not now know what to think on the matter."

Lucanus sat once again near Pilate. "You are not mad, my lord. These past few days have been like none other. This Jesus of Nazareth is like none other."

"You just said 'Jesus of Nazareth *is* like none other,' Lucanus! Is that what you believe—that he still *is*?"

Lucanus nodded. "As I have said, my lord, if any man can live after death, then Jesus of Nazareth *is* that man."

Pilate rose again from his chair and walked to a table at a far end of the room. "Lucanus, come here and look at this. Tell me what you make of it."

Lucanus walked to where Pilate stood holding a large linen cloth. "What is this?"

"This is the shroud the body of Jesus was wrapped in. It was all that was left in his tomb, except for that piece of cloth still on this table and that bronze coin. Look at this shroud and tell me what you see, Physician."

"Lucanus took the cloth from Pilate and could not believe his eyes. "I don't understand—this is the image of the prophet!"

"Is it blood? Is that what makes the portrait on this cloth?"

Lucanus examined the cloth closely, rubbing it with his thumb. "No, this is not blood. It is as if it has become a part of the cloth. It does not rub off."

"Well, what is it then if it is not blood?" Pilate demanded.

"I have never seen the likes of this, my lord. It looks almost like a burn from a fire, but there is no damage to this cloth." Lucanus put his face close to the cloth and sniffed. "There is no scent of smoke either. This is not from fire, it is not of blood, and it is like nothing I have seen before."

Pilate picked up the smaller cloth from the table and handed it to Lucanus. "What about this?"

Lucanus examined it carefully. "This is blood, my lord, see? Look at the difference between the two. On this smaller cloth, the image runs. It is uneven, and the cloth is damaged by the stain. But here, on the shroud, it is all different. The image is defined, the features of the prophet's face are clear, and there is no damage to the cloth. Even this bloody smaller cloth that covered his face did not alter the clarity of the image that is on this shroud!"

Pilate spoke softly. "How could this have happened, Physician? Could someone have painted this upon this cloth?"

Lucanus shook his head. "No, like I have said, there is no damage to the cloth, so this is not paint. There is no answer that I have for this, unless—" Lucanus stopped abruptly.

Pilate looked at his physician in surprise. "Tell me what you are thinking, Lucanus. Unless what?"

Lucanus thought for a moment before answering and then looked directly into Pilate's eyes. "There is no answer that I have, my lord, unless this image was created by some means beyond our ability to understand at that moment when Jesus of Nazareth returned from death."

34

Dad

"It was Friday morning, January 14. I will always remember that day. It was such a beautiful morning, Katie. I had arrived in New Orleans the night before and got to the house just as it was getting dark. Dad wasn't home, but he often was off somewhere doing something. I made myself some dinner and retired early. I woke up shortly after daylight, and when I went downstairs to get some coffee, I noticed Dad still wasn't home. I made the coffee and then caught the streetcar to the French Quarter. I was taking a little walk around and ended up strolling along the Riverwalk along the Mississippi River when I felt the vibration of my cell phone."

Katie looked at Trevor as he spoke and noticed his gaze seemed to be upon something far away. It was a beautiful morning, and she had joined him on the brick patio in the large yard behind his house. There were a number of beautiful trees and shrubs surrounding the property, which made the place private and quiet, except for the sound of birds happily chirping. Trevor's mood seemed sad this morning, and she noticed tears welling up in his eyes. She realized she had never seen him look as vulnerable as he did at that moment.

"I looked at my phone and saw it was my brother Rob calling. It was unusual that he would call instead of text, but I really didn't think much about it when I answered. I could tell by his voice something was wrong. I remember to this day exactly what Rob said."

"Trevor, you need to call Mom. It's bad. It's really bad."

"I asked what was wrong—what happened. He told me it was Dad, and I needed to call Mom. I could hear his voice breaking. I didn't yet know what happened, but somehow, I knew at that moment I'd never see Dad again. I found Mom's number in my phone, and when I called her, she answered right away. I explained Rob had called, and he was really upset but only said whatever happened was bad." Trevor looked at Katie. "I remember exactly what Mom's words were too."

"It's your dad, Trevor. He's gone."

Trevor sighed and looked up at the sky. "I knew what *gone* was euphemistic for. I swallowed hard and somehow found my voice to say I couldn't believe it, but she confirmed it was true. She told me he was in Grand Forks doing some kind of research at the university. They talked the day before when he stopped by the hospital where Mom worked, and they had lunch together. She said he and a friend from his college days were working on some project together. When he didn't show up at the university that morning as planned, his friend contacted the hotel where Dad was staying. They found him just sitting on the floor by the bed in his room. Mom told me Kyle was already on his way to Grand Forks, and Rob was trying to book a flight. I told her I had just returned to New Orleans, but I'd book a flight as soon as I could. Mom hadn't called Grandma and Grandpa yet—she didn't know how to tell them about Dad. I promised I'd take care of it, that I would call Uncle David to let him know so he could call Aunt Heather and Aunt Claudia and tell them. I figured one of them would go out to the farm and tell Grandma and Grandpa. I thought it best Grandma and Grandpa were told about Dad in person. I couldn't believe how calm I sounded through it all. I was in shock, I guess."

Katie reached out and touched Trevor's hand. "I'm so sorry."

"That's how I found out about Dad. I just kept walking by the river, not believing what happened. I realize everyone must die, but somehow, it just doesn't seem real when someone close to you does—especially when it happens so suddenly and unexpectedly. I never did find out what Dad was researching that would take him back to North

Dakota. I was always going to find that friend of his and ask, but I never got around to it."

"I'm sure this was difficult for you to share with me, Trev, but I'm glad you did."

"I think of Dad all the time, Katie. Everything seems to remind me of him, and now, with all this going on in his house, it's almost becoming an obsession."

Katie looked at Trevor, visibly concerned. "Does it help any to talk about this, Trev?"

Trevor nodded. "It does, Katie. Dad is in a cemetery back home in Grand Forks. He was cremated, but since it was January, we didn't have the inurnment service until later that summer. It was the Fourth of July weekend. Rob caught another flight back from New York, Kyle drove up from Saint Paul, I went back from New Orleans, and we all stayed with Mom at her house across the river in Minnesota. I remember we went out to buy some fireworks. Dad loved to set off fireworks for us when we were kids. We even ended up getting busted." Trevor smiled. "Just as my brothers set off the last big display, a policewoman came up the driveway and asked us if we were about finished. She was nice about it though. Dad would have enjoyed that."

"That was nice that you had the fireworks in your dad's memory."

"There is a recently built columbarium in the Catholic cemetery in Grand Forks, not very far from the University of North Dakota. A number of my mom's family are buried in that cemetery, including my grandma and grandpa on her side. At the little service, I placed Dad's urn into a niche in the top row of this new columbarium. Then each of us put a little memento inside the niche with Dad's urn before the niche was closed. Mom and I decided to each buy niches next to his." Trevor smiled and looked at Katie. "Mom said since we are all tall people, we should all be in the top row."

"That's wonderful, Trevor, but didn't you tell me your mom and dad had divorced?"

"Yes." Trevor nodded. "But I think Mom and Dad loved each other in spite of all the unhappy things that had happened between them. They always seemed to enjoy seeing each other over the years when Dad came for a visit, and we spent a number of holidays together, sort of like it used to be when my brothers and I were kids."

"That's remarkable, Trevor. It's nice to hear you all were able to remain fairly close."

"Mom said the columbarium was actually Dad's idea. When we were there for the inurnment service, we noticed that our niches are only a few steps away from the grave of my older brother, Troy."

Katie reacted in surprise. "I forgot that, Trevor! You did tell me you had an older brother who died shortly after he was born."

"Yes. Troy died shortly after birth, so none of us ever had a chance to know him. But we would put flowers on his grave every Memorial Day. Sometimes I would take walks in the cemetery and stop there—just out of respect and to let Troy know I thought about him. Now, when I go back up North for a visit, I'll stop and spend time with both my oldest brother and with my dad."

Katie smiled softly as she looked at Trevor. "What a thoughtful thing for you to do."

"I know Mom and Dad stopped there often over the years to visit Troy. I think Kyle and Rob did too. We are all family after all. We will always be family. But, Katie, listen to this. Here is this columbarium, and our niches in it directly face Troy's grave, only a few steps away. But there's more. This columbarium is cross-shaped with four ends, each of which features a life-size engraved portrait of one of the four Gospel writers. The end ours are in features an engraved portrait of Luke."

Suddenly Katie felt a chill. "That's quite a coincidence!"

"Do you really think that is a coincidence, Katie? I wonder." Trevor looked away with that sad and distant look once again his eyes. "I really wonder."

35

Lucanus Asks for Help

LUCANUS STARED IN awe at the Second Temple of Jerusalem, without doubt the largest religious complex in the known world. It took Herod the Great nearly twenty years to build it, and here it stood as a crowning accomplishment among all the other architectural achievements Herod had managed during his violent and bloody reign. The great fortress of new walls surrounding Jerusalem and the citadel that guarded the temple—which Herod called Antonia in honor of his patron, Mark Antony—had all been part of Herod's ambitious building program. In Jerusalem alone, Herod had also built a market, a new royal palace, an impressive building for the Sanhedrin, and an amphitheater. Herod also built in Jericho and Samaria and constructed new fortresses throughout Judea, including Masada and Herodium, where Herod would eventually lie buried.

Apart from the temple, perhaps Herod's greatest achievement was the creation of a brand-new port that Herod named Caesarea in honor of Emperor Augustus. Caesarea had a market, an aqueduct, baths, villas, a circus, official buildings, and pagan temples. Herod, much to the dismay of his own Jewish people, had preferred Greek influences, which were present to at least some degree in all his building projects. Caesarea was, indeed, a magnificently Greek city.

Pontius Pilate, his wife, Claudia, and his half legion would soon return there—not any too soon for Pilate, who never tried to conceal the fact that he did not like Jerusalem. This time, however, Lucanus would not return with Pilate but would remain behind to learn what he could about the real Jesus of Nazareth. Somehow he would get reports of what he discovered to Pilate.

Lucanus made his way up the steps of the temple and found a place to sit as he thought about why he was there and what he needed to do. Jesus had been here, in this very place, just before he was taken by members of the Sanhedrin. Jesus was beaten and mocked by Sanhedrin guards, spit upon by some of their members and followers, and then taken before Pontius Pilate, where they demanded he be crucified. Pilate had first tried to convince the crowd the matter was their affair and sent them to Herod Antipas, the son of Herod the Great.

Pilate and Herod had never liked each other. Herod resented Pilate as procurator of Judea, and Pilate thought little of Herod and considered him, if anything, a thorn in the side of Rome. Certainly, Herod Antipas was not as powerful or as intelligent as his father. Herod the Great, in the last years of his reign, had fallen in disfavor with Rome. Just before his death, he had decided two of his own sons were not worthy to rule in his place, and he had them put to death. Emperor Augustus, who had once considered Herod the Great his friend, divided Herod's client kingdom into separate parts when Herod died. Caesar Augustus would eventually insist on a much stronger Roman presence throughout the region. Rome would no longer tolerate an independent client king like Herod the Great had been. For nearly twenty four years—ever since Augustus removed Herod's son Archelaus for his incompetence—Rome had appointed a series of procurators and stationed Roman soldiers in the region to protect the interests of Rome. Pilate was now entering his fifth year as prefect.

Lucanus recalled how Pilate looked upon the man Jesus standing before him in the judgment hall—the face of the prophet swollen and beginning to bruise from the beating his own people had given him. These same people now voiced their rage and their charges against him and demanded Pilate put him to death. In that moment, learning Jesus was from Galilee, Pilate saw the interest of Rome might be better protected if Herod Antipas decided the man's fate. Herod, however, merely continued the mockery of Jesus by dressing him in one of his own purple robes, proclaiming him a "king" and sending the prophet and his accusers back to Pilate. It appeared to Herod that Pilate had finally recognized the importance and authority of his rule when he sent the matter of Jesus of Nazareth to him. Herod apparently never realized Pilate simply wanted no part in deciding the prophet's fate. So, that very day, through Herod's misunderstanding of Pilate's real intentions and purpose, the enmity between the two men faded, and they no longer thought quite as ill of each other.

Once again, Jesus stood before Pontius Pilate. No matter how hard Pilate tried to get Jesus to defend himself, Jesus would say nothing in his own defense—almost as if, it seemed to Pilate, Jesus *wanted* to die. Certainly, that is what those bringing him there wanted, his own people angry and insistent that Jesus be crucified. Pilate tried to dissuade the growing crowd and save the life of Jesus—even to the point of having him scourged to the brink of death in order to shock them into letting him live. But all was in vain as the crowd continued to grow and become more and more agitated as the morning progressed. Finally, to keep the peace and to avoid a potential riot, Pilate believed he had little choice but to give them what they wanted.

That was little more than ten days ago, and Pilate was now deeply tormented by what he had done—what he had allowed the Sanhedrin to do—to an innocent man. Pilate had asked Lucanus, as his physician and friend, to find some answers for him. So, here at the Second Temple of Jerusalem,

Lucanus would begin his search for Pilate's answers. He knew he had to go back to the beginning, perhaps as far back as to when and where Jesus was born. The first person he wanted to talk to was a member of the Sanhedrin—the Jewish council that had plotted and demanded the death of the prophet and who had inflamed many of their followers to demand the same. This man, this member of the council, was one who had tried to save Jesus by trying to persuade the others they were wrong about him. But why did he?

This man had spoken to Lucanus at Golgotha, where Jesus had just died upon a cross. There was something about this man Lucanus couldn't explain. There was something about the passion with which he spoke and what he had said that Lucanus could not forget. So he reluctantly agreed to this man's request to help him meet with Pontius Pilate. The man wanted to ask Pilate if the body of Jesus could be released to him so his family and followers could give Jesus a proper burial. Although Jesus, his family, and followers appeared to have no money, this man was certainly a man of means. He had offered his own tomb—a tomb he had prepared for his own burial one day—as a burial place for Jesus.

Lucanus looked up and saw the man he had come to speak with step out of the temple and into the morning sun. Lucanus rose to his feet and walked toward the man, who now saw him as well and began walking in his direction. Lucanus was about to have his chance to ask Joseph of Arimathea if he would now help him in return.

36

The Visit

"Trevor, wake up."

"Dad, is that you?" Trevor sat up on his bed as he fumbled for the lamp and turned it on. As his eyes adjusted to the light, Trevor was startled to see his father sitting on a chair near the window. "Dad, am I dreaming?"

Trevor's dad smiled. "You will think so later, Tad, but this moment between us is very real."

"But, Dad, you're—"

"Right here, and I am very much alive, Trevor. Although you haven't been able to see me or talk to me before now, know that I have never left you. My mortal form has ceased to exist, but that is all."

Trevor sat on the edge of his bed and looked at his dad closely. He looked so real, but he had to be dreaming. "I see you, Dad, just as you were. How is that possible?"

"You see me as you last remember me. I will always be recognizable to you, as you will be to me."

"Dad, I have so much I want to say to you! I love you, Dad, and I miss you. My heart has ached so much since you went away. We all miss you."

Trevor's dad rose from his chair and walked toward him, sitting down beside him on the edge of the bed. "That is the one thing about earthly death, son, that is so difficult—not being able to tell those who have yet to experience it that everything is all right."

"But, Dad, I don't understand. How can you be telling me this now if you couldn't tell me then?"

"Let me ask you this, son. When you first heard about what happened to me, did you try to let me know that *you* were all right?"

Trevor shook his head. "But I wasn't all right! And how could I tell you anything? You were gone!"

Trevor's dad smiled. "You see? You weren't all right because you didn't have faith! You didn't try to talk to me because you didn't believe you could."

"Why didn't *you* tell *me* all of this right away? Why didn't you tell Kyle or Rob or Mom? If you have never left us, why did you let us hurt so much after you died?"

"Trevor, I couldn't tell you anything that would have eased the hurt any of you felt because it is what *you* believed at that time that mattered. I didn't like seeing any of you sad because I love you, and I knew things would be all right in time—and the time will come when we will again be together, all of us, and we will never part from one another ever again."

"What are you trying to tell me, Dad? We were never all that religious growing up. Are you saying that if we believed in heaven, we would have known everything would be all right and we would have been 'all happy' when you died?"

"No, Trevor, I'm not saying that. There is always sadness when someone's earthly presence ceases to exist. Why? Because our physical presence here and now is all we know. To know anything else requires faith, Tad, and faith is one of the most difficult attributes to attain for most people." Trevor's dad smiled and touched Trevor's shoulder. "I wish your mom and I *had* been more religious with you and your brothers when you were growing up. We tried, you know. We didn't go to church as a family very often, but you and Rob graduated from Sacred Heart Catholic School. Kyle would have graduated from there too if I hadn't moved you all halfway across the state so I could take that state's attorney position. Oh, Tad, you will never know how much I came to regret that move. I was weak and not thinking clearly, a common problem for mortals, I suppose. I had always hoped that you all forgave me for the way that turned out."

"It wasn't easy to do, Dad. We felt you deserted us. I know you tried to keep us in your life, and we saw you fairly often. I suppose I spent more time with you after the divorce than Kyle and Rob did. I know you were usually there whenever we needed you, but it just wasn't the same after you divorced Mom."

Trevor's dad nodded. "I know, son. My heart breaks even now to think back on my foolish and selfish mistakes. If only I had known then what I was to know later—but I didn't, and what's done is done. But I never stopped loving you and your brothers *and* your mom, and I never will."

"We will always love you too, Dad." Trevor suddenly thought of something. "Dad, have you seen Troy?"

Trevor's dad smiled. "I have indeed! I was surprised that he looks just like I had pictured him to look—not as an infant, but as a little boy. I have also seen many relatives and friends I have known and loved."

Trevor walked to the window then turned and looked at his dad. "Tell me more. What's it all like?"

"Tad, some aspects are not very different from what you know already, and yet it all seems new and fresh and wonderful. The major differences are that there is no sorrow, no worry, no sickness, and no pain, only an abundance of love and happiness. Time is no longer of any consequence."

"Do you mean all the stories the priests and ministers tell are true?"

Trevor's dad laughed. He had not heard his dad laugh in more than a year, and it made Trevor smile. "Oh, Tad, you would ask that! Not at all! I have learned there is often far too much hype and guesswork coming from some of the clergy. Certainly, some of what they speak about is true, or close to being true, but it is all so different from anything one might expect. There are times when something is so beautiful it cannot be described accurately, and one needs to experience it for oneself to fully appreciate and understand it. This is one of those times."

"If we are to believe and have faith, how can we know what to believe and have faith in if the clergy can't even get it right?"

"They have some of it right, but when they start embellishing for dramatic effect or for their own purposes, they often stray from truth."

"What is the truth, Dad?"

Trevor's dad rose to his feet. "Tad, remember that Roman coin I gave you—the one you wear on the silver chain around your neck?"

"Of course, I remember it! I wear it most of the time."

"That coin is the key to your understanding."

"Dad, I have been having these strange dreams…"

"I know you have, son. That is part of the reason I am here." Trevor's dad looked at him seriously. "You have always looked at things with an open mind, Trevor. Since you were a little boy, you were always curious and interested in learning. There is much to learn in these dreams you are having if you consider them deeply. Just remember, your coin is the key and to trust in Luke."

"My coin is the key and trust in Luke? What does that mean?"

"Tad, read the Gospel according to Luke. I will always be with you, son. Trust in Luke...trust in Luke...trust in Luke...."

"Trevor, are you all right?"

Trevor opened his eyes and sat up on a leather wingback chair at his desk in the library. On his desk, he saw a half-empty glass of bourbon and a Holy Bible opened and marked with a swizzle stick. Katie was standing at his side.

"Yes, I must have dozed off."

"What were you saying? 'Trust in Luke?' Was that it?" Katie asked.

Trevor looked down at the Bible where it was marked and saw that it was open to the Gospel according to Luke. Trevor looked up at Katie and smiled. "Yes, Katie. *Trust in Luke.*"

37

Back to the Beginning

"I thank you for speaking with me. I know this is an uncomfortable time for anyone to speak about the crucified prophet."

Joseph of Arimathea looked intently for a long moment at Lucanus and could tell there was sincerity in his face. "Come and sit over here in the shade of this olive tree." Joseph motioned to a marble bench a few feet away from where the two were standing. In a moment, they were seated and sheltered from the bright heat of the sun. "You are correct. It is a troubled time we find ourselves in so soon after the crucifixion of Jesus. Most here at the temple try to convince one another that Jesus was a malefactor and deserved death, yet many are afraid. They have heard the stories of Jesus coming back from death and walking among us here in Jerusalem. They have no explanation for those stories, or for other things that have happened, like the hours of darkness or the tearing apart of the temple veil." Joseph nodded. "They are truly afraid and are beginning to ask among themselves questions for which there are no answers."

Lucanus looked at the olive leaves as they reflected bright specs of light from the morning sun then looked at Joseph and sighed. "What do you believe in all of this, Joseph?"

"I have known Jesus since he was a small child. I have observed marvelous things concerning Him for more than thirty years, and I knew very early on that Jesus truly is the Son of God."

"Jesus *is* the son of your God? Have you seen him, Joseph? Have you seen Jesus alive again?"

Joseph shook his head. "No, I have not, yet I have spoken with several who have, and I hope soon I too will be blessed to see him."

"Joseph, I must ask this question, and I intend no disrespect in asking it. Those who claim they have seen Jesus alive again, how do you know what they tell you is the truth?"

Joseph gently smiled at Lucanus. "Why would anyone say they saw Jesus if they had not?"

Lucanus was uneasy at the question and more uneasy about the answer he was about to offer Joseph. "I have heard Jesus spoke when he was alive that he would live again. Could it be there are those who want people to believe Jesus lives again when in fact he does not?"

"What of the body no longer in the tomb?"

Lucanus shook his head. "There are those who say the body of Jesus was taken from the tomb by his followers and buried secretly outside the walls of Jerusalem."

"What about the guards placed on duty at the tomb by your procurator, Pontius Pilate? Is that not why Pilate had the guards posted there—to prevent anyone from taking the body to make it seem Jesus had risen *if* he had not?"

"There are those who say the guards fell asleep on their watch, and when they awakened, they discovered the body missing."

Joseph shook his head. "A Roman soldier who falls asleep on watch is put to death, is he not? Were any of these sleeping soldiers put to death by Pontius Pilate?"

"No."

"Do you not see? I know the discipline of the Romans, and I have heard stories about Pontius Pilate. If the soldiers had fallen asleep as some claim they did, Pilate would not have hesitated to have them all killed." Joseph shook his head. "The body of Jesus was not taken by anyone and buried somewhere else. Jesus has risen from the dead, and he lives again just as he said he would."

Lucanus knew Joseph was right about what would have happened to the soldiers Pilate posted guard if they had indeed fallen asleep on their watch. He also remembered his conversations with Pilate and the reason Pilate asked him to learn all he could about this Jesus of Nazareth. Yet, if Jesus had returned from the dead, why didn't he appear openly to everyone in Jerusalem as he had before? Why would Joseph of Arimathea *not* be among those who claimed to have seen Him? "Joseph, of those you have spoken to who claim to have seen Jesus, is there one you have no doubt about believing?"

"Lucanus, I have no doubt about believing any who claim to have seen Jesus because I believe in Jesus. Yet, if you want to satisfy yourself about the truth, I will introduce you to one very special person who has seen Jesus alive again. Once you have spoken with her, you too will believe—even without seeing Jesus again yourself."

Lucanus shook his head. "I would welcome speaking with this woman you say is among those who have seen Jesus risen from the dead, but I have my doubts a conversation with one person could make a believer out of anyone—let alone me. I intend to trace everything accurately and establish with certainty all that has occurred."

Joseph rose to his feet and smiled knowingly. "Come then. I will introduce you, and you will believe."

Lucanus stood, and the two men stepped out once again into the heat and brightness of the sun and walked down the steps of the temple and into the busy street market. "Just who are we going to see whom you are so certain will make me a believer, Joseph?"

"She is a relative of mine." Joseph looked at Lucanus and put his hand upon his shoulder. "Her name is Mary, and she is the blessed mother of Jesus."

38

Buried Alive

As Judah awakened, he realized he could not move his arms or his legs. There was nothing but darkness surrounding him, and he could hear nothing. It was difficult for him to breathe, and he felt as if he would choke on sand if he breathed too deeply. He was able to move his head just a little, and as his eyes adjusted to the darkness, all he could see were some rocks and a few branches of a bush a few inches from his face. As he tried to remember what happened, he could recall the massive wall of sand coming down upon him as he tried to find some shelter.

Apparently, there was just enough space among the rocks and within the branches of this bush to trap some air for Judah to breathe. Judah realized, of course, there was not enough air to keep him alive for very long. He had to try to move—to dig himself out of this sand-made grave before his time ran out. Judah could move his fingers, and he tried to claw some sand with his hands, but it was no use. He could not move his arms at all. A wave of fear came over him as he realized he was going to die—buried alive in this sand—all because he would not listen to his friend Caleb.

He knew Caleb would come looking for him, but the air would run out long before Caleb could find him. Judah thought about his mother and worried about who would take care of her now. Caleb would see that she got the money for his sheep, but that would not last her long. As Judah began gasping for air and feeling like he was about to pass out, he thought of the golden chest. *How foolish I am!* he thought. *I should have listened to my friend.*

As Judah drew his last breath of air, his lungs full of burning pain, he felt sand pouring down upon his face. As he began choking, he could feel his left arm moving, being pulled upward. He felt a sudden jerk in his shoulders, and at once, he was breathing fresh-smelling cool air. He now felt both his arms and the rest of his body being pulled upward and out of his sandy grave. Within a few moments, he was lying on his back, and he could see the stars above him—high in the dark and windy sky. He tried to sit up, but a strong hand pushed him back down.

"Caleb, is that you?" Judah's eyes were watering as he brushed the sand from them and tried to see who had saved his life. "Who are you? Thank you!" Judah listened but heard nothing but the wind. As he turned his head to look around him in the darkness, he was at once struck with fear in the cold desert air. There, standing very near him, was a man dressed in ancient Roman robes and armor! Judah struggled to find his voice. "Who are you?"

The man just stood there for a moment in the darkness, looking at Judah as if he did not understand what he was saying. Then he took a few steps and seemed to be looking around him, as if he was trying to remember something. Finally the man turned to look once again at Judah. Although Judah could not quite make out the man's face, he could see a subtle smile. In an instant, the man who had saved his life was gone—seeming to just vanish before Judah's eyes, leaving Judah alone, frightened, and shivering in the cold desert air with nothing but a blanket of stars in the night sky to comfort him.

39

The Riverwalk

It was late afternoon when Katie found a parking spot a few blocks from Decatur Street in the French Quarter and started walking toward Decatur and the banks of the Mississippi River. She wasn't sure if she would find Trevor here or not—particularly at this time of day when growing throngs of people usually began spilling into the French Quarter and all the eclectic shops located along Decatur Street and the Mississippi River. However, since she couldn't find him at home or in Audubon Park, she figured there was at least a better-than-average chance she might catch him at Café du Monde, where she knew he was fond of having coffee. He told her he would often go there to think before immersing himself in a walk either along the river or through the French Market. Katie knew that right now Trevor had a great deal to think about.

This area along the Mississippi River was the scene of the 1984 World's Fair—just a couple of years before it became a favorite tourist attraction known as the Riverwalk. The famous French Market, often touted as America's oldest public market, began at Café du Monde and ended some six blocks later with a large flea market at the other end. She knew that if Trevor was there having coffee and she missed him, finding him wandering through the crowd would be difficult, if not impossible.

As Katie reached Decatur Street, she patiently waited to cross at a crosswalk instead of trying to save time by jaywalking, like many tourists and even some of the locals were known to do. Although accidents were not all that common, they occasionally did occur. As Katie began crossing the street, she smiled as she thought of the first time she and Trevor stopped at Café du Monde. Poor Trevor didn't quite know what to think about the pigeons that occasionally visited patron tables, scavenging for morsels and crumbs that might be left behind from someone's beignets. It was not something familiar to him in the Midwest, although he did recall a similar experience he had at Coney Island when he visited his brother Rob in New York City. It seemed to Trevor that the pigeons at Coney Island were every bit as bold as the ones at Café du Monde. She remembered how much Trevor spoke about that trip and all the places in New York City his brother Rob had taken him to—the museums, the Empire State

Building, Times Square, and of course, Broadway. He hoped to return there again one day.

A young woman was sitting on the sidewalk outside the café, playing a guitar and singing some unrecognizable tune. Passersby tossed coins and an occasional paper bill into her open guitar case, seeming not to care all that much about what she was playing—not that she seemed to notice much herself, staring out across the street and looking almost as if she were in a trance. Many would-be musicians actually made a very good living doing just what this young woman was doing, or so Katie had always heard. Of course, there were many itinerant trades practiced along these ancient streets, including painting, sketching, selling various items tourists couldn't bear to live without, and even telling fortunes with tarot cards and palmistry.

Katie tossed a dollar into the open guitar case as she brushed by the young singer and stepped inside the café.

Café du Monde itself was not very large, certainly nothing fancy, but its reputation for coffee and beignets superseded it; and there were so many people sitting, standing, and walking about that it was difficult for Katie to tell if Trevor was there or not. As she walked toward the back, looking from table to table and occasionally being bumped as she made her way through the crowd, someone put a hand on her shoulder.

"Looking for anyone in particular, or are you just here to feed the pigeons?"

Katie turned and smiled at her friend. "Trevor! I'm glad I found you, or you found me. I wasn't sure you'd be here, but I thought I'd take a chance and try to spot you."

"Actually, I just got here myself, and I was looking for a table when I spotted you. I'm not having much luck at it either, as you can see."

"Well, maybe I just brought you some luck!" Katie motioned to a young couple getting up from a small table just behind Trevor.

In a moment, after brushing off some powdered sugar from the chairs, they were seated where the young couple had been.

Trevor smiled. "I guess you did bring me some luck. I had about given up on finding a spot today. There seems to be even more interest in beignets today than usual." Trevor gently pushed the young couple's abandoned plates and cups to one side of the table, brushed away some powdered sugar from the table, and was immediately amused at a pigeon strutting quickly to the table near his feet to investigate. "Looks like we already have a little guest."

Katie laughed. "I know how you love these little pigeons stopping by for a crumb or two. I'm guessing you come to see that as much as you enjoy the coffee and beignets."

"You're right—it's the ambience of this unique place, I suppose. I like watching people and trying to figure out where they might be from and what they might do for a living. Of course, like you say, the coffee and the beignets are pretty tasty."

A waiter stepped up to the table and picked up the dirty plates and cups. "Ready to order?"

Trevor thought it must have already been a long day for the waiter since he appeared tired yet nonetheless friendly in the way he asked the question. "Katie? Why don't you go ahead?"

"I'd like a couple beignets and some hot chocolate."

The waiter didn't bother to write it down. "You, sir?"

"I'd like coffee and a couple of beignets."

The waiter was gone without a further word.

Trevor chuckled. "The waitstaff must all have fantastic memories, no?"

Katie smiled. "I can't imagine how they do it—there are so many people. But it seems most of the staff have been here a long time."

"Ah, I'll just bet you could be right about that. It's hectic, I'm sure, but it must be a fun place to work, right where a lot of the tourist action is." Trevor leaned back in his chair. "So, mother hen, how come you came around looking for me today?"

Katie looked intently at her friend. "I'm worried about you, Trev. You have been more preoccupied than usual, and I seem to remember you told me you'd be home today. I stopped by your house first, and when you weren't at home, I went to Audubon Park. This was the last place I could think of to look for you. I knew you prefer coming here in the morning, so I wasn't sure if I'd catch you here this late in the day, but I thought it worth a try."

Trevor shook his head. "Katie, either you are a mother hen, or you've become a stalker!" He laughed aloud as the waiter returned with hot chocolate, coffee, and beignets. Trevor paid the waiter, telling him to keep the change, and he left as silently as he had come. "You don't need to worry about me, Katie. We've been through all this, haven't we? I just need a little time to sort some things out. These past few days have been rather bizarre, don't you think?"

Katie couldn't deny that statement. "I know, but I still believe there has to be a reasonable explanation for all of this, don't you?"

Trevor took a bite of beignet and sipped his coffee. "I don't know, Katie. What I do know is since this all started, my dad has been on my mind nearly every waking hour, and when I'm asleep, I find myself surrounded by toga people. I'm beginning to seriously wonder if I am losing my mind."

"Oh, for heaven's sake, Trev, you're not losing your mind!"

"Well, let's just say I wouldn't want to tell too many people about all that has been happening. That little episode at the cathedral was certainly not a normal and sane thing to happen, was it?"

"You dozed off because you were tired, and you were dreaming again! It didn't help that Father Archer kept you up so late the night before. I am sorry about that."

Trevor leaned forward in his chair, lowering his voice. "That's another thing. What's up with all this painting business? First, a painting gets modified at the university with the apparent addition of a Roman official of some kind who just happens to look like my dad. Later, at the house, your friend Father Archer sees a painting of the Nativity and thinks there's something strange about it, only to discover a few minutes later that my dad's old paintbrushes in his room have fresh wet paint on them. Then, if that isn't enough, a short time later, that very same painting somehow falls off the wall so I'll be sure to notice it again. Looking at it, I realized it has been mysteriously modified! On closer inspection, I find the three kings have been painted over, and the paint was still wet—just like the painting at the university earlier in the day." Trevor laughed nervously. "You haven't taken up painting lately, have you, Katie?"

"Of course, not," Katie sighed. "What do you think it could be?"

Trevor shrugged. "I have no clue, unless it might be your ghost."

"Don't even joke about that, Trev! What do you think we should do?"

"What do I think *we* should do?" Trevor quipped, grinning as he took another sip of coffee. "If I were you, I'd finish my hot chocolate and beignet and run in another direction."

"I'm not deserting you in this, buster, and if this were the other way around, you wouldn't leave me to face it alone either. I'm in it for the long haul."

"Well, I appreciate that, Katie, I do. However, I'm thinking it may not be as serious as it all seems. The whole painting business and ghostly apparitions aside, do you remember what your Father Archer suggested that just might explain it all—or at least, might explain a big part of it?"

Katie leaned forward. "I'm not sure I do. What did he say?"

"Well, when we were talking at the house when he and that Dr. Gallagher came by, he suggested that my thinking so much about my dad and my being surrounded by so many of his things throughout his house might explain some of what I've been experiencing in my dreams and otherwise."

Katie looked empathetically at her friend. "I do remember that, and it sounds like a reasonable explanation for some things, I guess. It could explain why you have trouble sleeping, but like you said, how would that explain the paintings? It sure wouldn't explain the voices we both heard or what I saw that first night I stayed in your house." Katie sat back in her chair. "Do you really think we could *both* be imagining all of this because you have been thinking so much about your dad?"

"As far as *I* am concerned, it's possible, I suppose. If I think about it, all these things seem to be related somehow to my dad—the things he was interested in and what he was working on toward the end of his life. I don't know yet how it might explain what *you* have heard and seen. It occurs to me that I'm not sure I have ever allowed myself to grieve or fully adjust to the notion that my dad is gone from this world."

"Gone from this world?"

Trevor nodded. "I don't know what you believe about the notion of life after death, Katie, but I'm seriously beginning to question what I thought I believed on the subject."

Katie put down her hot chocolate. "Do you think there is life after death, Trevor?"

Trevor sighed. "Katie, until a few days ago, I would have said no and have given the question very little thought—but now I can't say that." Trevor leaned forward, now almost whispering. "I saw my dad, Katie! I spoke with him!"

Katie gasped and put her hand to her mouth.

"Unless there is some explanation I'm missing, as surely as I sit here talking to you, my dad lives again!"

40

The Coin

Trevor shook his head as he watched Katie drive away. *What she must be thinking*, he thought. *Maybe I should have just kept that part about believing my dad lives again to myself for the time being.*

"Excuse us, sir."

Trevor looked at an elderly couple trying to make their way past him on the crowded sidewalk where he was standing. "I'm sorry," Trevor said apologetically. "Excuse me." Trevor stepped into the street to let them pass. As he watched them go, he smiled sadly to himself. *Too bad Mom and Dad couldn't have grown old together like those two.*

Trevor stepped back into the pedestrian traffic and made his way toward the French Market. It wasn't that he ever bought much there, but he did enjoy watching people and looking to see if there was anything new for sale—something different from the usual fair of tourist items. As Trevor walked along, occasionally being bumped by someone in the crowd, he thought about his dad. It seemed like he was thinking about him all the time now. There were just so many unanswered questions, so many things left unsaid between them. He didn't have a chance to tell his dad good-bye—to have a few last moments with him to say how much he loved him.

Did I really see Dad in the house, or was that just a dream too? It seemed so real, so convincing, and with all the strange things that were happening, Trevor worried about whether he was becoming delusional. Katie looked troubled when he told her about it. She didn't say anything, just looked at him as if she hadn't heard him correctly. She hardly spoke at all when Trevor walked her back to her car. She had tried to get him into the car and let her take him home, but he told her he wanted to stay for a while—that he had some thinking to do.

Trevor changed his mind and decided not to walk through the French Market. He crossed the street and kept walking. It wasn't long before the crowd thinned out and there was only an occasional person or two whom he encountered. Soon he found himself on Esplanade Avenue, and a few minutes later, he was standing up against a wrought iron fence, looking at the old US Mint—the only mint to have produced both American and Confederate coins. Trevor marveled at the old building. His dad had told him this was the only Southern mint to resume operation after the Civil War. It closed as a mint for the final time in 1909 and was now the Louisiana State Museum.

As Trevor stood there thinking about the history of the place and how much his dad enjoyed telling him about it when they had walked by the site some years before, he reached inside his shirt and pulled out the Roman coin his father had given to him. *I wonder what the building was like where this coin was minted?* Trevor asked himself. *I wonder if it was minted in Rome.*

"Your coin was struck in Jerusalem, Tad."

Trevor turned, startled at hearing his dad's voice; and there he was, standing alongside him, leaning against the wrought iron fence. "Dad!"

His dad smiled. "Sorry to give you a start. I heard your thoughts, and I wasn't thinking about being—well, you know—the way I am now."

"You mean you are really here? I'm not dreaming?"

"Like I told you at the house, Tad, you will think later that you are dreaming, but these moments between us are very real."

Trevor shook his head. "But, Dad, I just don't understand how any of this is possible! I must either be dreaming or hallucinating!"

Trevor's dad looked at him intently. "There is nothing wrong with your perception, son, although I understand why you or others might think my being here with you is impossible."

Trevor reached out and touched his father's arm, and realizing—at least for the moment—that his dad was real and not imagined, he embraced him. "Oh, Dad, I just don't understand any of this!"

"I know, son."

A young couple turned the corner and was walking toward them on the sidewalk. Trevor stepped back from his dad and looked in the young couple's direction. "Can they see you too?"

"No, they can't." Trevor's dad sighed. "Only those who knew me before my death are able to see me now, and then *only* if they truly believe they can see me again."

"But how do I see you, Dad? In spite of what we've been told in church, I've not been a big believer in an afterlife."

"You do see me, don't you? We've been talking to each other, haven't we?" Trevor's dad smiled. "If so, you must believe, Tad, but then you do have a rather special gift."

Trevor looked puzzled. "What special gift would that be?"

"You can see and hear things, Trevor, which most others can't. You think you are dreaming, but you are actually living in the moments of your thoughts—just as you are doing right now."

"Dad, you've lost me. What are you talking about?"

"Trevor, when you tell your friend and others that you don't know what the dreams you have been having are about—that you don't understand what they mean—you aren't being completely truthful."

"I'm not lying, Dad! I have no clue what any of these bizarre dreams I have been having mean!"

Trevor's dad smiled. "You do. You just don't know you do. You aren't allowing yourself to understand your dreams—not yet."

Trevor shook his head as he leaned against the wrought iron fence and stared at the old US Mint. "So you are telling me these dreams I have been having about Romans, religious figures, and other random people talking and whispering—you are telling me I understand what it all means, but for some reason, I'm not admitting it?"

"Something like that. Trevor, think about the first voice you hear in these dreams. Is it a man's voice or a woman's voice?"

"Dad, I don't know!"

"But you do know! Think!"

Trevor looked up toward the sky, closing his eyes for a moment. He could hear a clock ticking—the clock in his dad's house. "It is man's voice. He's talking to a woman."

"Go on, Tad, what does the man say?"

As Trevor tried to remember, suddenly he could hear the man's voice: *"He doesn't know. He's lying again."*

"That's it, Trevor!"

"That's it? What's it, Dad? What the man's voice says makes no sense at all!"

"Sure, it does. It is what I have been telling you all along! You have been denying what you know of these so-called dreams because you really do know much more about them than you realize!" Trevor's dad grabbed his shoulders and looked directly into his eyes. "You know much more about these dreams than you are allowing yourself to know. Some of what you are dreaming reflect memories of things you know—things you have either experienced or you are currently living through, mixed together with other things you are just now learning about or beginning to understand!"

Trevor stepped back and leaned against the fence, looking into the street. "Whoa, Dad, you can't expect me to wrap my brain around all of this! How would something like that even be possible?"

"You are standing here talking to me, aren't you—you know, your dad? I'm the same dad who died and was cremated and whose ashes you yourself put into the columbarium niche bearing my name, right?"

Trevor allowed himself to gently slide down the side of the wrought iron fence and sit on the grass, drawing his knees to his chest. "I must be losing my mind."

Trevor's dad sat down on the grass beside him. "Do you remember the story in Luke's Gospel when, after Jesus rose from death, he appeared before the remaining apostles gathered together in Jerusalem? They were all afraid, Trevor, and they thought they were seeing a ghost and not really seeing their risen Lord. But Jesus showed them his pierced hands and feet, told them to touch him, and he even ate with them to show he was really there with them."

"Yes, Dad, I remember hearing that story and believing that is all it was—*a story*. We were never that religious. You don't expect me to buy all that religious gibberish, do you?"

Trevor's dad laughed. "Well, you should know now, sitting here and talking to me, that it is *not* religious gibberish! I am here with you in a similar way that Jesus was there with his apostles nearly two thousand years ago. They were full of doubt then, just as you are full of doubt now—and that is the point! Don't you see? They were being dishonest with themselves by appearing not to believe in what they heard and saw—by disbelieving what their own senses were telling them was true. There *is* eternal life for those who die! Trust your senses, Trevor. You have been given a very great opportunity here. Faith is very difficult to achieve without some tangible proof. Often we refuse to allow our own belief and trust in that proof, even though it is all around us and inside us. All we need to do is look for it."

Trevor looked at his father a long moment. Whether he was having a mental breakdown or not, Trevor had to admit what his father was telling him seemed to make some sense. "Dad, why me? Why am I able to sit here and see you and talk with you? Why am I having and living these so-called dreams?"

"Do you remember what I said before leaving you yesterday?"

"Yes, something about my coin being the key and to trust in Luke. I remember asking you what that meant, but you didn't tell me. You just told me to read the Gospel according to Luke—that you would always be with me and to trust in Luke."

"Yes, Trevor, I will always be with you, and you must trust in Luke. Read his Gospel and compare it to the others. The Gospel according to Luke will provide you with the truth." Trevor's dad sighed. "The coin I gave you, son, *is* the key. I didn't realize it at the time I gave it to you, however. I knew it was a special coin—one of a few coins minted in Jerusalem by Pontius Pilate in the eighteenth year of the Roman Emperor Tiberius, which would translate to about 30 CE. I thought the coin truly one of a kind because of a mint error on it and the fact it was likely in circulation when Jesus was crucified by Pilate in 30 CE. I later learned it is much more than that! It is in part because of your coin, your own uncertainty about life after death, and my desire to help you find the answers that you have been living these experiences you have become a witness to."

"But, Dad, that couldn't mean every person who has one of these coins—and I assume more than this one

I have survived through the centuries—is having these experiences?"

"No, son, but the coin you have is *truly* one of a kind. Your coin is more special than I could have ever possibly imagined when I gave it to you, something I learned about and was trying to do more research on at the time death parted us."

Trevor looked at his father. "What was it you learned about my coin?"

"There has been much research on the Shroud of Turin—you have heard of that surely?"

Trevor nodded. "Yes, the linen shroud some believe was the burial cloth of Jesus, which supposedly shows his image on the cloth."

"That's right. A few years ago, another image was discovered on the shroud, one which has been overlooked and isn't mentioned very much. The visible image of a coin was discovered over one of the eyes of Jesus! This newly discovered image has been identified as an error coin, minted by Pontius Pilate in Jerusalem in the eighteenth year of the Roman Emperor Tiberius. The eighteenth year of Tiberius would be 30 CE—the year Jesus was crucified!"

Trevor suddenly felt a chill come over him. "So this coin appearing over one of the eyes of the image on the shroud is like the coin you gave me?"

"Look at your coin again. Do you see the small error of extra metal that runs through one of the letters?"

Trevor looked at the coin and, after a moment, could see a tiny bit of extra metal running through one of the letters just like his dad said. "I see it. It looks almost like it is a crack in the coin, doesn't it?"

"Considering the way coins were minted two thousand years ago, that is truly a unique error, likely one of a kind." Trevor's dad touched his son's shoulder. "Trevor, the very coin that once rested on one of the eyes of Jesus closed in death—the newly discovered image of a coin visible on the Holy Shroud of Turin—I am convinced *that* coin, Trevor, is the coin I gave to you for Christmas, this very coin that you wear upon your neck!"

41

Mary

As LUCANUS WALKED alongside Joseph of Arimathea, he marveled at how briskly Joseph was walking for a man of his advanced years. The area they were now walking through was one of the poorest in Jerusalem.

"I have asked Mary many times to stay with my wife and with me, but she prefers to stay in a simple dwelling provided by a friend of hers she has known since she was a child."

"Provided by a friend of hers?"

"Yes. Her friend, named Joanna, who is married to the steward of Herod himself."

"Herod!" Lucanus looked at Joseph in disbelief. "Did not Herod Antipas harbor enmity with Jesus? He was also responsible, I have heard, for the death of another prophet—the one some called John the Baptist—was he not?"

"Yes, Lucanus, Herod held enmity in his heart for Jesus and was responsible for the death of the Baptist. But you must understand Herod has no idea the wife of his steward ever knew Jesus, that she helped to support his ministry, or that she provided a small house for Jesus and Mary to dwell in when they were in Jerusalem. Joanna's husband, Chuza, does not even know."

Lucanus shook his head. "I have heard Herod Antipas does not have a stable mind. This all seems to me a very dangerous friendship indeed."

"Sadly, that is so, but God protects Mary."

Lucanus reacted in surprise. "Your God protects Mary? Why did your God not protect Jesus and the Baptist?"

Joseph sighed. "Lucanus, you do not yet know there is reason for all that has happened and what is yet to happen. In time, you will have answers to all your questions." Joseph stopped and pointed to a modest low-built earthen dwelling with the typical dirt and straw roof. "There is where we will find the mother of Jesus."

Lucanus walked the few additional steps to the door and waited as Joseph tapped gently upon the well-worn wood with the grip of his staff. "Mary, it is Joseph. I have brought someone I would like you to meet."

The door slowly opened, and a beautiful woman with dark and sad eyes stepped out into the sunlight. Lucanus was surprised at how young and beautiful this woman was.

This woman appears to be too young to be the mother of the prophet. Surely this must not be Mary.

"Uncle Joseph!"

Joseph reached out and touched Mary's shoulders and smiled gently at her. "Mary, I'd like you to meet Lucanus. He would like to know about Jesus."

Mary looked at Lucanus closely for a moment and then smiled. "I have seen you, have I not?" Mary thought a moment and then nodded. "Yes, you were there on the hillside some distance away when Jesus was crucified. I saw you kneeling there, and I wondered who you were."

Lucanus again felt the shame he had first felt that day when he had, at Pilate's bidding, painted the sign that was hung upon the cross of the prophet. When Jesus, as he hung dying upon his cross, fixed his eyes upon him, Lucanus remembered growing weak and falling to his knees in his shame. "Yes, I *was* there. I am sorry for your loss and for the pain you must feel."

"Please, come inside if you wish. I can offer you some cool water and some bread."

Lucanus looked at Joseph, who nodded his approval. "I would like that," Lucanus replied.

Mary turned and went back inside, and Joseph motioned for Lucanus to follow. Soon they were all sitting on large flat stones that were set alongside a low wooden table. Mary placed a loaf of bread upon the modest table where a goatskin pitcher of water and several clay cups had previously been placed. When Mary seated herself upon one of the stones across from Joseph and Lucanus, she poured water into a cup for Lucanus then for Joseph and finally for herself. Joseph then tore a piece from the loaf of bread and gave the loaf to Lucanus, who tore a piece from it as well and then handed the loaf to Mary. Lucanus looked about the room. There was a place at one end to cook and a doorway leading to what looked like another small room. Except for a few meager furnishings and personal items, there was very little else for him to take notice of.

"Has Joanna been by to see you, Mary?" Joseph asked, breaking the silence.

"She was here earlier and has gone to market. She wanted me to go with her, but I had a feeling I should stay." Mary smiled. "It is good I did stay, is it not so, Joseph?"

Joseph nodded. "Yes, Mary, it is so." Joseph turned to Lucanus. "Lucanus, what would you like Mary to tell you about Jesus?"

Lucanus looked at Joseph then at Mary. "I…I don't know quite how to start. Joseph has told me some incredible things about your son, yet there is so much more I would like to know about him." Lucanus sighed. "Would it be proper to ask you some things? I know this is a sad time for you."

Mary looked at Lucanus for a long moment. "I am sad for others, but I am no longer sad for myself. You can ask me anything about Jesus you would like to ask."

Lucanus swallowed hard as he thought again about the most burning questions he needed answers to. "Forgive me, but perhaps the greatest question I have is the one I should ask you first." Lucanus looked at Joseph, who smiled and nodded his head.

"Go ahead, my son," Joseph spoke softly. "I believe I know the question you want to ask Mary. It will be all right."

Lucanus looked at Mary, and at that moment, he thought he could see a radiance about her face—as if light was shining down upon her. He felt a shiver run through him as he began to wonder just who these people really were. "Do you believe your son, Jesus, lives again?"

Mary looked at Lucanus then at Joseph and again turned her eyes toward Lucanus. "I *know* He lives. Jesus has always lived and will live always."

Lucanus thought about Mary's answer for a moment then spoke softly—almost in a whisper. "Tell me if you can, how it is you can possibly *know* this?"

"Jesus came here to me, in this very place, the morning he rose from his death upon the cross." Mary looked at Joseph. "That is why I didn't go to the tomb with Joanna and the others later that morning, Joseph. I knew Jesus was no longer there."

Lucanus reacted in surprise. "You actually saw him here in this place *after* he had died?"

Mary smiled. "Yes, I saw Him, Luke, here in this place. He spoke to me and told me to mourn no more."

Lucanus could hardly believe what he was hearing, yet Mary looked so sincere, and he could see in her dark eyes she was telling him the truth. Suddenly he recalled the name she addressed him by. "You called me Luke?"

Mary smiled. "I did. I know your name is really Lucanus, but you should know the entire world will know you by the name Luke."

Lucanus shook his head. "I do not understand how that can possibly be. I have no position that would cause the world to ever know I existed."

"You will be known throughout the world to the end of days as Luke. You will find your way." Mary looked at Joseph. "Have you not told him, Joseph?"

Lucanus turned his attention to Joseph, whom he had forgotten for a moment was even present. "Tell me what, Joseph?"

"You have begun your journey, Lucanus, by coming here and speaking with Mary, the mother of Jesus." Joseph smiled. "Remember what I told you on the hill as Jesus died upon his cross? I told you that, being an educated man, perhaps you would write what you have heard and observed about Jesus one day. You are hearing, and you are observing, and now you must write it all down so the people will know the truth. It is your writing that Mary is referring to."

Lucanus swallowed hard. *How can they know Pontius Pilate has asked me to write down everything I learn about the prophet and that is my whole purpose for staying in Jerusalem for a time?* "If you please, what do you know about my writing anything concerning your Jesus? I am not a Jew."

"I know you are not a Jew, Luke," Mary said softly. "And I also know that you cared about Jesus, and you are here to know more about him. Is that not your real purpose for being here, so you can write it all down as it really happened?" Mary smiled. "I trust you will write accurately of Jesus so those who read what you write can know the truth about him."

Lucanus was in awe at Mary's words. "How can I *know* the truth? I was not an eyewitness to anything but his trial before Pilate and his death upon the cross. I am not a Jew, and I am not minister of his words or his deeds. Would not his followers be the better ones to accurately set down all these things in writing?"

"Because you are not a Jew," Joseph said quietly, "you are less likely to concern yourself with what has been written before. You will not look for reasons to write things that are not accurate about the life of Jesus on this earth, about his death at the hands of his own people, or concerning his resurrection from the dead solely to show fulfillment of prophecy."

Mary looked at Lucanus, and he could still see that radiant light upon her that he had noticed earlier. She smiled as she spoke. "You are an educated man, Luke. Only but one or two among the followers of Jesus have the ability to even read or write their own names."

Lucanus shook his head. "I must tell you that I am a Roman citizen. Joseph knows I am physician to Pontius Pilate and have been of his household for a number of years. Before the trial and crucifixion of Jesus a few days ago, I barely knew Jesus but for a few mumblings among those close to Pontius Pilate and among those in the service of Herod. I do not think I am the one who should be writing down anything for you or for your people about Jesus." Lucanus thought again about what Pilate had asked him to do—to find the truth about this Jesus, whatever that truth might be, and to report his findings back to him in Caesarea. "What I learn about Jesus and what I write about him may not at all find favor with you or with your people."

Mary smiled that gentle smile Lucanus was beginning to know, and he felt strangely calmed by that smile. "I know in my heart what you learn and what you write will find favor with us and with the entire world. I trust in you, Luke, and I will help you in your quest for truth."

Lucanus sighed. He knew now in his heart what he must do. "So my name is to be Luke?"

Joseph laughed aloud and patted his shoulder. "If Mary says your name is Luke, then Luke is your name from this day forward."

Mary, smiling, reached across the table and touched Luke's hand. "I know this hand of yours will write well, and I do hope the name Luke pleases you? It is God's will."

Lucanus looked at Joseph then at Mary, whose gentle smile made him realize he actually felt comfortable with the name, although he wondered at what Mary just said—that this was *God's will*. Luke was not very familiar with the God of the Jews. "The name Luke does have a certain quality to it and does not displease me." Lucanus shook his head and laughed. "Very well, you may call me Luke, and Luke is the name I shall use when I write about your Jesus. Now, tell me, where do we begin?"

Mary took a sip of her water and looked at Luke. "Let us begin at the beginning."

42

Stories to Tell

As Judah sat on the side of the hill, he could see Caleb walking in the distance down below him among the sheep and the donkeys. He could see Caleb was looking for the grass that was no longer there but covered in sand. Judah felt weak as he got to his feet and struggled to walk down the hill toward his friend. He was never so glad to see anyone before as he waved at Caleb and tried to shout hello, but his throat was dry and sore, and his words were barely more than a hoarse whisper. All at once, Caleb looked up and saw him! Judah could now see Caleb waving back and running up the hill, slowed down by the fresh sand.

"Judah! You are alive! I was so very worried. You were out here with nothing to protect you in that terrible storm!"

Judah smiled at his friend as he tried to walk toward him, collapsing to his knees in his weakened state. Caleb reached out and caught him, easing Judah back into a sitting position on the sandy hillside. Caleb quickly unhooked the strap of his goatskin water pouch and pulled the stopper out, offering the water to Judah. "Here, drink this—but slowly."

"Thank you," Judah said weakly as he took the water and drank deeply, beginning to choke.

Caleb pulled the goatskin water pouch back from Judah. "Drink slowly so you do not choke!"

Judah nodded. "Yes, thank you. I am just so very thirsty." This time, he drank slowly, in small sips, and he seemed to feel much better almost at once.

"How did you survive the storm, Judah? Did you find a cave?"

"No." Judah shook his head. "I almost had the golden chest free, and I did not see the great wall of sand until it was upon me. I was buried in the sand, Caleb, and I just knew I would die! I thought about my poor mother and about you and our animals and about how you were right that I was being so foolish about that golden chest."

Caleb nodded. "You are all right now. That is what is important." He looked farther up the hill, where he had first seen Judah. "Where is this chest you almost lost your life for? Is it up there?"

Judah started laughing weakly and then began to cough. Caleb reached out and grabbed his friend's arm. "I am all right, just weak, Caleb. I will be strong soon."

Caleb sat by his friend. "Why do you laugh when I ask about the chest?"

Judah shook his head. "You were so right, Caleb, about everything. There is something about that chest. I do not know where it is—it is buried once again beneath all that sand. I left it to try finding what shelter I could when the wall of sand came upon me. This morning, at daylight, I saw nothing around me for miles but sand."

Caleb sighed. "I am sorry, Judah. I know you wanted to have that chest—that you thought it was gold and we would be rich shepherd boys."

"Caleb, I learned last night that *we are* rich shepherd boys! We are alive, and thanks to you, we have our animals. Today is the first day of the rest of our lives, Caleb!"

"I am happy to hear you say so. But, tell me, are you finished looking for this chest?"

Judah nodded. "You were right about it, Caleb—it is either very good or very bad. I am thinking it is good, but I am also thinking the man it belongs to guards it well."

Caleb sat forward as if he hadn't heard correctly. "What do you mean when you say 'the man it belongs to guards it well'?"

"He is a very strong man, Caleb. You are not going to believe what I am about to tell you! I was dying, Caleb, buried in sand where I couldn't move and could barely breathe. Air was running out, and at the moment all was going black, I thought you had found me! You were there digging and dragging me out of my sandy grave." Judah looked at Caleb with wonder in his eyes. "I think this man must have been a Roman soldier—he was dressed in ancient robes and armor like we have seen in books! It was this man who saved my life last night! I think the chest belonged to him, Caleb! He seemed to be looking around for something. Then as he looked at me, I thought I saw him smile, although I could not see his face very clearly in the darkness. Then as quickly as he was there, he was gone. I have not seen him or the chest since."

Caleb got to his feet. "Can you stand? We need to find some grass for the animals somewhere. If you can stand, we can get you to one of the donkeys, and you can ride."

"I can stand."

Caleb helped Judah to his feet.

"I did not think you would believe my story," Judah said.

Caleb smiled as he helped Judah walk slowly down the hill to where the animals were. "I do believe your story, Judah, and I want to hear more of it."

Judah looked at Caleb in surprise. "You really believe my story as incredible as it is?"

Caleb nodded. "I do believe you, and I trust you will believe me."

"Believe you about what?"

Caleb looked at his friend seriously. "It seems, my friend, you and I both have incredible stories to tell."

Dr. Gallagher's Idea

"Here you are." Dr. Gallagher's secretary smiled as she handed Katie a bottle of water and a glass. "My name is Brenda. Dr. Gallagher is on his way."

"Thank you, Brenda," Katie replied as the secretary returned to her desk. Katie sat quietly for a moment, just looking out the window at the street ten stories below. There was a lot of traffic today—more than usual, Katie thought. She began regretting coming to Dr. Gallagher's office without an appointment. Dr. Gallagher was out, but the secretary offered to call him. Katie had reluctantly agreed, but only because she was really worried about Trevor. Apparently, the former priest thought it important enough to leave the meeting he was in and hurry back to the office to meet with her. Now second thoughts set in, and she wondered if it was all such a good idea.

There was the jingle of a bell as the door opened, and a man stepped into the reception area and walked toward the secretary's desk. He noticed Katie look up at him as he walked in but turned his attention immediately to the secretary. "Is Joseph in?"

"I'm sorry. He's not, Mr. Wright. He is on his way but does have an appointment when he arrives."

The man turned his attention briefly to Katie then concentrated once again on his conversation with the secretary. "Any idea when he might be free? This is quite important!"

"I'm not sure, but you are certainly welcome to wait if you like. He doesn't have any other appointments after this next one for the rest of the day."

"The day is almost over!" The man's impatience seemed to grow. "Look, just tell him to call me when he's done, will you? I can't be sitting here until midnight, hoping I'll get a chance to talk to him."

The secretary smiled patiently. "I can certainly do that, unless you'd care to just make an appointment for another time while you are here?"

"You aren't listening! I told you this is important! Have him call me as soon as he's done, please!"

The man looked again at Katie—this time, she thought, with contempt—as he walked to the entrance and opened the door to the hallway outside. A moment later, he slammed the door behind him, and he was gone.

As Brenda looked at Katie with a soft and apologetic look, Katie got to her feet, still holding the unopened bottle of water and the glass the secretary had given to her. "I'm sorry. I shouldn't have barged in here without an appointment. I think I should just be going."

The entrance door opened, ringing the bell once again; and this time, it was Dr. Gallagher, who stepped inside with a grin and his hearty Irish laugh. "Well, well, I see you've sworn off soft drinks now, as well as the nectar of the gods, and you have resorted to water!"

Katie smiled back, a bit embarrassed. "I'm sorry to interrupt your meeting and drag you back here. I just thought you might be in your office, and I could talk to you for a few minutes."

"Think nothing of it, my child! That meeting was about as boring as any I've ever been to! You saved me! Come on into my office and sit down. Are you sure you don't want something tastier than water? Frightful stuff that, unless you use it to bathe or wash your car with it."

"Water is just fine," Katie replied. "Thank you so much for taking the time to talk to me without an appointment."

"No worries, no worries." Dr. Gallagher laughed. "Come on in."

"Excuse me, Doctor," Brenda said as she stood up behind her desk. "But did you happen to notice Mr. Wright when you came in just now?"

"Dan? No, I didn't see him. Was he here too?"

"Well, for a few moments. He seemed a bit edgy and said he had to talk to you about something important. I offered him an appointment, but he was adamant that you call him as soon as you were finished with your other matters."

"Bah, he's always edgy—like he's suffering heartburn from some marginal meal," he said, looking at Katie, smiling. "Or drinking too much water." Doctor Gallagher laughed loudly, as if only to himself. "I'll be sure to give him a call after I've had a chance to visit with Miss Katie here."

"I can wait if you want to call him now," Katie offered.

"Nonsense! You were here first, my dear! Come in, come in!" Dr. Gallagher opened the large mahogany door to his office and motioned for Katie to enter.

A few moments later, she was seated on one couch, and Dr. Gallagher seated himself across from her on another and poured what she assumed was whiskey from a decanter that was on the low coffee table between them.

"Now then," Dr. Gallagher said with a wink, "you have your water, and I have my *fruit juice*." He took a sip from his glass. "Ahhh, one of life's little pleasures. Now, tell me what's on your mind this lovely but late New Orleans afternoon!"

Katie looked at her watch and saw it was after five o'clock. "Oh no, I'm so sorry. I didn't realize it was this late. I should have known, of course, but I guess I wasn't thinking. I—"

Dr. Gallagher laughed. "Hold on, young lady, hold on! You're talking so fast I'm having trouble keeping up with you!"

"I'm sorry, Doctor."

Dr. Gallagher smiled. "There's nothing to be sorry about. I often meet with people after hours—this is what I do! Now, slow down, relax, sip your water—if you must drink that vile stuff in front of me—and tell me what brings you here to chat."

"You probably already know it's about Trevor. I left him a little while ago, down in the French Quarter. I have to tell someone how much I am really worried about him."

Dr. Gallagher nodded knowingly. "I know you are, and quite frankly, so am I. There is something going on with him. That is certain. Just *what* that something is, though, is a puzzle indeed."

"Doctor, he told me this afternoon that his father is alive again—that he's talked to him!"

Dr. Gallagher seemed unaffected at what Katie just told him as he sat quietly, looking at her and sipping his drink. He then leaned forward and spoke in a low and serious tone, "Katie, what Trevor told you might very well be the truth."

Katie was momentarily dumbfounded but managed to find her voice. "How can you possibly say that? Trevor is worried he is losing his mind, and I have assured him he isn't, but now I'm beginning to wonder a little about you!"

Dr. Gallagher laughed then realized Katie was not quite amused. "Katie, do you remember when you and Father Archer came here and you first told me about Trevor?"

"Of course, I do."

"Do you remember my theory about what might be going on with him?"

Katie nodded. "Yes. I believe you said you thought Trevor could talk to the dead."

"I said I believed Trevor could *communicate* with the dead, Katie, as well as if he were communicating with the living."

Katie shook her head. "I'm not sure I understand your point. Talk or communicate, what's the difference? It's crazy to think about either way!"

"No, Katie, it's not crazy at all. You are a good Catholic girl. You believe in communication with the spirit world, or else you wouldn't pray."

"Come now, Doctor, that's entirely different!"

Dr. Gallagher shook his head. "No, it's not entirely different at all. You believe you can pray, ask for forgiveness or for blessing, and you will then receive the forgiveness or the blessing you asked for. If you didn't believe that, why would you do it? The mind is marvelously complex. If we believe in something strongly enough, it becomes very real to us. Yet if this were all it was with Trevor, I wouldn't be as concerned as I am about him. But Trevor presents a whole different dimension to it all. He not only appears to have the ability to communicate with the spirit world—and I do mean more than simply talk—but I believe Trevor can actually see and interact with those who have passed on! What is even more intriguing to me is that he seems to have the unique ability to actually share his connection with those around him, the ones closest to him, those he knows and trusts—like you. This is why I believe you were able to hear the voices and see the apparitions Trevor heard and saw while you were at his house."

"So you *do* think all of this has something to do with the house?"

Dr. Gallagher poured himself another drink from the decanter and again sat back on the couch. "I think Trevor's house may be the center of these experiences he has been having—perhaps where this all started—but house or no house, I don't rule out Trevor's ability to communicate with the spiritual realm in any other place at any other time."

Katie thought a moment. "So that could explain how he could see and hear things at St. Louis Cathedral?"

"Precisely, and I would venture to guess anywhere else he might happen to be. We need to somehow figure out a way to have him connect with these spirits and maintain that connection until these experiences he has been having can be played out or explained more fully. I'm thinking this would be the only way he will be able to free himself from what apparently, and for whatever reason, has been building in his mind since he first began having his dreams.

"But didn't we already do that when you hypnotized him at his house?"

Dr. Gallagher shook his head. "No. Trevor made a contact all right, but we couldn't maintain it. *Something* or *someone* interfered and broke the connection—perhaps because of a question I asked that somehow inadvertently changed the focus."

Katie sighed. "I don't understand. Why can't you just try hypnotizing him again?"

"I could and I may if Trevor is willing, but I am a bit hesitant to do so. There was definitely a second presence who was manifest during that session. I wasn't quite prepared for that, which was my fault. This second presence appeared to me to be very strong and trying to hide something from Trevor, or perhaps protect him from something. We weren't able to identify that presence, Katie, and I do not want to inadvertently put Trevor in any danger or in some type of unknown situation."

"Can such things really happen? I thought that was all movie stuff?"

"It *is* movie stuff, yet there are many things that happen in this world of ours that comprise what we could refer to as *movie stuff*," Dr. Gallagher spoke with caution. "Katie, when your friend Trevor tells you his dad is alive and he has talked to him, I have no doubt Trevor believes he is telling you the absolute truth. Trevor is not *losing* his mind. He is *using* his mind in ways the rest of us do not fully understand. Not only that, but as close as Trevor and his dad obviously were, I would venture his dad is likely an integral part of all this. After all, what Trevor seems to be dreaming about are things Trevor told us his dad was interested in and doing research on at the time of his death."

Katie felt a sudden wave of fear come over her. "Do you believe that Trevor's dad has returned from the dead?"

Dr. Gallagher gently smiled. "Katie, I have believed for a very long time that when there is a death in this life, only the body dies, not the person. The person is the spirit component of the body—the soul. The body is really nothing more than a mere shell for the soul. Think of it. Does the person really change from youth to old age? The body does, of course, but what about the person?" Dr. Gallagher winked. "I feel much the same as I did when I was younger, but I'm reminded things have changed every time I see this shell of a body I'm trapped in. When the body or the shell dies, I believe the person lives on and is very much alive in spiritual form."

"But how can that be?"

"My dear, to explain beyond what I have just suggested to you would only be conjecture. Know that it is faith that will sustain us when we have such questions. If we allow it to, faith will comfort and guide us until the time comes when we will learn the mystery of life after death firsthand."

Katie sighed. "You sound more like a priest than a doctor."

Dr. Gallagher laughed. "You have to remember I still consider myself a little of both."

"So what do we do now? Do we ask Father Archer again if he'd be willing to do an exorcism?"

Dr. Gallagher shook his head. "No, at least we won't ask him yet. I have just thought of something else we might try first to get to the bottom of all this and offer Trevor some protection at the same time! After all, it has often been said there is safety in numbers."

Katie sat forward. "What are you thinking, Doctor?"

Dr. Gallagher drank the last of his drink. "Katie, would you be kind enough to find Trevor? I'd like the two of you to join me for dinner later this evening. Do you have my cell phone number? I believe I gave it to you when we were all at Trevor's house the other night."

Katie nodded as she looked through her cell phone directory. "I think so. Yes, here it is."

"Good." Dr. Gallagher rose to his feet, walked to his office door, and opened it for Katie. "Could you also call Father Archer and see if he can join us as well? How does Muriel's sound, say eight o'clock or so? See what time is good for all of you and let me know."

Katie stood and walked toward the door, calling Trevor on her cell phone as she walked. "I'll do my best."

"Good, good. Meantime, I better call that fellow who was here earlier without an appointment." Dr. Gallagher laughed at his own little joke as he gave Katie a little wink. "I'll see you later."

As Katie walked out into the reception area, she heard Trevor's voice as he answered her call. "Katie? 'Sup?"

44

Going Out to Dinner

TREVOR HEARD THE grandfather clock downstairs in the foyer mark the six o'clock hour. As he finished shaving and washing his face, Trevor wondered what Dr. Gallagher had in mind this time. Reaching for a towel, he patted his face dry then splashed a small amount of aftershave lotion in his right palm and rubbed his hands briskly together, patting his face and neck. *Katie will be here shortly*, he thought as he took his clean shirt from the hanger on the bathroom door and put it on. He wondered whether he should tell them about his dad—that he had seen him and talked to him, not once but twice! *No, they'll think I should be committed.* He wished they could see his dad and talk to him as well.

There was the sound of someone walking up the stairs. *Odd, I didn't hear Katie come in!*

"Katie, is that you? I'm almost ready." Trevor finished buttoning his shirt and noticed that Katie hadn't answered yet as he stepped out into the hallway. "Katie?" As Trevor made his way down the hallway to the front stairway, he could see there was no one there. *I could swear I heard someone walking up the stairs!* Trevor walked down to the foyer and could see the entrance door was closed. He opened the door and stepped outside onto the porch. Katie's car wasn't anywhere in sight. Trevor smiled. "Dad, was that you?" As he looked around and listened, hearing nothing, he suddenly felt a bit foolish. *There's no one here. What's happening to me?*

He sat down on the porch railing and looked down St. Charles Avenue. A streetcar was making its way lazily downtown. It was the start of a pleasant evening, warm but not too warm. There was a gentle breeze that made the yard and garden come to life with the pleasant scent of flowers and freshly mowed grass. Trevor remembered the smell of grass and freshly mowed hay from the Midwest. When he was a boy, he and his brothers would often spend time at the farm where his dad had grown up. Grandpa had sold the land surrounding the homeplace, and the farmers who had bought it had an alfalfa field nearby. Trevor had always enjoyed the smell of freshly mowed hay.

The sound of Katie's car horn brought Trevor back to the moment. As she pulled into the driveway, Trevor got to his feet and locked the front door to the house before walking down the steps and to the driveway.

"Waiting long?" Katie asked, leaning out the open window of the driver's door.

"Not at all. I just came out on the porch before you pulled up." Trevor opened the passenger door and got into the car. "So what's this all about?"

As Katie backed her car into the street and began driving down St. Charles, she turned to Trevor. "I really don't know for sure—something about an idea Dr. Gallagher has to help figure out what is going on with you these days."

"He's not planning to hypnotize me at a restaurant, is he?"

Katie laughed. "No, I don't think that's the plan. I'm guessing he just wants to talk to you about things."

Trevor turned to Katie, a serious look on his face. "You told him about my telling you I saw my dad, didn't you?"

Katie suddenly felt like maybe she had done something wrong. "Yes, Trevor, I did. I'm sorry, but I—"

"That's all right, Katie," Trevor said reassuringly. "Because I had thought about telling Dr. Gallagher and Father Archer about that myself. Of course, I decided against it." Trevor laughed. "You just made things easier. I just hope they don't throw a net over me at dinner."

"Trevor, Dr. Gallagher said he believes you."

Trevor reacted in surprise. "He told you that?"

"Yes, he did. He's even got me convinced." Katie smiled. "Well, almost anyway. He sounds pretty convincing. I'm sure he'll be anxious to discuss it all with you over dinner."

Trevor sighed. "I'm feeling anxious about that discussion myself. I hope he isn't just planning to humor me while you and Father Archer swoop over me with the net."

Katie chuckled. "Don't be silly. No one is going to swoop over you with a net."

"I wish I was as sure about that as you are."

"The Quarter is going to be crazy tonight. Maybe we should park in the ramp and walk? It's a nice evening for it."

Trevor nodded. "I agree." Trevor pointed to a side street. "Maybe we should turn here before Canal Street. We may get there a little quicker."

"Good idea." As Katie signaled and turned her car onto the side street, a woman suddenly stepped away from the curb and into the path of the car. Katie slammed on her brakes, and just as suddenly as she had appeared, the woman was gone.

"What's the matter?" Trevor asked in a startled tone. "Why did you hit your brakes like that?"

Katie looked at Trevor in surprise. "Didn't you see that woman who stepped out in front of us? Where'd she go? I didn't hit her, did I?"

Trevor looked out the windows around the car. "What woman? I didn't see anyone!"

All of a sudden, Katie felt a shiver and goose bumps. "My God, Trevor, it was *that woman!*"

Trevor looked at his friend, confused. "What woman, Kate?"

Katie put her hand on Trevor's arm. "The woman whose ghost I saw in your bedroom!"

A New Plan

Dr. Gallagher looked thoughtfully at Katie for a long moment before he spoke. "So you believe this woman you saw—the one who stepped in front of your car on the way here tonight—was the same woman you saw the other night at Trevor's house?"

"Yes, I am certain of it. As soon as I saw her, she vanished! Just ask Trevor!"

Trevor smiled nervously as he put down his coffee cup. "Well, it's true that when Katie called my attention to what she had seen, when I looked for the woman, she was not there."

Father Archer looked puzzled. "So you didn't see the woman at all, Trevor?"

"No. But from the way Katie hit her brakes and the conviction she has in her story, I'm certain she saw something."

The waiter arrived with the meals each of the four had ordered, and after a few moments, everyone had their dinner before them.

"This certainly looks good." Dr. Gallagher picked up an open bottle of wine from the table. "Anyone care for a little fruit of the vine?"

Katie held out her glass. "I'd like some please. Thank you."

Dr. Gallagher laughed. "Well, our little Irish lass has finally decided to abandon her soft drinks and turn that water she was drinking earlier into wine!" As he poured the wine for Katie, Father Archer picked up his glass as well.

"As long as you're pouring, Joseph."

As Dr. Gallagher poured wine for Father Archer, he looked at Trevor. "How about you, son?"

Trevor shook his head. "No, thanks, not now anyway. I think I'll just stick with the coffee for the time being since I haven't been sleeping anyhow."

"Ah, well, my boy, that is why I wanted to see you all tonight." Dr. Gallagher poured himself a glass of wine and put the bottle back on the table. "Here's to getting at the bottom of Trevor's little dilemma."

Trevor smiled sheepishly as Dr. Gallagher, Father Archer, and Katie toasted their wineglasses toward him.

"Well, that would certainly be wonderful if we could pull it off."

"Eat up, everyone. Dinner is on me." Dr. Gallagher picked up a piece of shrimp, dipped it in some cocktail sauce, and took a bite out of it. "Tell me, Trevor, what do you know of the term *environmental context*?"

Trevor thought a moment then shook his head. "Well, taking the words at face value, I suppose the term refers to the surroundings that influence a person's development—something like that."

"Very good, Trevor, very, very good! That is precisely what it refers to—the familiar external surroundings of our environment that influence how we develop and fashion what we know and what we think about."

"So basically, if I was raised in ancient Rome, I would speak Latin, write Greek, and wear a toga?"

Dr. Gallagher laughed aloud and nodded. "Precisely! You have it, my boy!"

Katie looked confused. "Have what, Dr. Gallagher? I'm not sure I understand any of this!"

"Let me explain, my dear," Dr. Gallagher replied. "If we can put Trevor into just the right environmental context and, having done that, try hypnosis once again, I think we just might have more success in learning what these dreams of his are all about."

"Sure, Katie," Trevor quipped. "We'll just find a time machine somewhere and transport ourselves back a couple thousand years."

"Well, I don't think we have to go to that extreme," Dr. Gallagher said, showing his big Irish grin. "But we do need to make Trevor *think* he's back to the time period of his dreams."

Father Archer had remained silent, eating his dinner and listening to what the others had been saying. But now he felt he needed to become part of the conversation. "Tell us, Joseph, if you can, just how do you think we can accomplish this little charade?"

"That's where you come in, Donald. How's your steak?"

Father Archer took a sip of wine. "Fine, fine. How is it I come into this exactly?"

"Come, come, Donald! Think for a moment about what we've been talking about here!"

Trevor and Katie looked at each other then at Dr. Gallagher and Father Archer. Suddenly Father Archer smiled and nodded. "I think I follow you now, Joseph. By heavens, it just might work at that!"

"That's the spirit, Donald! I knew you'd think this was a brilliant idea!"

"Well," Father Archer said cautiously, "let's hold off on how *brilliant* this is until we know if it will work or not."

Katie couldn't take the suspense any longer. "Oh, please! Will one of you tell Trevor and me what you're talking about? This is driving me crazy!"

"Tell you what," Father Archer said with a sly wink at Dr. Gallagher. "Something I have been working on since Hurricane Katrina destroyed a number of churches throughout the Gulf may be just what we need. So far, Joseph is one of only a few I've shown it to. Let's finish our dinners before they get cold, and we'll fill the two of you in on what we have in mind."

Trevor smiled. "You priests sure enjoy drama."

Dr. Gallagher laughed. "Drama is a must, dear boy! As I had suspected, Donald has just the place in mind for our little environmental-context experiment!"

46

The Sanctuary

Father Archer turned into the large parking lot, drove forward to the front of an old church, and stopped near the door. "Well, we're here, and it looks like it will be a beautiful morning."

Trevor looked out the passenger-side window and could see the sun just peaking up over the horizon. "A great day for time travel," Trevor quipped as he looked at Katie sitting in the backseat and winked. "Are we all going, or am I the only one with a ticket on this little adventure?"

Katie smiled. "If I can go with you, you bet I'll go!"

Father Archer chuckled. "I don't think any of us will be going anywhere but inside St. Agatha's." Father Archer opened his door and stepped out, fumbling for a key among the dozen or so he had dangling from his key chain. "Joseph said he would meet us here at daybreak, so he should be arriving at any moment."

Katie and Trevor each got out of the car as well. The air was a bit cool this morning—a bit unusual for this time of year. Trevor rubbed his arms to shake off a little chill and looked at the church. "So this was one of the churches damaged in the hurricane? It doesn't look too bad."

"Yes, it was—but it wasn't damaged beyond repair, just enough where the archdiocese decided not to reopen it. Many of the parishioners were displaced because their homes were damaged or destroyed, and repairing or rebuilding them wasn't a desirable option for many of them."

"So you bought it to fix it up, Father?" Katie asked.

"Yes, I did, and for very little money. My largest expense was to prove the structure safe and sound enough to save it from the wrecking ball—that and, of course, payment of the taxes on the property." Father Archer sighed as he looked with pride at the old building. "But to me it was all well worth it. This was my parish when I was a boy. I served as an altar boy here, and it was where I found my calling to the priesthood." Father Archer looked deep in thought as he stepped up to the door and put a key into the lock. "My parents attended this church from the time I can remember until the ends of their lives. I had to save it if I could."

"So this is where you store things you collect? Do I have that right, Father?" Trevor asked.

"Well, in a way, Trevor. It is where I store certain things I collect and arrange them in a somewhat special way, which I'm about to show you."

"Dr. Gallagher is here!" Katie announced as Dr. Gallagher drove up alongside Father Archer's car, shut off his engine, and stepped out.

"Good old, Joseph. Right on time." Father Archer turned the key in the lock and opened the door. "Good morning!"

Dr. Gallagher smiled his familiar Irish smile. "Top of the morning to all of you, and a glorious day it looks to be!"

As the four of them stepped inside, Father Archer switched on the lights. It was a beautiful church with high Gothic arches and ancient lamps hanging down from chains high above their heads. There were beautiful stained glass windows, with colorful rays of light streaming through them on the east side of the church. As they walked farther inside, Trevor noticed there were no pews, but instead, there were little scenes that had been created by the careful placement of dozens of religious statues, large potted plants, and various settings that had been constructed to represent scenes from what all appeared to be the time of Christ.

"This is fantastic!" Trevor said as he stepped between two Ionic columns supporting a large arch at the entrance to the main part of the church. "You have done all of this yourself, Father?"

"I've done a lot of the work, but I did hire some workmen to do much of the construction and heavy lifting right after

I acquired the church and began collecting most of what you will see." Father Archer smiled at Trevor. "Now you know why I was so interested in that stained glass window your dad found and installed up in his room. He beat me to the punch on that one!"

Katie looked in awe. "This church is wonderful! I've never seen anything like this before, Father. What a terrific idea!"

"Thank you, Katie."

"You have done a lot since you first showed me your sanctuary, Donald. I am impressed," Dr. Gallagher said.

Father Archer pointed to a large working water fountain, surrounded by living plants and several stone benches. "Come, let's sit down and discuss how we hope to accomplish what we are here to do."

As Trevor and Katie sat together on one of the benches, Trevor noticed for the first time how serene and peaceful the setting was. He felt strangely relaxed and at home here and, for a moment, almost forgot where he was or why he was there.

As Father Archer and Dr. Gallagher sat on the bench facing Trevor and Katie at an angle, Father Archer smiled. "What I have tried to do here is create a scene for each of the most important moments in the life of Jesus. After Katrina and Rita, when the archdiocese struggled with deciding what to save and what to let go, I began collecting statues and artifacts that weren't going to be used anywhere else in the diocese and brought them here. I didn't realize at the time just how many things were going to either be sold or discarded. At first, my intent was to simply store them until they could be integrated back into the diocese at a later time, but then it occurred to me I could do something unique and important with all of it. It all became quite an enterprise indeed. There aren't very many who have seen my project yet—Joseph is one of the few, and now the two of you. I wanted it all to be finished first, but as you will see, I'm still working on it all."

Dr. Gallagher shook his head. "I had no idea you have done so much with this, Donald. I can hardly believe my eyes!"

"It is a labor of love, that is for sure." Turning his attention to Trevor, Father Archer looked interested in what his reaction might be. "What do you think of all this, Trevor?"

"I don't know exactly, but I seem to have a real feeling of peace and tranquility in this place."

"That is good," Dr. Gallagher replied. "That is very, very good!"

"Are we going to try hypnosis again?" Katie asked.

"That's up to Trevor," Dr. Gallagher answered. "How do you feel about that prospect, young fellow? Are you willing to give me another chance at getting to the bottom of these dreams of yours?"

"Well, that's why I'm here, I guess. That's why we're all here. So what's the plan?"

"The plan is to place you under hypnosis with your Roman coin once again—I do hope you have it with you?"

Trevor reached inside the collar of his shirt and pulled the chain and coin up over his head and handed it to Dr. Gallagher. "I'm rarely without it. Here you go."

"That's fine, just fine. Thank you."

"Joseph and I talked about this earlier," Father Archer explained. "And I believe he will be doing this a little differently this time."

"Oh?" Trevor asked.

"Yes, Trevor," Dr. Gallagher replied. "Once I have put you under hypnosis this morning, I don't intend to ask you any leading questions. By that, I mean I will only speak with you about things you yourself talk about."

"How will that work exactly if you don't ask me questions? Don't you have to ask the questions?"

"Typically, yes, but this is a bit of an experiment we are going to try—here in Donald's magnificent sanctuary. You see," Dr. Gallagher continued excitedly, "that is where the concept of environmental context comes in. Instead of asking you questions about your dreams, you will have the opportunity to step into some of the scenes you are dreaming about."

"I'm sorry." Trevor shook his head. "You mean by being in this old church, I'm going to think I'm actually a part of my dreams?"

"Not as much being in the church," Father Archer explained, "but more by being exposed to the scenes I have created inside it. It occurred to Joseph first, then to me, that many of the scenes I have created here, which I have designed to reflect certain stages in Christ's life, are similar to the ones you have described as being a part of your dreams."

"That's right, my boy!" Dr. Gallagher exclaimed. "For example, there is the painting at your house of the Nativity that, somehow, was partially repainted. You mentioned a painting of the Crucifixion at Loyola that was partially repainted and had the likeness of your father in it. You also mentioned Christ coming to life, on a crucifix that wasn't really there, during your recent visit to mass at St. Louis Cathedral, and you told us the name Pontius Pilate is mentioned in your dreams."

"Among the scenes I have created here, Trevor, there is one of the Nativity, as well as one of Pontius Pilate condemning Christ to death, and of course, there is one portraying the Crucifixion itself. There are also quite a number of statues depicting various persons from the Bible." Father Archer looked at Trevor and Katie. "Joseph and I believe, once you are under hypnosis and you walk through these scenes, you may see something that will trigger a memory or some explanation as to what these dreams mean to you and why you might be having them."

"Oh, that sounds so exciting, Trevor," Katie said excitedly. "I can hardly wait to have you try this!"

"I'm willing to try," Trevor answered consciously. "But it sounds a little like a *Twilight Zone* episode to me. Dr. Gallagher, do you really think this will work?"

"I've never tried anything quite like this before, so I can't be certain, but I believe there is a very good chance it may—particularly since you, shall we say, 'acted out' a scene from the Crucifixion when you were in the environmental context of mass at St. Louis Cathedral recently."

Trevor appeared embarrassed. "Oh man, please don't remind me of that!"

"You saw something that day that made you do and say what you did and said, but the problem is you don't remember doing any of it, or why you did. Under hypnosis, it is my hope, if you have another such experience, you will remember it."

"So once you hypnotize me, you are going to turn me loose to wander around the scenes Father Archer has created in this old church, hoping I see something that turns me into an ancient Roman?"

Dr. Gallagher laughed aloud. "In a manner of speaking, yes, except we will be walking right there with you—silently and unobtrusively, of course—observing what you do and what you say."

"So I have your word you won't let me wander off or do something crazy?"

"Don't you worry about that, Trevor, "Dr. Gallagher said assuredly. "The three of us will take good care of you the entire time."

"Well, then, should we get started? The sooner we get to the bottom of all this, the better."

Father Archer looked at Katie then at Dr. Gallagher. "I guess we're all ready?"

"Perhaps the best starting point would be the scene of the Nativity, Donald, would you agree?"

"That certainly sounds like a reasonable place to start—especially since a painting of the Nativity proved to be a somewhat dramatic focal point in Trevor's recent experiences. The Nativity scene is right over here."

Together, Trevor, Katie, and Dr. Gallagher followed Father Archer around one of the large supporting columns, and soon they were all four standing before a magnificent life-size Nativity scene. As Trevor looked at the life-size figures, his attention was immediately drawn to the face of Mary, the mother of Jesus. As he stared at the statue, he suddenly thought he noticed Mary's eyes move—as if she were looking back at him!

"Are you ready to begin, Trevor?" Dr. Gallagher dangled Trevor's coin from his hand.

Trevor looked again at the face of Mary, and her eyes looked the same as when he first saw the statue. He realized his imagination must have been playing tricks on him. He smiled at Katie and Father Archer then turned his attention once again to Dr. Gallagher. "Yes, I'm ready."

Dr. Gallagher lifted the chain and held the ancient coin before Trevor's eyes as he began twirling it back and forth in rhythmic motions. Some of the colored rays of light from the stained glass windows behind them reflected on the coin, and Trevor soon found the coin becoming obscured by a gentle fog.

Katie noticed her vision was becoming blurred and saw that Father Archer seemed to be frowning. He began rubbing his eyes as if he too were experiencing the same sensation. She tried to speak but found, to her utter surprise, she could not!

Trevor reached out and touched the wooden railing separating him from the Nativity scene as it too became more and more obscured. He focused his attention entirely on the coin as it twisted gently back and forth, back and forth, back and forth—as it seemed to be moving away from him. He began stepping toward the coin, which was almost lost now in the thickening fog. He stepped more quickly as he could barely make it out. He continued walking toward the coin, quickening his pace in the thickening fog, trying to keep it in view; but within just a few moments, it was gone!

Trevor stopped and looked around. He was now entirely surrounded by fog, but he thought he could hear a female's voice. "Katie, is that you? Dr. Gallagher? Father Archer?"

There was no answer. "Where is everyone?" He made his way cautiously toward the sound of the female's voice and abruptly came to an unexpected stop as he bumped into someone—no, *something*! He could now see a light! It was very faint, but it grew stronger and brighter as he looked at it.

As the fog began to clear, he could see that he was standing outside an open window. Inside, there were three people—two men and a woman. The three appeared to be seated on large flat stones at a table in a small room, and the woman was speaking, but in a language he could not understand. She was beautiful, and Trevor realized the light he had seen was actually some type of warm glow that seemed to be present about this woman's face. He became mesmerized at the very sound of her voice, and to his surprise, he could now understand clearly every word the woman was saying.

How It All Began

"It was yet in the days of King Herod when a most wonderful voice spoke to me as I was resting at my parents' home in Nazareth. I was startled at first, for I saw no one. Then there he was, telling me not to fear him, calling me by my name, yet I had never seen this man before. He told me he was the angel Gabriel, sent to give me wonderful news because I had found favor with God."

Luke looked at Mary for a long moment, not quite knowing what to say or how to say it. He looked at Joseph, who sat quietly without concern of any kind. "Mary, are you saying you were visited by an angel?"

Mary smiled. "I was visited by the angel Gabriel, Luke. Gabriel told me I would conceive a son who would be called the Son of God, and I was to name him Jesus. I did not understand since I had never been with a man, although I had been promised in marriage to a wonderful man named Joseph. Gabriel told me all things are possible with God and that my kinswoman Elizabeth had also conceived a son in her old age and was in her sixth month. Gabriel then left me to reflect upon all he had told me."

Luke sighed. "I am sorry, but you are telling me you saw an angel—a celestial being sent by your God?" Luke turned to Joseph for help. "Is this what you are hearing as well, Joseph?"

Joseph nodded. "I understand what you must be thinking, Luke. I myself have yet to see an angel, but I know in my heart they do exist, and if Mary says she has seen Gabriel and he has talked to her—"

Luke stood up, covered his face momentarily with his hands, then looked with all seriousness at Mary. "I am not a Jew, and I know nothing of Gabriel or angels or people coming back from death. I am having great difficulty understanding any of this, let alone believing any of it. I really have my doubts I can write the story of your Jesus—it is just all too beyond what I know and understand or what I am capable of believing."

Joseph stood and put his hand on Luke's arm. "Please, sit and listen to the rest of Mary's story. You will begin to see why Jesus is the Son of God and understand why he came to us and why what has taken place had to happen."

Luke could see the sincerity in Joseph's face, and as he nodded and sat down once again, he looked across the table at the mother of Jesus. "I am sorry, but I am a man of reason and of certainty. If I were to tell anyone this story, I would be thought to have lost my senses."

"Hear my story, Luke—the story of Jesus, the only Son of God and born of me who is truly blessed among all women. I promise you will find all the reason and certainty you seek."

Luke shook his head as he looked at Mary—that radiant glow once again visible about her face. Strangely, he felt foolish and calm all at once. "I am sorry. Please, forgive me and tell me more."

"It was late December when I traveled to see Elizabeth. I needed to speak with her since we were both destined to give birth to sons—she in her old age, and I a virgin betrothed to a man who knew nothing of my secret. I stayed with Elizabeth for three months until her son was born. She and her husband, Zacharias, named the boy John. It was at about the same time word of King Herod's death reached the town, and there became much concern among the people as to what would happen. I left Elizabeth and her newborn son, and I returned to Nazareth to be with my own family. By the time I arrived, I was nearly in my fourth month, and I knew there would be much to explain to my family and to Joseph, my betrothed husband. At first, then—like it is with you now— it was difficult for anyone to believe what I told them. I could tell Joseph was deeply hurt, but he believed me and defended me against those in the village who spoke against me. Joseph had a good heart and a strong will, and he took me for his wife."

Luke nodded. "He must have cared for you very much. I am sure it was a difficult time for both of you."

"There was much more difficulty for us all to endure. Because of Herod's death, Emperor Augustus ordered a census before deciding whether he would appoint a new king to take Herod's place. Quirinius, the governor of Cilicia and also coregent governor and military commander in Syria, conducted that first census after Herod's death. On his orders, Rome's presence was greatly increased throughout the region to keep order as more and more soldiers arrived throughout the summer. Augustus would order a second census ten years later when Herod's son Archelaus, who had been appointed by Augustus to rule over Judea after the first census was completed, had been removed by Augustus and exiled to Gaul."

Luke immediately recognized the name Quirinius. He had seen Publius Sulpicius Quirinius once, nearly ten years before, at Caesarea. Quirinius had been a trusted friend of Caesar Augustus and was a favorite of Tiberius, who was the stepson and successor to Augustus. Quirinius had no fewer than four legions at any given time under his command. When Quirinius died in the eighth year of Tiberius, the emperor asked the senate to decree a public funeral praising his years of service to Rome. "I recall Quirinius was a powerful man who was admired and trusted by Caesar Augustus because of his ability to command order."

"Those days following Herod's death were days of fear. No one knew what Rome would do. It was near the beginning of my ninth month when Roman soldiers first came to Nazareth and posted the decree from Caesar Augustus. In that decree, each family would need to be enrolled for the census, and each family must travel to the patriarch's ancestral home. So Joseph and I set out from Nazareth to his ancestral home of Bethlehem that September. The trip to Bethlehem, which should have taken four or five days, took Joseph and me a full week because of my condition."

"That was a most difficult time for Mary," Joseph of Arimathea said softly to Luke. "Since she was already so close to the time she would give birth to Jesus."

"It was difficult for Joseph too. We had a poor little donkey Joseph used for carrying lumber and tools. Instead, that gentle animal carried me. I rode most all the way, yet we would have to stop often to rest. We had very little food and almost no money." Mary smiled. "I know Joseph went without eating many times on our journey so I could have more to eat. I even saw him feed a small portion of food meant for him to our little donkey. He was truly a kind and gentle man."

"Did Joseph have family in Bethlehem to help you once you arrived?"

"No, Luke," Mary said, shaking her head. "We were all alone when we arrived, and it was late. We had planned to stop along the road, as we had been doing, and continue on into Bethlehem when it was daylight. But it was very near my time, and I knew Jesus was about to be born."

Joseph of Arimathea reached out and put his hand upon Mary's hand. "God was with you, Mary."

"Yes, He was. When we arrived at Bethlehem, Joseph tried so desperately to find a place for us to stay, but there were so many people. Joseph was told about a sheepfold with a small cave we might find shelter in, just outside of town. By the time we reached the cave, I knew my time was very short, and God's son would soon arrive. There were a few sheep and cattle there, and Joseph gathered some hay and made a place for me to lie down. It was there, beneath the stars in a small stable, among the animals, that Joseph and I welcomed our Lord Jesus as he was born into this world."

"You and your husband were all alone in that stable? There was no midwife or anyone else to help you deliver your child?"

"God was with us, Luke." Mary smiled gently at him. "In the heavens, there was the singing of many angels during the time Jesus was born. Soon after, a young shepherd boy was the first to come into the cave, followed by several other shepherds. The shepherds told us they heard the voices ringing through the night sky as they watched over their sheep. It was at that time the angel of the Lord appeared to them and told them not to fear, that a savior had been born in Bethlehem and they would find the child wrapped in swaddling clothes, lying in a manager, and there would be peace on the earth and goodwill among men. Then, as the angels left them, the shepherds came to Bethlehem to see the child for themselves, and they found us in the place where Jesus was born. The shepherds told us their story, which I have kept deeply inside my heart for all time since."

Luke marveled at the story of the simple birth of the prophet—the very same prophet some were saying had returned from death! "What did you do? Surely you could not stay in that cave with your child!"

"We did stay there with all the gentle animals until we were enrolled in the census a few days later. We then made our way to Jerusalem and stayed there for the circumcision and naming of Jesus until the days of purification and the presentation of Jesus to the Lord, according to the Law of Moses, were accomplished. Joseph had just enough money for the required sacrifice of two turtledoves at the temple, and it was after that we made our journey back home to Nazareth."

48

Luke Reports to Pilate

Pilate looked at Lucanus in disbelief. "You intend to write your reports to me under the name *Luke*?"

"Yes, the prophet's mother gave me the name."

Pilate shook his head and rose from his chair. "A Jewish woman gives you the name of Luke, and you take it as your own? Have you lost all senses?"

"I have given this some thought, my liege. Do you remember your concern about how I was to get my reports on Jesus of Nazareth to you without anyone suspecting what my purpose was or, more importantly, what your purpose was?"

"Yes, I do recall that. Go on."

"It occurs to me that by using the name Luke, my true identity might be well concealed."

Pilate looked at Lucanus with a frown. "And what is to be my identity? Perhaps you propose this Jewish mother of the prophet give me a different name as well?" Pilate scoffed. "Do not be foolish, Lucanus!"

Luke spoke cautiously, "My liege, I have come up with a name for you as well in this matter, which should not displease or dishonor you yet keep your identity a secret if any of my reports should fall into unintended hands."

Pilate looked at Lucanus with curiosity. "Is that so? What name might you have in mind for me in this matter?"

"My lord, all of my written reports to you after this day will be sent from Jerusalem to Caesarea by messenger. The chance someone unintended may read one or more of these reports before they reach you does exist. If the reason for these reports is misunderstood, it could mean trouble for you—for both of us."

"Do you think for one moment I do not know that? Imagine what Tiberius would do if he thought I was at all concerned about this prophet Jesus being *alive*?" Pilate shook his head. "But do not forget, Lucanus, there are few who are capable of reading anything."

"I know you are aware of the dangers, my liege, and I am aware there are few who read and write who may come in contact with these reports. However, it only takes a single person, does it not?"

Pilate sighed as he walked to a window and looked out over Jerusalem. "I suppose you are right. I question this entire plan, yet I must know, Physician, if this man Jesus is indeed *alive*—if it is indeed possible he somehow returned from death—as more and more people seem to claim."

"If you think I have lost my senses for writing by the name of Luke, you will likely be convinced of it when you hear my first report. My lord, the circumstances surrounding the birth of this Jesus of Nazareth are so incredible it is difficult for me to understand if such things could even take place. Yet his earthly parents were hardworking people of very modest means—not at all what one might expect for the arrival of a savior who is the foretold Jewish messiah and king."

Pilate turned from the window and took several steps toward Lucanus, a look of concern on his face. "Did I hear you right? Did you say 'earthly parents of a savior foretold as the Jewish messiah and king'?"

"I did, my lord."

Pilate sighed as he sat back down in his chair, looking at Lucanus for a long moment. "So are you now telling me Jesus of Nazareth was indeed the King of the Jews?"

Lucanus swallowed hard and looked at Pilate with caution. "My lord, some say he *is still* King of the Jews."

"That is what you must find out! I am still convinced when a man is dead, he stays dead. The thought a man can return from death does not seem at all possible." Pilate motioned to a chair across from the one he was seated in. "Very well. Sit down and tell me what you have learned thus far. But mind you, I am interested in facts, not in prophecy! I will call off this entire plan if I find that is all that you propose to tell me."

Lucanus sat in the chair across from Pilate. "I will tell you what I have learned from my meeting with Mary, the mother of Jesus, and her uncle Joseph of Arimathea."

Pilate sat forward. "Joseph of Arimathea is of the same blood as the prophet? So *that* is why he asked to claim the body of Jesus! I thought perhaps it was because the Sanhedrin wanted to be certain the prophet was indeed dead and they could know where he was to be buried so the soldiers could keep watch."

Lucanus spoke softly, "Joseph of Arimathea did not agree with other members of the Sanhedrin when they condemned Jesus and brought him before you demanding he be crucified. But he was only one man."

Pilate nodded. "I am not surprised. He seemed to be as good a man as there is in this terrible place. I could tell when he came here to ask for the body of this Jesus that he was not like many of these religious zealots. My first thought that night was to send him away and let the wild dogs take care of the prophet's remains as they have often done in the past with those who have been condemned to their death by crucifixion. But, Lucanus, I could see there was something about this man—something similar to what I had also noticed about this prophet Jesus—which caused me to release the prophet's body to him instead for a proper burial."

"I am pleased to hear you say that, my liege, because I too believe Joseph of Arimathea is not like other members of the Sanhedrin. He sincerely believes in what I learned from the prophet's mother. He himself tried to convince me that what I am about to relate to you is truth."

Pilate again felt a wave of fear race through his veins as he thought about this Jesus and all that had happened since he was crucified. He thought about the centurion Longinus and his story concerning the man of light he had seen outside the tomb on the morning the prophet's body had disappeared. This was indeed a dangerous path he and Lucanus were now traveling—looking at the possibility this prophet was some sort of savior even death could not destroy! If word got back to Rome about any of this— Lucanus was right about taking some precaution.

"Before you begin your report, *Luke*, since that is the name you choose in writing your reports, do you now care to tell me what *my* new name for purposes of receiving these reports is to be?"

Luke smiled. "It is a Greek name, my lord, a name of importance that also means 'loved by God.'"

"Loved by God!" Pilate looked displeased. "*What* God? You propose to give me a name that means 'loved by God'?"

"My liege, this would not be a public name—you and I are the only ones who would know to whom the name refers. Yet, if any of my reports should come into other hands, what better way to protect your true identity? The name would make it appear the reports are written for one of the prophet's own followers."

Pilate nodded his approval. "I begin to see more clearly now your reason." Pilate again thought about the dangers involved in secretly seeking information about the prophet. "Very well, very well—tell me, *what* is this Greek name?"

Luke smiled. "*Theophilus.*"

49

The Image

Trevor suddenly realized he was just standing somewhere, looking through a misty fog. He couldn't see anything or hear anything. His heart began to beat faster. *Am I dreaming again? The voice of this man Lucanus is familiar, yet I have no idea who this man might be. And what of this other man—is it indeed Pontius Pilate? This Lucanus called him lord and liege and mentioned something about the name Theophilus. I have seen this other man in my dreams before.* Trevor shook his head. *None of this makes any sense, but then these dreams never made any sense!*

Trevor reached out into the fog and took a few cautious steps, trying to get some bearing as to where he was. As he inched his way along, he listened for any type of sound that might help him figure out what was taking place. *Where am I?*

Suddenly there was a sound. Trevor stopped and listened intently. *Wait! I hear footsteps just ahead of me!* Trevor cautiously stepped forward once again, this time in the direction of the footsteps, trying to see something or someone he might recognize. As the fog seemed to dissipate, his eyes began to focus on a shadowy figure some distance ahead. As Trevor walked toward the figure, he could begin to see it was a tall man dressed in ancient Roman garb, walking briskly and beginning to disappear once again from view. Trevor picked up his pace, trying to keep the man in sight and get closer to him. *I must stop this man if I can*, Trevor thought. *I've got to find out what is happening here!*

Soon Trevor was within a few yards of the man, and he could now see it was this person Lucanus whom he had just witnessed talking to the man now apparently identified as Pontius Pilate in his dream! *I am still dreaming*, Trevor tried to convince himself. *But this all seems so real! I must find some answers this time!* Trevor called out to the man, "Hello! Wait for a moment, please! I would like to talk to you."

Abruptly the man stopped and just stood there for a long moment—looking straight ahead and keeping his back to Trevor. Then, just as Trevor reached the place where the man stood, the man slowly turned to face him.

Trevor stood silently as if in shock, unable to speak as a wave of fear came quickly over him. *How is this possible?* Trevor stepped back and shook his head. *No! It can't be!* As

Trevor stared in disbelief at the man, he at first thought it was his dad but soon realized it was not his dad at all, but rather it was as if he were looking into a mirror at the very image of himself!

Luke Speaks with Paul

As LUKE SAT in the shade of a few trees just outside Jerusalem, he could see dust clouds in the distance. It was nearly Passover once again, and Jerusalem was crowded with thousands of Jews arriving from throughout the region. Pilate and at least half a legion were returning from Caesarea to keep order during this often tumultuous time, as was his custom and the expectation of Rome. It had been a year since Luke had seen Pilate—and seven years since the prophet Jesus had been crucified.

Luke had learned much in those seven years and had sent a number of reports to Pilate, keeping him informed of it all. Those reports, all addressed to *Theophilus*, had gone unnoticed by anyone else so far as Luke was aware. Pilate, of course, had never sent any acknowledgement of receiving them; but each year, Luke managed an audience with Pilate inside his stone palace in the Antonia Fortress near the temple. It was at that time, each year, the two men would discuss the past year's events and discuss what Luke had learned and had written down.

Each year, during the first three years after the prophet's death, Luke had hoped to return to Caesarea with Pilate after the Passover. Each of those three years, Pilate had asked Luke to stay and continue his search for more and more information about Jesus of Nazareth. It seemed Pilate was never quite satisfied—as if he was looking for something Luke had just not been able to find. For the past four years, however, Luke had asked to remain in Jerusalem, and Pilate had agreed, so long as Luke continued the work he had started concerning the prophet.

Luke had learned much during his years spent in Jerusalem from those who had known Jesus firsthand— from the prophet's family, consisting of his mother and his uncle, to those who walked with Jesus and had loved him. Luke had even made the journey into Galilee, to the town of Nazareth, where the boy Jesus had grown into manhood. Jesus had visited Nazareth only once after he began his ministry; and after he read scripture in the synagogue where he had first read the ancient texts, those who had known him nearly his entire life—who had watched him grow and work alongside his father and, after his father's death, continue to work and care for his mother, those very people considered close to him in that little town—had tried to kill him on a nearby cliff. But somehow he managed to escape unharmed, never to return.

Indeed, that appears to have foretold his fate at the hands of his own people less than three years later when they took him to Pilate to be crucified. Luke learned much about the ones who betrayed him as well. Luke found himself wanting to believe in this prophet and struggled with his remaining doubts, for which he still sought desperately to find some answers. To his surprise, he had watched Pontius Pilate appear to become increasingly open and even receptive to the idea that, perhaps, what Luke had learned about the prophet's ministry and his return to life from death might possibly be true after all.

Pilate had confided in him on his last visit that his wife, Claudia, had become a devout follower of Jesus of Nazareth—quietly, of course—and she had pleaded with Pilate to do the same for the sake of his own salvation. Pilate, being a soldier and an official of Rome, could not risk taking such an action, even in secret and even if he were convinced, which at least up to the last time Luke had spoken with him, he was not.

Luke had written notes for himself of the history he was assembling concerning Jesus of Nazareth and his teachings—assembling those notes into more formal written reports for Pilate. The two men would discuss those reports each year upon Pilate's return to Jerusalem. He had shared some of his notes with Mary, the mother of

Jesus, and with Joseph of Arimathea. Joseph had told Luke there were others too who had undertaken a written record, some who had known and had followed Jesus. He named two—a man named Matthew and another named Mark.

Joseph was aware of some writings by Matthew but was concerned Matthew was writing more to show a fulfillment of prophecy from the scriptures than to write an accurate account of the actual life of Jesus. Joseph had mentioned several things from his reading of Matthew's writing that had simply not happened involving Jesus but, instead, were stories known from scripture concerning Moses, which Matthew had altered specifically to fit his narrative of the life of Jesus.

It was as if, Joseph surmised, Matthew was intent on portraying Jesus as a new Moses, who had come to deliver his people from the Romans, instead of Jesus bringing salvation for all mankind. Joseph also mentioned others who, in addition to Matthew and Mark, were apparently telling stories and retelling them—often differently from the way they had told them before. If these people were capable, they would also write them down. However, some of these people had not been the actual followers of Jesus when he was alive, and some had never known Jesus at all!

Joseph was pleased with Luke's writing and had often praised him for his accuracy. He admired how Luke had written from what he knew to be fact and how he had sought out the truth about Jesus from those who knew him best, like his mother, Mary. Joseph told Luke he was advantaged in being a Gentile—that he had not therefore been influenced by ancient scripture and prophecy when writing about Jesus, thus avoiding the temptation to alter his writing for the sake of some prophetic purpose. Luke was not sure whether his writing about Jesus would be preserved for future generations as Joseph believed, but for such possibility, he had tried to write his account accurately so anyone who might read it could rely on what he had written about this most remarkable prophet.

As Luke watched the massive dust cloud in the distance, he realized Pilate and the soldiers would arrive within a matter of hours.

"Deeply in thought, my friend?"

Luke turned, a bit startled, to see Paul sitting down beside him. "I was watching the dust cloud in the distance."

Paul nodded. "You know what that means, do you not, Physician? The Romans are returning."

"Yes. I suspect they will be here before nightfall."

"That is always bad, my friend," Paul said quietly. "Pontius Pilate and his bloodthirsty armies. Herod is bad enough."

"Unless there is trouble, it should not be so bad to have the Romans in Jerusalem. Rome simply wants to avoid any difficulty with so many in the city."

Paul looked with disdain at Luke. "You sound like a Roman when you say things like that! What is the matter with you? Have you forgotten the Romans killed our Savior?"

Luke thought back to seven years before, and he knew better. Pilate ordered the death of Jesus, but he had also tried desperately to save him. Luke knew this to be true, for he was there. "I am a Roman citizen, Paul, you know that. Even so, I am not taking the part of Rome in anything—I only say what is true about the reason for Pilate and his soldiers coming here."

"They murdered Jesus!"

"Paul, we have had this discussion before. It is true Pilate condemned Jesus to die, and it is true his soldiers crucified him, but it is also true that Jesus was brought to Pilate by his own people—your people—and they demanded Pilate put him to death."

Paul got to his feet. "I am painfully aware of what some of our people did, and I am ashamed of it just as I am ashamed of what I myself did before finding Jesus as my Savior and Lord. But I make no excuse for Rome and its legions. Rome is the root of evil in this land!"

"What of Herod?"

"Herod is in power because of Rome, is he not?"

Luke nodded. "He is. But you know as well as I that Rome holds Herod in check, as it did to less extent with his father, Herod the Great, before him." Luke smiled. "Come, sit with me and calm yourself, my friend. I am not a Jew, but I am not without feeling for the Jewish people. You know that, and you also know I have much interest in the prophet Jesus and his teachings."

"I do know that, Luke, which is why we are friends."

Luke laughed. "The fact that I write down your thoughts for you has nothing to do with our friendship then?"

Paul felt embarrassed. "You know I cannot write as well as you."

"Yet I write for you just the way you ask me to, do I not? I am teaching you how to read and write better, and you are learning, is that not true?"

"It is."

"Then believe me when I tell you that even though I am a Roman citizen, even though I am not a Jew, I am not against you."

Paul sighed. "You are right, Luke. You are right. I am sorry. It is just that I do not like Pontius Pilate and his Roman soldiers in Jerusalem."

Luke looked at his friend as he spoke, a serious tone now evident in his voice. "Was it so long ago, Paul, that you yourself had persecuted some of those you are now concerned may be troubled by the presence of Rome?"

Paul looked for a long moment at Luke and then nodded in sad agreement. "What you say is true, but unlike me, I doubt Rome will ever repent as I have done since the Lord Christ Jesus spoke to me."

"Give them time."

Paul put his hand on Luke's shoulder. "You are a Gentile, and you have a different view than I have. Perhaps time will change Roman hearts, though I have my doubt."

"What of Jewish hearts, Paul? Do you have no doubt you will make them all believers in the prophet Jesus?"

Paul sighed. He could not argue the fact that he, indeed, had his doubts about many of the Jewish people. "I will speak with you later. I have much to prepare before the Romans arrive."

Luke watched as Paul walked back toward the gates of Jerusalem. It was less than a year before that Paul had taken part in the stoning and death of a man named Stephen—an outspoken follower of the prophet's teachings—and shortly after that, Paul claimed to have heard the voice of the risen Jesus as he pursued other disciples of Jesus on behalf of the Sanhedrin. This fact is what drew Luke to him, to seek his friendship.

Paul was a man who had despised the followers of Jesus, who believed in nothing the prophet taught, and who certainly did not believe he had risen from the dead. Yet now he was a firm believer, not only a follower but a minister of the prophet's teachings—all because he heard the voice of the risen Jesus and became convinced of his resurrection from death! He was risking his very life being in Jerusalem—there was talk of several plots by his own people to kill him—but he had managed to conceal his true identity from them, at least for the present.

Like Luke, Paul had changed his name because of this remarkable prophet he and many others now believed in. As a persecutor of those who spoke about the prophet, his name had been Saul of Tarsus. Luke met Paul when Luke was speaking with Peter, one of the original disciples of Jesus. It was after that meeting Paul told Luke how he had pursued some of the prophet's disciples to Damascus. But as he drew near them, he was thrown from his horse in a blinding light; and as he fell to the ground, he heard a voice ask, "Saul, why do you persecute me?" When Saul could not see the man to whom the voice belonged, Saul asked who he was, and the voice answered, "I am Jesus!"

Saul was struck blind for three days and could not eat or drink. He was taken to Damascus and cared for there by the very ones he had persecuted. When he regained his sight after the third day, he too became a disciple of the Lord Jesus and took the name Paul. Had he not believed, surely this man, who had begun by persecuting the followers of Jesus, would not have become a follower of Jesus himself and risked certain death by returning to Jerusalem, proclaiming publicly the prophet's teachings and risking discovery! Paul certainly would not do this unless he had some proof that Jesus had conquered death—not only for himself but for all those who believed in Jesus and his teachings!

Luke feared it was only a matter of time before Paul's true identity became known. Luke and Peter had both urged Paul to leave Jerusalem. Luke wondered what it was his friend might have to prepare now that the Romans were returning and hoped, whatever it was, that it would not result in bloodshed.

Pilate's Return

As NIGHTFALL CAME upon Jerusalem, there was much confusion in the streets. Hundreds of people were there already to observe Passover, and as Luke watched Pilate and his soldiers enter the city, there were outcries from many who saw the return of a large Roman presence as a threat to their freedom and perhaps their very lives. Word had reached Jerusalem some months before that Roman soldiers had massacred some Samaritans who had peacefully been at worship. Luke knew nothing more of this but intended to ask Pilate about what happened when he next saw him. Herod too was back in the city, which added to the tension and the unrest. Some say he had become quite mad—not unlike his father, Herod the Great, had become shortly before his death only months before the birth of Jesus.

As Luke watched the last of the soldiers make their way to the Antonia Fortress near the temple, his thoughts drifted back to the last time he had come to Jerusalem with Pilate, seven years before when the prophet Jesus had been brought to the stone palace by his own people to be condemned to death. Luke had learned it was one of the prophet's own disciples—one of his original twelve, who was called Judas Iscariot—who betrayed his master to temple guards of the Sanhedrin for thirty pieces of silver. When Luke had later met the apostle Peter through Mary, the mother of Jesus, he learned from Peter that a field had been purchased with the blood-tainted coins, and Judas had fallen headlong upon the land to his own horrible death. That field was from that time forward known as Akeldama, or the field of blood.

Luke turned to go back to the small shelter he had lived in this past seven years, paid for by most excellent Theophilus—Pontius Pilate himself. Pilate had kept his word and had provided all Luke needed to survive in this inhospitable place so he could learn all he could about Jesus of Nazareth and perfect an understanding of it all by writing it down in an orderly way. There were few around him who could read or write; but many of those who could, aside from a certain privileged and learned few, read and wrote in Hebrew. Luke preferred to write in Greek.

He suddenly thought back to the time of Passover seven years before, when Pilate had ordered him to paint a sign to be placed above the head of the prophet on his cross. Pilate had told Luke to paint the words "This is the King of the Jews" upon the sign in Greek, Latin, and Hebrew. Pilate wanted to be certain anyone who *could* read would be able to read what he had written and tell others who could not read what the words were. Luke had always thought it was Pilate's way to cause shame to the Sanhedrin and all those who demanded Jesus be crucified. It was if to say, "Look what you have done to your King!"

"You there, you look familiar to me! What is your name?"

Luke, startled, looked up to see a Roman centurion on horseback only a few feet away. "My name is Lucanus."

"Lucanus! Pilate's physician! I thought that was you. Do you not remember me?"

Luke thought for a moment, and then he remembered the name of the centurion who had taken the place of Longinus seven years before. "Flavius, it is good to see you again."

"You appear to be doing well in this place, Physician. Pilate asked us to search until we found you. Come with me at once."

"Come with you now? I thought surely he would want to wait until morning, having just arrived."

"I have my orders. He told us to find you because he must see you now."

Luke nodded. "Very well, let us not keep Pilate waiting."

52

Recalled to Rome

"My lord, I have Lucanus with me."

Pilate turned and faced the two men. "Flavius, that was fast! Thank you. That will be all."

Flavius struck his armored breastplate with his right hand and gave a slight bow then turned and left Luke alone with Pilate. Luke was at once troubled by Pilate's appearance—he looked tired and had a gray pallor. "My liege, begging your pardon, you look tired from your journey. May it please you, could this not wait until morning so you might have some rest?"

"My physician still, I see. Come, Lucanus, sit with me. We have much to discuss, and there is little time." Pilate motioned to a chair then seemed to fall more than sit into one near it. "I am tired, but time will not allow a later meeting."

Luke took his seat near Pilate, an obvious look of concern on his face. "I do not understand—why is there no time to speak later?"

Pilate sighed as he poured two goblets of wine; then he offered one to Luke, which he accepted. "The new procurator, Marcellus, will arrive sometime later tomorrow. Once I have introduced him to Herod and officially given him command, I will be leaving with a cohort back to Caesarea."

Luke was taken by surprise at Pilate's statement. "Did you say *new procurator*, my liege?"

"I did." Pilate drank deeply from his wine goblet, and then he looked at Lucanus. "I have been recalled to Rome by Tiberius."

A new and deep concern for Pilate entered Luke's mind. "But why have you been recalled to Rome?" Luke asked, almost afraid of what Pilate's response might be.

"I wrote a letter to Emperor Tiberius about your Jesus of Nazareth. Apparently, I am no longer in Rome's favor as a result."

Luke looked for a long moment at Pilate, who seemed to have aged even in the few minutes Luke had been with him. "Why did you write such a letter, if I may ask?"

Pilate sighed deeply. "It began with the killing of those Samaritans at Mount Gerizim—surely word of that must have reached you here?"

Luke nodded. "Yes. Is it true, my lord, what they say happened?"

"It is true, I am saddened to admit. There was more to it all, of course. The Samaritans were armed with weapons, and there was some concern they threatened insurrection, but I was ultimately responsible for how it ended. There was a fairly large number of Samaritans who were killed—enough so there was a complaint taken to Vitellius, the Roman governor of Syria. Vitellius sent a report to Rome, and Tiberius was not at all pleased. Since I was already in disfavor with Tiberius over the Samaritan matter, and since I had for some months contemplated how I might send my letter about the Jewish prophet—which I felt I must at some time send anyway, you understand—I decided to send it along with my report on what occurred at Mount Gerizim."

Luke put down his goblet of wine, unable to drink at what Pilate just told him. Luke knew Pilate was likely in serious trouble over the Samaritan matter, and by adding a letter concerning Jesus with his report of it to Rome, Luke feared what might soon befall his benefactor and his friend. "What, if I may know, was in your letter about Jesus of Nazareth, my liege?"

"Lucanus, I have had seven long years to consider what I allowed to happen here. I have considered our conversations since and have read and reread the reports you sent to me about this Jewish Messiah. My wife, Claudia, has gone nearly mad over his crucifixion and death at my hands, and I have now come to believe in this Jesus as the Son of the one true God."

Luke was astonished at what he was hearing. Even he had not allowed himself to actually believe everything he had learned, although he had wanted to believe in it all and had struggled with it for the very same seven long years Pilate mentioned. "I do not know what to say to you, my liege. I am stunned at this revelation."

Pilate laughed as he poured more wine into his goblet. "I suspect you could not be more stunned than Tiberius. I hope this talk of returning from death through this Messiah is true. I suspect I will soon have the chance to meet the prophet once again—face-to-face in his kingdom this time, the one he spoke to me of on the day I ordered he be crucified. I only hope he is a stronger and kinder judge for me than I was for him."

Pilate took another drink of wine and looked at Lucanus with a resigned look. "I wrote in my letter how Jesus of Nazareth's own people delivered him to me, bringing charges against him that they could not prove to my satisfaction; yet I was so afraid of the great uproar they made in demanding his death—so afraid of an uprising I might not be able to control with so many in Jerusalem for their Passover—that I gave in to their wishes, which I knew to be unlawful and unjust! I explained how I ordered Jesus scourged to the brink of death and then ordered he be crucified even though I could find no just cause for the evil accusations made against him."

"But you tried to save him!"

"I tried to make myself and others believe so, but I could have saved him had I not been weak and afraid of what Rome might do if I allowed events to get out of my control. The only man, if you can call him a man, I saved that fateful day was Pontius Pilate! I never before concerned myself with killing if I felt it necessary or even convenient. But this man, this Jesus, was guilty of no crime, and I knew it! My wife begged me to leave the matter alone, and now I have lost her to madness over what I have done—or, perhaps better said, what I failed to do. I believe Emperor Tiberius is now convinced I too have lost my mind. Imagine me, Pontius Pilate, believing in the resurrection of a Jewish Messiah and Savior whom I now embrace as my own! You know my reputation for violence and for caring very little, if at all, for these people. I have dealt with problems by the sword and with brute force—not by kindness, understanding, and forgiveness. *That* was Jesus, *not* Pontius Pilate." Pilate shook his head and sighed. "What has become of me?"

Luke was nearly speechless, struggling to find words. "My liege, do you *really* believe in Jesus in the manner you speak of?"

"I do, thanks in no small part to you, Lucanus. You have done what I have asked, and you have found answers for many of my questions. You have accomplished much—beyond my expectations of what I hoped you might have learned. You have written your reports well, and I have kept them all. I myself have written down my own thoughts concerning your reports, our discussions, and what I remember firsthand of the events surrounding my brief encounter with this ambassador of truth. In my letter to Tiberius, I spoke of how darkness fell over the entire world at the time Jesus was crucified, how the sun was dark at midday and the stars appeared with no luster in them, how blood painted the moon, and how the great veil in the Jewish temple was torn in two."

Pilate looked at Lucanus with fear in his eyes. "Most importantly, I wrote of what Longinus said about the man of light on the day Jesus, the Son of God, rose from death and about people seeing him throughout Judea."

Pilate got to his feet and walked to a table, upon which was a golden chest. As he opened the chest, he turned to Lucanus. "Look at what I have! All of your reports are here, along with my own writings concerning these matters, the bloodstained napkin that covered the prophet's face in death, the crudely fashioned crown of thorns that tore flesh from his innocent head—which I myself found in the earth at the foot of the cross where he died—as well as the coin that fell from the shroud we found in his tomb. It is all here, except for the shroud with the image of Jesus upon it. That, dear Claudia has claimed for herself. She keeps it neatly folded with her most prized possessions. She rarely allows it out of her sight. She will sit for hours holding it upon her lap and praying for her salvation, and she continues to cry her sorrowful tears that I am forgiven my unpardonable crime."

Luke rose to his feet and walked to Pilate, looking into the open chest. Luke could see, written upon the chest, the very same words Pilate had ordered him to paint on the sign that hung above the head of Jesus on his cross. "My liege, the words on this chest and all the contents here seem very dangerous for you to have in your possession. I had thought you would have destroyed my reports once you had read them."

"You thought I would have destroyed them? No! These writings and the other treasures in this chest tell the story of Jesus of Nazareth. Lucanus, the story of this prophet must be preserved and told. It is a story I suspect is not yet finished, but I trust you will see it through, and you will finish it! I have brought this chest for you. You must both write and tell the full story of what has happened in this place so it is preserved for all time."

Luke looked at Pilate and wondered if, indeed, this was the same man he had known and had served for so long. "But how do you suggest I do this? Such a task is one for a true believer! I have struggled with it all, but I do not yet fully have your conviction or your faith."

"I do not believe you. You are lying to yourself to say so! What you have written here was not written by anyone but a true believer! His own mother gave you the name Luke. You told me so, remember? Luke is the name you write by! You know his mother! You watched him die on the cross I put him on! Who better than you, Lucanus, to write the truth of all this? But now, instead of writing reports for me, you will write the prophet's story. You will find your conviction and your faith—you had more than I in the beginning, as I recall. Perhaps it has become more evident to me now because I have come to realize the blood of Jesus is upon my hands and because my time outside *his* kingdom grows short."

Luke was troubled by Pilate's last statement. "What are you saying?"

Pilate sighed as he withdrew the coin that had been found in the tomb of Jesus and handed it to Lucanus. "Take this coin—one I had minted the year I crucified Jesus. You will look at this coin and remember me, but most importantly, you will remember Jesus, who rose from death in his tomb and left only this and his burial linens behind him." Pilate closed the chest and looked at Lucanus sadly. "Come back tomorrow afternoon, early before the new procurator arrives. I was told to expect him later in the day. I will have someone help you remove this chest tomorrow."

Luke persisted in his question. "My liege, you trouble me with what you are saying. What do you mean when you say your time grows short?"

Pilate returned to his chair, sat down, and poured another goblet of wine. "I have been a soldier in the service of Rome for so long I cannot remember having done anything else. I have dedicated my life to Rome, and I trust I have served as faithfully and as well as was my privilege and ability to do so. But now I must serve another master—as my dear wife, Claudia, once told me I must do if I am ever to find my salvation. I know what my being recalled to Rome means, Lucanus. If it were not for Tiberius, I doubt I would see Rome again. Were it not for Tiberius, I might not live long enough to return to Caesarea and my dear wife. Yet I have come to know this world does not matter, Lucanus. This world, as the prophet so clearly implied to me in this very place seven years ago, is not of *his* kingdom. *His* kingdom to come is what really matters, Lucanus!"

Luke looked at Pilate a long moment, at first not knowing how to respond to what he just heard. "You truly believe in all of what you tell me, my liege?"

Pilate finished his wine, and then he nodded, with what appeared to Luke to be a state of peace overcoming him. "Yes, Lucanus, I truly do. Unlike my judgment of the innocent and fearless Jesus for crimes he *did not* commit when he entered the kingdom of Rome, I am not innocent of my crimes, and I am fearful of His judgment when I enter into the kingdom of the one true God."

53

Stabbed in the Desert

Luke had trouble sleeping during the night even though he was extremely tired. What sleep he did manage to get was troubled by dreams—faces of people he had known in the past seven years since Jesus had been crucified. He dreamed of Pilate and of his wife, Claudia—she was dressed all in white, seeming to float just above the marble floor of the palace. In the dream, she posed a question to centurion Flavius, who was also in the room, but Luke answered her instead by saying, "He doesn't know. He's lying again."

Claudia confronted centurion Flavius directly, "Just answer the question."

Luke again responded for the centurion, almost as if to protect Claudia from what the centurion might answer, saying, "He doesn't know."

Claudia persisted, this time screaming her husband's name, "Pontius Pilate!"

Pontius Pilate! Yes, Pilate was mostly on Luke's mind as he thought deeply about the end of the conversation the two men had the night before. Pilate mentioned to Luke he had lost his wife to madness—perhaps that was why she was in the dream?

As Luke reached the gates of the Antonia Fortress, one of the soldiers standing guard looked without expression at Luke and barked a question at him, "What do you want?"

Luke didn't recognize the guard, but that was not unusual, considering there were always changes being made in the ranks. "I am here by order of Pontius Pilate, prefect of Judea."

"Marcellus is prefect of Judea. Pilate is no longer here."

Luke was at once stunned by what the guard said. Pilate had told Luke about how Marcellus was to be the new prefect, but why would Pilate no longer be at the palace? Where would he be? "There must be some error. Pilate asked me to come this afternoon for a chest. He must be here."

"I tell you he is not! I know nothing of a chest."

"Is centurion Flavius here?"

"Flavius is here."

Luke was relieved. "Would you find him and tell him I am here? My name is Lucanus, Pilate's physician."

The two guards looked at each other, and the first guard Luke was talking to turned and made his way into the stone palace. Luke could not imagine Pilate leaving so soon—and before Luke arrived to retrieve Pilate's important chest. Surely, Pilate would not leave before Luke arrived without at least telling the guards he was coming.

"Physician!" It was Flavius, walking with the first guard toward the gate. "Come, walk with me."

Flavius opened the gate, and Luke entered the courtyard and walked with Flavius toward the garden at the far wall—the garden where he had often seen Pilate, deep in thought, looking out over Jerusalem, or sitting with his wife, Claudia, in the shade of olive trees. When he and Flavius reached a large olive tree, Flavius leaned against it and looked seriously at Luke. "What can I do for you, Physician?"

"Flavius, after you brought me here last night, Pilate asked me to return this afternoon for a chest he wanted me to have. One of the guards at the gate just told me Marcellus is now prefect of Judea."

"He is, and between you and me, he is not one to ever let anyone forget it."

"I see." Luke nodded in understanding. "Tell me, Flavius, is Pilate still here?"

Flavius removed his helmet and sat down on a large stone near the tree he had been leaning against. He sighed as he looked up at Luke. "Pilate is gone. Marcellus arrived with about four hundred men. He met only briefly with Pilate. Then Pilate ordered me to prepare his horse. He left in full armor with one of the centuries Marcellus arrived with—about eighty men."

"He left for Caesarea already? But I was to meet him today! He was to give me an important chest."

"Lucanus, when Pilate left Antonia Fortress with Marcellus's men, there was a chest—a golden one—that they took with them."

"I don't understand."

Flavius motioned to another stone near the tree. "Sit, Lucanus. What I have to tell you is not easy. I know you were Pilate's physician, and I know also you were his friend."

Luke did not like hearing the words the way Flavius spoke them, nor did he like the tone in which they were spoken. He sat on the stone and looked at the centurion, almost afraid to ask the question burning in his mind. "Tell me, Flavius, what has happened here?"

"Pilate left with Marcellus's men very near the dawn. The chest you mention, if it was a golden one, they took with them. I placed it on a cart myself, Pilate's last order to me. About two hours later, the century returned—*without* Pilate and *without* the chest."

Luke felt a sudden wave of cold sweep over him. "What? What are you trying to tell me, Flavius? Are you saying…?"

"I am saying, Physician, Pilate is gone. He is no more."

"I don't believe it!" Luke jumped to his feet. "There must be some mistake!"

Flavius shook his head. "There is no mistake. I heard the men talking when they returned. Word reached Judea that Emperor Tiberius is dead. Gaius Caligula is now the emperor of Rome. With Tiberius dead, there was nothing to stop Caligula from ordering Pilate's execution."

Luke felt numb. "Pilate seemed to be aware of something last night. He seemed preoccupied with fate, but he mentioned nothing of the death of Tiberius or this new emperor Caligula."

"Pilate knew nothing about any of this last night. The news came with Marcellus this morning."

"But why would Caligula have Pilate murdered?"

"I do not know, Lucanus, other than what I have heard rumors of—some nonsense about Pilate having betrayed Rome—but I do know better than to ask. I trust you know better as well?"

Luke nodded. Flavius was right about the danger of asking too many questions. "You say you heard the men talking. What else do you know, Flavius? I must know what I can."

Flavius got to his feet and looked out over the stone walls—far into the distance beyond the city of Jerusalem. "What else do I know, Physician?" Flavius sighed as he put his helmet back on. "I know that with his golden chest, Pontius Pilate lies buried somewhere out there—stabbed in the desert."

54

St. Agatha's

"*Stabbed in the desert!*" Trevor looked at Dr. Gallagher in surprise. "Flavius? What…where…is this place?"

Dr. Gallagher, a look of astonishment on his face, put his hands on Trevor's shoulders. "Trevor, this is St. Agatha's. Do you remember coming here this morning with Katie and Father Archer?"

"Trevor? Who is Trevor? Who are you? Where is this place?"

Katie stepped close to Trevor. "Trevor, it's me, Katie. You remember me, don't you?"

Trevor looked blankly at her. "No. No, I do not know you!" He looked around at Father Archer and again at Dr. Gallagher. "I do not know any of you!" As Trevor spoke, he seemed for a moment to stumble. Then he collapsed to the floor unconscious.

"My God, do something!" Katie shouted hysterically. She dropped to her knees and began shaking Trevor. "Trevor, wake up! Trevor!"

Father Archer helped Katie to her feet as Dr. Gallagher knelt by Trevor and checked him over. "He's just fainted, probably from the shock of coming out the hypnotic trance he was under. Donald, is there any water here?"

"Yes, there is a water cooler just as you walk inside at the front of the church. It's where one of the holy-water fonts used to be."

Father Archer eased Katie down on a nearby bench and quickly went to get the water as Trevor groaned and began regaining consciousness. "That's good, Trevor," Dr. Gallagher said softly. "You just had a bit of a faint, dear boy. Can you sit up?"

Trevor put his hand to the side of his head as he sat up on the floor with Dr. Gallagher's help. "Yes, I think so. What happened?"

"Here you are, son." Father Archer handed a cup of water to Trevor. "Take it slowly now."

Trevor drank some water from the cup then looked up at Father Archer. "Thanks."

Katie got up from the bench she was sitting on and came and sat by Trevor on the floor. "Are you all right, Trevor? You scared me!"

Trevor nodded. "Yes, my head hurts a little, but I'm fine."

Dr. Gallagher looked at Trevor's head. "Ah. You do have a bit of a bump there, I'm afraid. It must have happened when you fainted and fell to the floor. Are you feeling dizzy at all? Any blurred vision?"

"No, not now anyway. It got a little foggy earlier." Trevor started thinking about what seemed to be another dream, but this time, everything had seemed so real, and he remembered it clearly. Trevor looked at Dr. Gallagher, Katie, and Father Archer and smiled weakly. "You won't believe what I've been dreaming!"

Dr. Gallagher laughed. "Yes, we will! We will believe you, Trevor, because, thanks to your remarkable ability, I think we *all* witnessed your dream right along with you—at least I know I did!"

Katie nodded. "So did I!"

"I did as well," Father Archer said as he stepped close to Trevor. "It was all fascinating and made sense of some things Christians and historians alike have wondered and argued about for centuries!"

"Really?" Trevor asked. "Like what?"

"Oh, Trevor! Where to begin?" Father Archer answered excitedly. "Explanation for conflicting Gospel passages, the Nativity, the judgment and crucifixion of Jesus, what became of biblical figures like Pilate, and—"

"Slow down, Donald, slow down!" Dr. Gallagher laughed. "This poor boy has had quite a morning and a bit of a faint. Let's give him a chance to fully rejoin us before bombarding him with everything we've learned today."

Father Archer nodded. "Of course. You are right, Joseph. I am sorry, Trevor, but this has been one of the most astonishing days of my life!"

Dr. Gallagher smiled. "My boy, I don't know if all we have learned here today will check out with scriptures and what histories have been compiled, but what you have discovered for us will open the doors for much more future study and debate."

"Let's not forget a renewed interest in the story of Jesus and the church, Joseph," Father Archer said excitedly. "I believe this will 'check out' with the scriptures and the histories that have been compiled these past two thousand plus years! It all seems to fit together like a jigsaw puzzle that we have just discovered more of the key pieces to. Trevor, do you realize what you have done?"

Trevor shook his head and smiled. "Do you mean besides fainting and making a fool of myself?"

Dr. Gallagher laughed his hearty Irish Laugh. "Oh, my boy, we need to write all of this down and do some serious study of all you have shown us here today. Donald is right—it all seems to fit together and make perfect sense!"

"I have to admit, it does, although it will certainly raise some eyebrows both inside and outside the church." Father Archer looked at Trevor. "Do you remember when you and I spoke late one evening in your house about your dad?"

"Of course, I do—it wasn't that long ago. You were quite the detective as I recall, especially when it came to those wet paintbrushes that you found in my dad's room."

"Yes, well, do you remember telling me your father came home one day all excited about something he had found in his research concerning the prophet Luke?"

"Yes, I remember telling you that. He said he had found something he felt certain would completely change what people believed about the notion of life after death."

"You told me it was Luke your father was researching. He had read and reread the two books attributed to Luke, and he even had a stained glass window of Luke installed in one of his rooms upstairs."

"That's right. He told me he couldn't believe that in nearly two thousand years historians, scholars, and those in religious vocations seemed to have missed something that was right there in front of them the entire time."

"Did you hear that, Joseph?"

Dr. Gallagher nodded. "I did indeed. What we witnessed here today through Trevor must be precisely what Trevor's dad was referring to."

"I hate to dampen the excitement the two of you seem to have with all this," Trevor said cautiously. "But wasn't this all just a dream? I mean, it seemed real enough to me, but was it real? How could it be? I believe my father got all of his information from research—not from dreams."

Father Archer spoke first, "Trevor, you make a good point about what we all witnessed here today being like a dream, but remember, you were under hypnosis. Because of your exceptional abilities, the rest of us were all able to share in what you experienced. All this was enhanced for you, perhaps for all of us, by these biblical scenes I have recreated over time in this church." Father Archer turned and gestured to all the scenes that had been constructed. "Look around you! As you stepped from scene to scene here at the old St. Agatha's, new and different information was revealed to you—to all of us— prompted, I presume, by what you saw in each of these scenes reconstructed here. We all saw and heard what took place in the amazing experiences you had here today, and we all were a part of it as if we were right there with you!"

"Wait a minute. What do you mean by saying 'right there' with me? Wasn't I *right here* with you in this church? Didn't you tell Katie when she asked you earlier about taking a trip that none of us would be going anywhere but right here inside St. Agatha's?"

"Yes, that is what I said, Trevor. Physically, St. Agatha's is where we have all been the entire time."

Dr. Gallagher smiled. "You transported us with your mind, Trevor, to a time two thousand years ago, and as a result of your extraordinary and splendid ability to do that and share the experience you had with us, it was as if we all were eyewitnesses to everything you saw and heard."

Katie looked at Trevor, Dr. Gallagher, and Father Archer. "This has been quite a day, but Trevor looks really tired. To tell the truth, I am too. I hate to break this up, but do you suppose we could continue this later when we've all had some time to think it through?"

"Absolutely, my child," Dr. Gallagher agreed. "We do need to take some time to rest and process what has happened here—all of us need to do that. When and where would you all like to meet up again?"

Trevor got up to his feet. "Well, you're welcome to come to my house tomorrow. It's Saturday, and I'll be home all day. Maybe you can somehow explain to me what it all means and why I am having these dreams in the first place. I mean, that's really what this is all about, right?"

Father Gallagher nodded. "I think I may be able to do that, Trevor, which reminds me." Dr. Gallagher reached into his coat pocket and withdrew a chain. "Here is your coin—the one your dad gave you. Whatever you do, don't lose it! If you think about all that has been revealed to us here today, I trust you will know why this coin is so important. I believe this coin is the key to why you have been having these dreams."

Trevor unexpectedly felt a chill as he looked past Dr. Gallagher and saw his father standing there, smiling knowingly at him. "*My coin is the key*! That is what my dad told me!" Trevor exclaimed.

Dr. Gallagher, Father Archer, and Katie all looked at Trevor, but he didn't notice. Trevor was looking past the three of them and now saw that his father was no longer there.

55

The Mysterious Woman

Katie awoke and looked at the clock on the bedside table. *Nine o'clock! I overslept. I promised to make Trevor breakfast!* Katie got up quickly, got dressed, and stepped out into the hallway, quickly walking toward the end of the hall. *His door is open. He's already up*, Katie thought in disappointment. She walked down the main staircase, and as she reached the foyer, she could see the front door was unlocked and open, with a gentle New Orleans breeze blowing through the screen door. Katie stepped out onto the porch and looked out upon the front yard to see if Trevor might be there.

"Good morning, sleepyhead!"

Katie turned, a bit startled, and saw Trevor standing at the far end of the porch. Before him was an easel with what looked like an ordinary board placed upon it. Trevor sat down on the porch railing and seemed to just be staring at what was apparently painted on the board.

"Good morning! I'm sorry about sleeping so late. Have you had any breakfast yet?" Katie said.

Trevor laughed. "No, I've been waiting for you. I thought you promised to make something mighty tasty for me this morning?"

Katie smiled. "I'll get to it in a minute." Katie walked toward Trevor. "I see you are taking up painting again! What are you painting?"

"Well, to begin with, I didn't paint this. I found it when I came out on the porch this morning. The other thing is, I have no idea who this woman in the painting might be. Come here and take a look."

Katie stepped up next to Trevor and looked at the board on the easel. "Trevor! She is beautiful!" As Katie looked more closely, she began to remember something. "She looks familiar for some reason, but I can't quite place her."

Trevor motioned to the paintbrushes and palette on a small table next to the easel. "The paint is still wet—just like the painting was upstairs and the one at Loyola chapel. It's truly a mystery how these paintings show up, and no one notices who is painting them or how. When I first saw this, I thought I recognized the easel and palette. I went upstairs to my dad's room, and sure enough, his easel and palette were gone! Funny thing is, I could see there were some blank canvases up there. I have no idea why anyone would paint on a plain board." Trevor looked at Katie with a puzzled look. "Now that you mention it, she does look familiar somehow. I think I must have seen her somewhere, but for the life of me, I don't know when or where it could have been."

Katie sat down on the railing beside Trevor. "Did you have any dreams again last night?"

"I don't remember dreaming about anything last night—and I certainly don't remember dreaming about this lady, whoever she is. I was pretty tired when you and I got back from our little experience at Father Archer's church museum yesterday."

"Trevor, this portrait is amazing! Whoever painted this has some real talent, don't you think?"

Trevor nodded. "Well, I'm no art critic, but I can't argue with you about that. I just can't imagine who could have painted this." Trevor looked at Katie and smiled. "You haven't been doing a little artwork on the side lately, have you?"

Katie chuckled. "No, it sure wasn't me. I *wish* I was able to paint like this. The only thing I ever tried to paint was something for my mother in grade school and some silly paint-by-number things. They were absolutely terrible!"

Trevor smiled. "I know what you're saying. I tried painting out here on this very porch with my dad, but I wasn't very good at it either."

Katie looked more closely at the portrait. The features were remarkably lifelike, and the colors were brilliant and perfectly matched. "I can't believe this, Trevor! This looks like a portrait by a master artist!"

Trevor looked at Katie, this time seriously. "Do you suppose this has something to do with what happened yesterday at Father Archer's old church?"

Katie suddenly felt a chill. "I don't know. But how *could* that be possible?"

Trevor got up from the porch railing and looked out over the front yard. "I wonder how any of what has been happening lately is possible." Trevor put his hand on Katie's shoulder. "Katie, there is something I didn't tell anyone yesterday. Just before we left St. Agatha's, I saw my dad standing behind Dr. Gallagher."

Katie looked startled. "What? I didn't see anyone! You're frightening me, Trevor."

"No need to be frightened of my dad." Trevor smiled sadly and sighed. "He was there for just an instant, but I had the feeling he was trying to tell me something by his presence."

"Really, like what?"

"I wish I knew, Katie. He just stood there smiling at me—like he used to do when I did something he was proud of."

"I'm sure your dad was always proud of you, Trevor. From what you have told me, he really must have loved you a lot."

Trevor smiled. "I know he loved my brothers and me, Katie. We never quite understood why he and Mom divorced, like I told you before, and we were damn mad at him for it. But we loved him too. We loved both Mom and

Dad very much. That's why the divorce hurt us so much." Trevor looked at Katie with a sadness she had come to know in him often lately. "I miss him. My heart still aches like it did when I first heard the news he was gone."

Katie looked at Trevor with a reassuring smile. "Someday you will be with him again, Trevor. I know you have your doubts, but I hope you believe that. I believe one day I will see my own father again."

Trevor nodded. "If I have learned *anything* in all that has happened lately, I have learned such things may *indeed* be possible."

Katie smiled. "I am so glad to hear you say that, Trevor! Just admitting it is possible is a good start, don't you think?"

"Katie, do you know what I'm thinking about right now?"

"What?"

"That tasty breakfast you promised me. I'd like to have time to eat it before Father Archer and Dr. Gallagher arrive. Weren't they coming by sometime today?" Trevor smiled. "Of course, you could cook up a bunch of stuff, call it brunch, and invite them to join us?"

"No, I promised *you* breakfast. Let me get right to it."

As Katie turned and walked back to the screened entrance of the house, Trevor sat down on the porch railing once again and looked at the freshly painted portrait. As he looked at it intently, he took a deep sigh and spoke softly as if he actually expected to hear an answer to his question: "Dad, are you doing all these paintings?"

56

Revelation

FATHER ARCHER AND Dr. Gallagher both looked in awe at the portrait that Trevor had found on his porch earlier in the day.

"This is indeed remarkable, Trevor," Father Archer said as he touched the edge of the wood the image of the woman was painted upon. "Do you know who I believe this is?"

"You have seen her?" Trevor asked, surprised.

"Many times, though never in person. I do hope to meet her face-to-face one day."

Dr. Gallagher smiled. "You're thinking what I'm thinking—that this is a portrait of the Virgin Mary, right, Donald?"

"That is precisely who I think this is a portrait of!"

Trevor looked at the two men and shook his head. "Katie and I thought she looked familiar. Yesterday at the church—this portrait does seem to favor the woman Mary in my dream or whatever that was!"

Father Archer looked at the painting again. "That's it, Trevor!" Father Archer said excitedly. "*This is* very similar in likeness to the Virgin Mary we saw yesterday in our experience at St. Agatha's!"

Trevor felt a chill as he looked at Father Archer and Dr. Gallagher. "What does all of this mean? Do you have any clues?"

"There could be an explanation," Father Archer began. "Which seems quite unlikely and yet points directly to what we all witnessed during your hypnotic trance yesterday."

"You know," Dr. Gallagher began, "this likeness of Mary is similar to many of the great paintings from the early centuries, except for two very interesting things. The first is that whoever painted this chose to portray the Holy Mother in a somewhat modern, twenty-first-century appearance. But what is even more interesting, the artist chose to use wood for this painting—and wood was almost exclusively used in the very earliest centuries, when artists did not use canvas."

Father Archer could barely contain his excitement as he exclaimed, "Of course! Artists used wood in the first century!"

Trevor shook his head. "I can't speak for Katie, but you've lost me."

"Trevor," Dr. Gallagher said, smiling, "St. Luke is the patron saint of painters and physicians. There is a very old legend that Luke knew the Virgin Mary and painted her portrait. I believe what we experienced yesterday would seem to verify that."

"Joseph is correct about the legend, Trevor," Father Archer continued. "This painting may be tangible proof that what we experienced yesterday was reality and not merely some type of mass hypnosis affecting all of us!"

Trevor was puzzled. "So is this portrait like the other portraits Luke painted of the Virgin Mary?"

Dr. Gallagher sighed. "Unfortunately, we have no idea, at least no definitive answer we could give you. You see, although the legend is a very old one—and a number of churches throughout the centuries have claimed they possessed a genuine portrait by Luke of the Virgin Mary—such claims could never be verified, and skeptics often dismiss the entire legend as myth. Of course, anything painted upon something other than wood would not even be considered as authentic, correctly deemed to have been painted much later in time and by someone other than Luke."

"Yesterday," Father Archer explained, "it became quite evident while you were under hypnosis that you somehow assumed the identity of St. Luke—at least, that is the best explanation we can come up with as to how you were able to share with us what St. Luke experienced nearly two thousand years ago."

Trevor looked at Katie and at the two men. "Are you trying to tell me we somehow brought Luke back to the twenty-first century with us, and he's opened an art studio on my dad's porch?"

Dr. Gallagher laughed. "Oh, you are a caution, my boy! Yet you may not be too far off at that. Someone painted this portrait and, whoever it was, painted it on a piece of wood instead of canvas."

Trevor shook his head and sat upon the porch railing. "This is all just too much for me, I'm afraid. Do you really believe in all of this?"

Father Archer sat beside Trevor on the railing. "What explanation do you have that you think we *should* believe in?"

Katie had been sitting quietly, listening to the three men talk, but now she could no longer keep her silence. "Trevor told me just this morning that if he has learned anything from what has happened lately, it is that anything is possible! Do you remember telling me that, Trev?"

"I do, but believing the spirit of a long-dead two-thousand-year-old saint is now painting portraits on my dad's porch is a little tough to buy into." Trevor sighed. "I have to be honest here. Until my dad developed his interest in this Gospel writer, I knew very little about him, except for hearing his name mentioned during readings at church now and then. As you all know by now, I haven't exactly been a church person. The whole business of an afterlife—of heaven and hell and being reunited with friends and loved ones someday—always seemed to be pretty unrealistic to me."

Dr. Gallagher nodded. "When I was a priest in my parish, I questioned my own faith, Trevor. I know what you are saying. It's a lot easier to not believe than it is to believe. But you were, by some means, given an incredible ability to witness the past, and somehow, you were able to share it with the rest of us yesterday. If only it were possible to reveal what we were blessed to witness with everyone!"

Trevor sighed. "We could write a book and title it *Revelation*."

Father Archer smiled. "That's a good idea, Trevor, and you may be just the one to write it!"

Trevor smiled. "But let's be honest with one another here. Who could possibly *believe* any of this? How do we know any of what we all seem to have witnessed yesterday at St. Agatha's was real?"

Father Archer spoke softly, "Did you know any of what was revealed to us yesterday beforehand? Did you hear about it or read it somewhere, or did you simply imagine the entire series of events in your own mind? If so, how could we all see and hear through you what Luke seems to have experienced nearly two thousand years ago?"

"Well, sure, I was familiar with some of it. How many times have we heard the story of the Nativity or that there was a Gospel writer named Luke or there was a bad guy named Pontius Pilate?"

Dr. Gallagher nodded in agreement. "That is true, Trevor, as far as you go. But you shared other things with us—things I doubt you could have known beforehand, things Donald and I have never heard of before. What you witnessed and what you somehow were able to share with the rest of us was very likely a two-thousand-year-old reality! I have no explanation for it. I have no religious, scientific, or plausible explanation for it at all, yet I know in my mind and in my heart it happened and we all witnessed it. This is why your dreams have all seemed so real to you—why you at times became a part of them and found yourself walking in your sleep. How else can we explain current things like the appearance of this amazing portrait or the changes in the painting upstairs in your house and at Loyola chapel? Yet, even though I have no explanation of *how* all of this is happening, I do believe I can pinpoint *why* it is happening."

Trevor looked at Dr. Gallagher with interest. "I'd love to hear it. Let's start with the painting upstairs and that painting at Loyola. What is your theory for those little mysteries?"

Father Archer spoke first, "If I may, I have a theory of my own for the changes in those two paintings. We are talking about Luke. In Luke's Gospel, he describes the Nativity the way we witnessed the Holy Mother tell him about it during our experience at St. Agatha's. Luke portrayed the teachings of Jesus as having special concern for the poor and needy—those who were downtrodden. For example, in Luke's Gospel story of the Nativity, he does not mention wealthy kings, only poor shepherds who visit the manger. Matthew, on the other hand, does not mention lowly shepherds, only wealthy and powerful kings who seek the Christ child. If we can believe the spirit of Luke is responsible for this portrait on your porch, we can also assume his spirit might be responsible for painting over Matthew's kings in the Nativity scene, because according to Luke, the kings weren't even there!"

Dr. Gallagher smiled. "That certainly sounds reasonable as far as the Nativity is concerned, Donald, but what about the painting of the Crucifixion at Loyola University?"

"As I understand it from Trevor, the addition of another figure was painted into the scene of the Crucifixion at Loyola. I believe that figure is the spirit of Luke himself, perhaps through the spirit of your father, which is why the figure appeared to you as your dad. I suggest the reason was to give you a clue as to what we would learn later at Saint Agatha's—that Luke was there at the time of the Crucifixion and he saw Jesus die on the cross."

"Speaking of Luke and of your father," Dr. Gallagher said, "as far as we can tell from what you have told us, your dad died quite suddenly and unexpectedly. His death left a number of things unsaid between you, leaving a tremendous void in your life and a deep sadness in your heart. You had a number of things in common with your dad—your memories, this house, what you knew about his work concerning Luke near the end of his life, as well as all the things he left you, like that Roman coin you wear on the silver chain around your neck. You were raised Catholic."

"You were an altar boy like your dad, and even though you say you weren't religious and haven't been a churchgoing person, you remember much of what you were taught in the church. Important things—those things that, if true, would mean one day you'd be reunited with your father—became an obsession deep in your subconscious mind. You began having dreams shortly after your dad died, and what did you dream about? You dreamed about the crucifixion and death of Jesus, but most importantly, you really wanted to know whether the resurrection of Jesus really happened. You had to know the answer to that, and your dreams became focused on those who were there, who could convince you the resurrection of Jesus really occurred."

"After all, the resurrection of Jesus is the cornerstone of Christian faith. Why? Because if true, all of us have the promise of being raised from death and living again with Jesus and all those we know and love in this life. You wanted desperately to have the chance to say those things to your father that were left unsaid between you. You wanted desperately to be with him again one day, to see your brother Troy and to be with all your loved ones again in a new life without death and parting."

Trevor looked at Dr. Gallagher for a long moment then at Katie and Father Archer, who sat quietly, thinking about what had just been said.

"I can't argue with you that all of this doesn't make perfect sense, because it really does. You are right. I did want answers after my dad died, but you are telling me I wanted those answers so badly I somehow managed to find them?" Trevor shook his head. "How could I possibly do such a thing when no one else can?"

"Who is to say no one else can? There are many who have found Jesus and answers to their salvation in a variety of ways. You do have a distinctive ability that, as I said, I can't fully explain, although I truly wish I could. What I do know is that this gift of yours is so very special. You are somehow able to transcend time itself and even share your experiences with those near you," Dr. Gallagher answered.

"What about my dad? Did I really see him and talk to him, or was I imagining that with this *unique gift* you are so convinced I have?"

"I have little doubt you really saw him, Trevor. I believe you saw him in a similar way to how we all saw the Virgin Mary, Joseph of Arimathea, St. Luke, Pontius Pilate, St. Paul, the people of Jerusalem, and the Roman soldiers from two thousand years ago when we were at St. Agatha's yesterday. We saw them, and we heard them speak to one another. We learned answers to questions that have been puzzling us for centuries."

"Tell me, if you can—will I continue to have these *experiences* you speak of?"

"That is a very good question, Trevor. If you allow yourself to believe in what you have been blessed to witness and to share with the rest of us, I suspect you will have found many of the answers you so desperately wanted after your father died. As a result of obtaining those answers, there may be no need for you to further experience those things you have been witness to since your father's death."

"I told Katie about something earlier this morning, but I haven't told you or Father Archer about it yet. Yesterday, just before we all left St. Agatha's, I saw my dad there at the church. He was standing just behind you, and he was smiling at me—like he used to do when he was proud of me for something. He was just there for a moment, and then he was gone. Do you think I will see him again?"

Dr. Gallagher sighed. "In this life, I don't know, Trevor. Now that you have some of your answers, your dad may simply wait until he sees you again in God's kingdom." Dr. Gallagher put his hand on Trevor's shoulder. "What are your thoughts concerning your dad?"

Trevor smiled sadly. "It did seem to me at the time he may have been telling me good-bye, at least for now."

Katie reached out and hugged Trevor with tears in her eyes. "Oh, Trevor, you will see him again! I know you will, and I know now I will see my father again one day too!"

"Dr. Gallagher and I are in the process of checking out some of the things we learned from our wonderful experiences at St. Agatha's yesterday. May we come back again in a week or so to visit with you and Katie about what we discover? If our suspicions are correct, we may be able to give you some additional assurances that will help you in your faith." Father Archer said.

Trevor and Katie both nodded their approval.

"That would fine," Trevor answered. "I'd like that." Trevor pointed to the portrait. "Do you want to take that portrait along with you and check that out too?"

Father Archer looked pleased. "That would be wonderful, Trevor, if you would permit us to take it. We'll take good care of this portrait, won't we, Joseph?"

"Absolutely, we will! Thank you, Trevor."

Trevor smiled. "Oh, one other thing—maybe you should take the easel and all the other painting materials along with you as well. I don't think I have any more boards lying around the house, and I don't want to come out here some morning and find our mysterious artist has painted images all over the porch."

Epilogue

Trevor poured a cup of coffee with his left hand as he dialed a phone in his right. He took a sip of coffee while listening to his call ringing, waiting for his brother on the other end to answer.

"Hi, Trev!"

"Hey, Rob! How are things in New York?"

"They're fine. What's on the agenda in New Orleans for today?"

"Well, my old college friend Katie and a couple of new friends I made recently are stopping by in a few minutes. They are all happy about some research they have done concerning those dreams I was having some time ago."

"Yeah, I remember you telling me about that. Are you still having those dreams?"

Trevor sipped his coffee. "No. I've been sleeping a lot better too. Whatever was causing them seems to have stopped."

"That's good. I was beginning to worry about you. Kyle and I were just talking about that the other day."

"I need to call Kyle too, but he's always so busy—I never know when he's on call or at a medical meeting somewhere."

"Yeah, he's pretty busy. How about you? Are you teaching summer school?"

"No, I'm taking the summer off."

"Cool."

"Rob, I know you're busy, so I'll keep this short. I called because I wanted to ask you something. Are you still planning to go back to Minnesota this summer to spend some time at the lake with Mom?"

"Yeah, in July, I guess. I think Mom plans to rent a cabin at that same place we usually go. Kyle was trying to figure out when he could take a week off, so Mom is sort of waiting to hear back from him. I'm good pretty much anytime that month. Are you planning to come?"

"It would be nice to get out of New Orleans's humidity during July! I need to talk to Mom about it, but I hope to come up there for a couple of days. I've really got a lot to tell all of you."

Rob's voice sounded concerned. "Really, is everything okay?"

"Everything's fine." Trevor paused a moment, thinking about what he was going to say. "Rob, I need to tell all of you something about Dad. It's all a little difficult to believe, but I think you will all feel much better about the way things are once I tell you what I need to tell you."

"Okay, Trev, whatever you think. If you want to talk about this before we go to the lake though, let me know. You're sure everything is okay?"

"Everything is fine, Rob."

"That's good, Trev."

"I love you, Rob. I'll let you get back to what you were doing."

"I love you too, Trev. Let's plan something. Give me a call after you talk to Mom."

"I will, Rob. Later."

"I'll catch you later, Trev."

Trevor put the phone down on the counter and sipped his coffee as he walked through one set of pocket doors into the dining room. Then he went through another set of doors as he stepped into the foyer. He opened the front door and pushed open the screen as he stepped out onto the porch and into the early-morning daylight.

"That was pretty amazing timing!" Katie smiled as she walked up the steps. "I didn't even have to ring the doorbell."

Trevor laughed. "Father Archer and Dr. Gallagher won't have to ring it either. They're just pulling up into the driveway."

Katie turned and looked out into the street. "Wow, everyone has arrived right on time."

Trevor and Katie stood at the top of the porch steps as Dr. Gallagher and Father Archer got out of the car and made their way up the front sidewalk to the house. In a few moments, they were all comfortably seated on the porch in the fresh morning air.

"Before we get started on what we found out," Father Archer began, "Joseph has some exciting news he'd like to share with you."

Dr. Gallagher grinned and laughed his hearty laugh. "Well, I don't know how exciting it will be for the two of you, but it is very exciting for me! I have decided to return to the priesthood."

"That's wonderful!" Katie exclaimed as she got up from her chair and gave Dr. Gallagher a hug.

"When did you decide this?" Trevor asked.

"I'll tell you, my boy," Dr. Gallagher began as Katie returned to her chair. "I decided this shortly after our experiences at St. Agatha's a week or so ago. I am now convinced that my being a priest is my true calling and how I can best serve God from now on."

"So do we call you *father* now instead of doctor?" Trevor asked, smiling.

"I'd like that. I'm looking forward to hearing that distinction once I'm officially wearing my collar again, thanks in no small part to you, Trevor."

"Well, Trevor, Joseph and I have been busy doing some checking with various sources and some people we know concerning your revelation at St. Agatha's. We have even more exciting news for you! Much of what we witnessed together that day appears to be not only possible but probable! At least, there is nothing we have been able to find that can refute any of it convincingly."

"That is exciting, isn't it, Trevor?" Katie said cheerily. "Tell us what you found out!"

"Well, to begin with," Father Archer answered, "let me give you one example. According to the account Mary gave to Luke, the Annunciation—when the angel Gabriel told Mary she would conceive the Son of God—occurred in December. Shortly after, Mary went to visit her cousin Elizabeth, whom Mary was told had conceived a son in her old age, and stayed with her for the next three months until Elizabeth's son, John, was born in the month of March. Mary returned to her home in Nazareth upon hearing the news of King Herod's death at about the same time of John's birth. Based upon the writings of Josephus and other ancient sources, King Herod died in late March or early April of 4 BCE—the same year Jesus is believed to have been born. Mary tells Luke in your revelation that Jesus was born in September, not in December, when we traditionally celebrate the birth of Jesus at Christmas."

"Even though it has been thought for quite some time that Jesus wasn't really born in December," Dr. Gallagher continued, "there was some difficulty pinpointing which month he actually was born in. Then there is the matter of the census, which was the reason Joseph and Mary had to make the trip to Bethlehem in her ninth month. There is no record of any Roman census in 4 BCE, although there is a record of a Roman census in 6 CE. Luke has been criticized as being incorrect for writing there was a census in the year Jesus was born and for writing it was when *Quirinius was governor of Syria*. Other ancient sources suggest Quirinius wasn't governor of Syria until 6 CE. But—as we all learned while we were at St. Agatha's—Mary told Luke that Quirinius was governor of Cilicia, which bordered Syria, and he was also *coregent* of Syria at the time." Dr. Gallagher smiled. "The research Donald and I have been doing seems to confirm this is not only possible but is highly probable! At the very least, our research has offered nothing that convincingly contradicts this new information!"

"That's right," Father Archer agreed. "And as far as the census is concerned, Rome was very meticulous and methodical in the way the empire was administered. It makes perfect sense that Caesar Augustus *would* order a census when Herod the Great died! That would be the most efficient way for Rome to learn what it needed to know about Herod's kingdom before deciding who would take Herod's place. Augustus decided to split Herod's kingdom between Herod's three sons—but not allowing any of them the title of king that had been claimed by their father.

"Antipas became tetrarch of Galilee and Perea, Philip became tetrarch of lands east of the Jordan, and Archelaus became ethnarch of Judea, Samaria, and Idumea. However, ten years later in 6 CE, because of the inept rule of Archelaus,

Augustus removed him. Once again, Rome would conduct another census before replacing Archelaus. Augustus appointed a Roman administrator named Coponius as the first in a series of Roman procurators. Twenty years later, Pontius Pilate would be appointed to this position."

"Think of it," Dr. Gallagher exclaimed. "King Herod dies in March of 4 BCE, and it takes some time for Caesar Augustus to learn of it in Rome and more time to issue a decree that a census be taken to learn the true state of affairs in Herod's kingdom. Who better than Quirinius to conduct the census and maintain order while it is being conducted? As a result of the census, Quirinius became well-known throughout the region and was the perfect historical marker for Luke to refer to when writing about the Nativity of Jesus!"

"It was important to Luke to accurately mark these events in the times they happened. When Luke wrote of the Annunciation to Mary and of the birth of John, he wrote 'in the days of King Herod'—because Herod was still very much alive—in order to accurately and forever mark the time in history. Since Herod died in March of 4 BCE, around the time of John's birth, he was nearly six months in his grave when Jesus was born in September. Luke referred to the most prominent figure in Judea at the time Jesus was born—*Quirinius*, who was conducting the census decreed by Caesar Augustus. As governor of Cilicia and coregent of neighboring Syria at the time, Quirinius would have provided Luke with the perfect historical time marker for the birth of Jesus," Father Archer added.

Dr. Gallagher clasped his hands together and smiled. "Luke was absolutely correct in what he wrote, Trevor! Everything fits together marvelously and makes more sense than ever before! All this reinforces the certainty of what is written in Luke's Gospel—just as Luke promised in his prologue to it!"

Trevor shook his head. "I'm all happy that you are so excited about this, but what does it all really mean? I'll admit you provide an interesting history lesson, but what assurances do we really have that all the things Luke wrote about are accurate?"

"That is a great question, Trevor!" Dr. Gallagher replied, trying to contain his excitement. "If all the basic things Luke wrote prove to be accurate, as we are learning more and more is the case, there is no reason for us not to trust in Luke with regard to all things that he wrote about Jesus."

Trevor, upon hearing the words, remembered his dad telling him the same words, and he spoke those words aloud, "*Trust in Luke!*"

"Exactly, my boy," Dr. Gallagher exclaimed. "Trust in Luke! Remember what we all witnessed at St. Agatha's? All the writers in the Bible, all of them were Jews—all but one. Luke alone was a Gentile. We have learned through your revelation at St. Agatha's much that will allow us to have faith that Luke gave us an accurate and reliable account in his writings."

"Hold on," Trevor protested. "How can what we learned at St. Agatha's allow us to have faith that Luke's account is all accurate and reliable? I was under hypnosis! I was having dreams, remember? Dreams!"

"Yes, but what prompted those dreams, Trevor? Do you remember our earlier discussion of my theory on that?"

Trevor nodded. "Yes, and that does seem to make sense. I haven't had the dreams since. But to say that what was contained in those dreams is somehow—pardon the expression—*gospel* seems to me to be over-the-top."

"Luke gives us assurance we can rely on what he wrote. To paraphrase from Luke's prologue, he says, 'It seems good to endeavor to understand everything anew and write an orderly account that would assure certainty of all that had occurred.' Luke is the only Gospel writer to write such a prologue. It has been believed by some down through the centuries that Luke talked with many who knew Jesus and who had witnessed his ministry in order to accurately write his account—most likely beginning with the Virgin Mary herself." Dr. Gallagher smiled reassuringly. "Don't you see it? It all fits together, Trevor. What we witnessed at St. Agatha's is truly a remarkable revelation! So far, it all checks out as being not only possible but probable!"

"By all this, you are *actually* saying if Luke wrote it down, then we can believe whatever he wrote is accurate?"

"From what we already know of Luke, what time and history have already proven, and from what we are still learning? Absolutely, we can!"

"We have learned much more, Trevor," Father Archer continued. "For example, *Theophilus* is the name to whom Luke addresses his writings. The true identity of Theophilus has been a mystery for two thousand years, but it has often been thought that Theophilus must have been someone in an official capacity during Luke's time and perhaps a person who even financed Luke's work. Now we can't rule out that Luke knew Pontius Pilate, and Pontius Pilate was *Theophilus*!"

Trevor shook his head. "But if I understand things correctly, and I'm no Bible scholar, you are making this connection based primarily on what we all witnessed at St. Agatha's!"

"That's true, but the connection makes sense, considering all we do know from the New Testament and other sources, and there is no evidence that convincingly disproves it! The new pieces of the puzzle all fit together!"

"I have a question," Katie interrupted. "What about Pontius Pilate? Did he really become a believer in Jesus, and was he really stabbed in the desert because of it?"

"There have been many theories and much conjecture about what happened to Pontius Pilate after the Crucifixion of Jesus," Father Archer continued. "Pilate is thought by some to have converted to Christianity. He is even considered a saint in the Greek Orthodox and Coptic Churches. It is also believed Pilate wrote a letter concerning Jesus to Emperor Tiberius—and that letter may very well have contributed to his disappearance from history—although there appears to be more than one version of Pilate's letter in existence. This, of course, casts some doubt as to which letter, if any, might be the genuine letter written by Pontius Pilate or whether the genuine letter written by him has yet to be discovered," Father Archer replied.

"That is all true, Donald." Dr. Gallagher nodded. "But what is extremely remarkable is that Pontius Pilate—whose name is remembered primarily because of his judgment of Jesus and his act of condemning him to death on the cross—this once-powerful Roman procurator, simply disappeared into the mists of time under a shroud of mystery. We have learned a tremendous amount of valuable information through our experience at St. Agatha's, and the accuracy of what we experienced there is proving to be sound. Wouldn't it be wonderful if Pilate's golden chest of holy treasures, which he had intended to give to Luke, might actually be found in the Judean desert one day!"

Trevor shook his head. "This is really becoming too much, don't you think? You are actually suggesting a golden chest filled with writings and religious artifacts exists somewhere in the Judean desert?"

Father Archer smiled. "This is a lot to take in all at once, and there is so much more to talk about. Let's just say for now that all of this—as we had hoped when we spoke last on this porch of yours—should prove to give us a great deal of faith in the accuracy of Luke's writings. I believe we have fresh, new assurance that what is written by Luke concerning the life, crucifixion, death, and resurrection of Jesus is all an accurate account—an account that can be relied upon. Once we trust and believe in the certainty of Luke's writings, we can trust and believe we will live in God's kingdom! It is there we will be reunited with all those we have known, loved, and lost during our mortal lives."

Trevor looked at Katie, who smiled back at him with a reassuring smile. Then he looked again at Father Archer and Dr. Gallagher. "I do want to believe in all of this, Father. I do. In fact, I was just talking to my brother Rob before you all came by this morning. I told him I had a lot to tell him, my brother Kyle, and my mother. I had no idea *just how much* I would have to tell them until these past few minutes. I have to admit, what you are sharing with us this morning all seems pretty compelling. I do want to know everything!"

"Me too," Katie said excitedly. "I'm really happy about *knowing* and not just *hoping* I will see my dad again someday!"

Dr. Gallagher got to his feet. "How about we all go out and get something to eat—my treat! Then we can talk as much you like."

"It was your treat the last time," Trevor remembered. "So I believe it's my turn."

"Nonsense, my boy." Dr. Gallagher laughed heartily. "Have you forgotten? I'm about to renew my vow of poverty! You better let me treat all of you while I can still afford to do it!"

"You'll get no argument from me." Father Archer chuckled. "Lead the way, Joseph. I've worked up a mighty appetite."

Upstairs, in the second-floor hallway, just outside Trevor's room, Trevor's dad stood silently, looking out the window at the scene below as Trevor, Katie, Dr. Gallagher, and Father Archer walked down the steps of the porch and into the yard, making their way toward Dr. Gallagher's car. He looked down at the little boy who was holding his hand, then smiled as he stooped down to pick up his firstborn son.

"Is Trevor all happy now, Daddy?" Troy asked.

"Yes, Troy. Trevor seems to be much happier now."

The two of them looked out through the window and watched as Trevor got into Dr. Gallagher's car. *I hope you find some peace now, Tad. I know you can reassure Rob and Kyle and your mom that we will all be together again one day—never to part from one another ever, ever again. Troy and I will be waiting for all of you. Live your lives, and we'll be together soon enough. Always remember, son, death is only the beginning. I love you, Trevor.*

As the warm rays of the morning sunlight streamed softly through silky curtains and traveled silently and swiftly down the second-floor hallway, there was just the sound of the rhythmic *ticktock*, *ticktock*, *ticktock* of an unseen clock echoing throughout the empty house.